PE**N**

S**U**

Twice short-listed for the Booker Prize, Paul Bailey has been the recipient of the E. M. Forster Award, the Somerset Maugham Award, an Arts Council Award, a George Orwell Memorial Prize and a Bicentennial fellowship. He is also the author of *At the Jerusalem*, *Trespasses*, *A Distant Likeness*, *Peter Smart's Confessions*, *Old Soldiers*, *An Immaculate Mistake* and *Gabriel's Lament*.

PAUL BAILEY

SUGAR CANE

PENGUIN BOOKS

PENGUIN BOOKS

Published by the Penguin Group
Penguin Books Ltd, 27 Wrights Lane, London W8 5TZ, England
Penguin Books USA Inc., 375 Hudson Street, New York, New York 10014, USA
Penguin Books Australia Ltd, Ringwood, Victoria, Australia
Penguin Books Canada Ltd, 10 Alcorn Avenue, Toronto, Ontario, Canada M4V 3B2
Penguin Books (NZ) Ltd, 182–190 Wairau Road, Auckland 10, New Zealand

Penguin Books Ltd, Registered Offices: Harmondsworth, Middlesex, England

First published by Bloomsbury 1993
Published in Penguin Books 1994
1 3 5 7 9 10 8 6 4 2

Printed in England by Clays Ltd, St Ives plc

FOR JEREMY TREVATHAN

E forse io solo
so ancora
che visse
(And perhaps I alone
still know
that he lived)

Giuseppe Ungaretti: 'In memoria'

ONE

I work with human genitals. For twenty years, I have examined innumerable penises and vaginas. I am a venereologist, and I practise at St Lucy's, in London.

In the few months that I knew the boy who entered my life while Anthony Innocent was dying, I had no cause to look at him in a professional capacity. He seemed to be fit enough, in his shadowy way. Neither his 'sausage' nor his 'nectarine' was to be my concern.

What concerns me now, and I suspect always will, is something so fragile, so insubstantial, that I think I fear to write about it. I am used to making the exact diagnosis and offering – when I can – the effective prescription. But not in his case. With Stephen, alias David, alias Richard, alias Andrew – and who knows how many other aliases? – I am suddenly clumsy: as awkward in my mind as I was in my body on that terrible Sunday when I broke, by accident, my mother's most treasured possession.

I see that I have called him a boy, even though he must be almost as old now as his friend, Anthony Innocent, who died at thirty-four. Perhaps it's because he allowed me those glimpses, and they were only glimpses, of his craving for enchantment that I find myself unable to account him one of us – by which I mean, I suppose, the acceptably or unacceptably mature, the

3

responsibly or irresponsibly grown-up. There were times he seemed attached to me, like a child to its mother. Yet I never asked him what he wanted, or what I could do for him. I assumed that he would tell me himself – in his own slippery fashion, in a rare unguarded moment, when a barrier or two had fallen.

I remembered, this morning, another brief and strange attachment. Marcus, as I shall call him, remains unique among my patients in that he wasn't really a patient at all.

'You're clear,' I told him on his second visit to the Special Clinic at St Peter's.

'Clear?'

'There's nothing wrong with you. You're clear. You're clean.'

'I can't be.'

'You can be. You are.'

'I don't have gonorrhoea?'

'Exactly. You don't have gonorrhoea – or anything else. The tests have proved negative.'

'Does that mean,' he asked, 'that you aren't going to treat me?'

'Of course it does.'

'Not even a pill?'

'Not even that.'

'You are absolutely, totally sure – I mean, you are one hundred per cent certain – that I am not suffering from gonorrhoea?'

'I am sure, and I am certain.'

'Despite the pain in my – ?' He pointed a finger at his crotch.

'Yes, despite your pain.'

He did not appear pleased. 'If that's the best you can do for me, then I suppose I shall have to be satisfied.' He offered me his hand. 'Thank you, Doctor, and goodbye.'

He was back at the clinic a month later.

'I have reason to believe I have contracted syphilis,' he announced. 'Good reason.'

4

'I'm listening.'

'I don't wish to shock you, Doctor – shocking you is far from my intention, I must insist – but I need to state the brutal truth. And the brutal truth is that I have availed myself of the services of a prostitute.'

I assured him that he hadn't shocked me, and noticed how disappointed he looked.

'And that,' he continued, feebly, 'is why I'm here.'

'When was this encounter?'

'Two weeks ago. On a Tuesday, to be precise.'

'And you are showing symptoms already?'

'Yes, I am,' he replied. 'There is, I regret to say, pronounced trouble down below.'

'A discharge?'

'Definitely.' He nodded. 'Yes, definitely.'

He had not contracted syphilis, just as he had not contracted gonorrhoea. I informed him so in as dismayed a voice as I could muster, for I now realised what I could hardly believe – that he wanted to be cured of diseases it was impossible for him to catch. I likened him to those men and women who confess to murders they have not committed. His appetite for vicarious notoriety was as perverse, if not as public, as theirs.

'You are absolutely sure I don't have the pox? Please pardon my vulgarity.'

'I am absolutely sure, and you are pardoned instantly.'

On his next visit, he refused to be examined by my colleagues, insisting that I, and I alone, understood his predicament.

'It is Dr Potocki who is treating me. No one else will do.'

He had to wait nearly five hours for the benefit of my 'unrivalled knowledge'.

'What's the matter?' I asked, briskly ignoring his flattery.

'It's problematical, Doctor.'

'Problematical? In what way?'

'Well, it might be syphilis, or it might be gonorrhoea.'

'Might it?'

'It's one or the other. It has to be. You'll know which it is.'

'Perhaps.'

'It's been elusive up until now, but I have every confidence that you will find it today.'

'It' stayed elusive. 'It' went on evading detection. He came to see me again and again, and again and again I affirmed that I had found nothing wrong with him.

(Why did I never tell Marcus he was wasting my time? I think because I rather admired his persistence. I even began to anticipate our consultations with something like pleasure. They became my entertainment. I feared the day, which did not arrive, when I discovered his imagined 'it' to exist in reality.)

'Pray forgive my impertinence, Dr Potocki, but are you, by any chance, married?'

'Yes, I am.'

'I am not, as you are aware. I have failed in my determined efforts to take the plunge. A mere paddle in the shallows is the extent of my achievements, matrimonially speaking. Alas, I consort only with loose – or should I say louche? – women in a middle age that is otherwise fusty.'

I looked at cherubic Marcus and denied myself a smile.

(Some months later, when I heard that Marcus, *my* Marcus, was pestering another doctor at another clinic, I was overcome with an absurd anger. I felt rejected; betrayed, even. 'But *I* wasn't irritated by him,' I shouted at my bemused superior. 'I didn't consider him a pest. *I* showed him respect and concern.' I did not add 'He has no right', as my feelings were urging me to.)

Those thirty or so sessions with Marcus, with Marcus's fantasies, took place while I was living in hell.

Yes, I was married.

On the grubby piece of paper the boy held out to me were scribbled the names of ten London hospitals. He had put ticks alongside those he had already been to in his search for Tonio. He'd heard word on the circuit, he said, that Tonio was ill – no, more than ill – and being looked after by doctors, and he wanted to know if it was in this place, St Lucy's.

'Have you got Tonio?'

Had we? I didn't think so.

'Tonio *who*?' I asked. 'Tonio *what*?'

'He's just Tonio.'

'No one's just Tonio.'

'It's funny, the rest of it. It's Daily Something. Tonio Daily Something.'

I led him into the ward, the better to convince him that we weren't harbouring his Mr Daily Something, his mysterious Tonio.

But it was there he found him – in the wasted form of Anthony Innocent, in the bed nearest the door.

'Tonio?'

'He can't see you,' I said. 'He's lost his sight. You'll have to speak louder.'

'I'm here, Tonio,' he almost shouted.

'Who's here?'

'Me. It's me, Tonio.'

'Not Sugar Cane?'

'Yes.'

'My star pupil.'

'Yes, Tonio.'

'You've left it late.'

'I'll stay with you. I'll stay till whenever.'

And stay he did, until Anthony Innocent's inevitable death. No sooner had they been reunited than Tonio lost consciousness. There was to be no exchange of memories.

'I'm sorry,' I said, and added, hesitantly, 'Sugar Cane.'

'I can't allow that,' was his quick response. 'I'm Stephen to you and nothing else. Understand?'

It was my mother's idea to have me christened Esther. 'Such a beautiful English name for my beautiful little girl' was the phrase with which she presented me to her friends, whose own little girls were not quite so beautiful. 'And it isn't common. It is even rare. She will not have to change it when she becomes a famous ballerina.'

I was seven, almost eight, when my mother learned that I was not 'cut out' for ballet. 'It isn't her fault, Countess

Potocka,' my teacher, Madame Vera, explained. 'Blame nature instead.'

'What do you mean? Nature has made my Esther beautiful. Everyone is agreed.'

'They have not looked at her feet.'

'Her feet? Her feet have nothing the matter with them. She has no bumps or hard bits.'

'Her feet are already too big, Countess. And her hands as well, I'm afraid. Esther is growing rapidly, at a far quicker rate than the other children. Her body will not develop into the kind that is cut out for Aurora and Giselle. That much I can safely guarantee.'

'We can afford to pay you, the Count and myself.'

'Please listen to me carefully, Countess. I am a woman of principle. I do not accept money under false pretences. Esther's feet do not inspire me any more.'

'Inspire you? Feet inspire you? Why should only her feet inspire you?'

'Calm down, Countess. Because I teach from the feet upwards is the answer to your question. Do you understand what I'm saying?'

'No, I do not. I shall never understand your "feet" and "inspire" nonsense. I will pay you double. I will advise my husband, the Count, to send you a cheque.'

'Then you will be advising him in vain. I shall tear it up.'

'Mummy,' I intervened, finding courage in Madame Vera's resistance to the woman who did not dare to call herself a countess at home. 'Mummy, I don't want to learn dancing. I don't want to be a ballet dancer. Really and truly I don't.'

'You are not old enough, Esther, to decide your future. I want you to be a ballerina.'

'The child is right, Countess Potocka. Her heart is not in the dance and never will be.'

'First you say it's her feet and then it's her hands and now you bring up her heart. What can I ever do to persuade you?'

'Nothing, Countess. Nothing in the whole wide world.'

I became, then, what I had not been before – her ungainly daughter, whose hands and feet were not to be trusted. I was

8

still her beautiful Esther in public, though: 'It seems that her beauty is not *cut out* for the ballet. But she will turn heads when the time comes. Important heads, too.' Yet I was not forgiven for not inspiring Madame Vera, for not having my heart in the dance, for denying her the pleasure of sitting in a box at some grand theatre or opera house on the occasion of my debut as Aurora, acknowledging the wild applause that was her due as much as mine. 'You are *prima* and *assoluta* at last, Esther, and all thanks to me and my ambition for you.'

(I visited my mother this afternoon, at the nursing home in which I placed her ten years ago. I see her once a month, dutifully. I talk, but she hears nothing. I told her today that I am pregnant, and that the father-to-be is a man named Gabriel. The alarming news failed to stir her out of her waking sleep, as I knew it would. It is only food she recognises. The dullness leaves her eyes when a meal, any meal, is set before her, and returns again when the last, the absolutely last, morsel has been consumed. She has no table manners now, no etiquette. I can't, I don't, eat or drink with her.)

Anthony Innocent died, and his friend left St Lucy's, and it seemed that they would join a thousand others in the recesses of my mind – to be remembered, if at all, by chance, by association.

Then, early one summer morning, the boy I understood I was to address as Stephen sidled up to me in the street outside the hospital. He was wearing an electric-blue suit. I think I gasped with astonishment at this show of vulgarity.

'Hello, Doctor.'

'Stephen, is it?'

'If you like,' he replied. 'Stephen I'll allow.'

'Are you off to a wedding?'

'Me? Wedding? What wedding would I ever go to?'

'It's your clothes. They're so – so *flash*.'

'Bright, you mean.'

'Bright, then.'

'Nothing wrong with a touch of colour.'

'Of course not.'

'Does no harm.'

Except to my eyes, I refrained from saying.

'You can have this if you want it,' he mumbled, pulling out a small, leather-bound book from one of the suit's capacious pockets. 'Take it, will you?'

I took it from him.

'Is this a present, Stephen?'

'If you like.'

'Thank you.'

There was no title on the book's spine: just VOL. IX, embossed in gold. As I was opening his curious gift, he slid away. He did not hear my startled 'Where on earth did you get this?' when I discovered that I was now the owner of the ninth volume of George Chapman's translation of Homer's *Iliad*, published in London in – it was a minute or two before I managed to add up the Roman numerals – 1620. 'Where, Stephen?'

I find I have to return to that long-buried day, the day of my departure from Madame Vera Carter's Académie de la Danse (Méthode Petipa), the day my abiding inability to please Maria Potocka perhaps began.

'You are refusing, are you, my husband's, the Count's, money?'

'I am, indeed. It would not be well spent, I do assure you.'

Madame Vera stooped to kiss me goodbye, as was her custom at the end of a lesson. My mother forestalled her, however, and snatched me out of her embrace, shrieking, 'Do not touch her, you hypocrite! Leave the bitter pill unsugared!'

(My mother needed no dramatist to provide her with exit lines. They came to her as the occasion demanded. My father, the cause of so many of them, kept a special notebook in which he recorded his favourites. She would slam the door behind her, and then he would wait until he was certain she wasn't coming back before jotting down the latest of her last words. 'That was a particularly fine example,' he would remark with an appreciative smile.)

The bitter pill she commanded Madame Vera to leave unsugared puzzled me so much that I asked her what it was. Was it a medicine? I persisted. Was it like cod-liver oil? 'For a girl with big feet you are walking too slow,' she snapped. 'Pick the large things up.' I stopped instead, and stamped them on the grass. We were in Regent's Park, 'breathing in God's clean air'. Why was the pill bitter, and why wouldn't she let Madame Vera put sugar on it? 'I shan't budge till you tell me.'

My mother glowered at me. 'The bitter pill is the bitter pill that woman, that soi-disant dance teacher gave me today, which she tried to sugar-coat by kissing my daughter.'

But when did Madame Vera give Mummy the bitter pill? Was it in a bottle, or was it in a packet like the ones Daddy took for his pain? Was it white, or did it have a colour?

'Esther, Esther, Esther, the bitter pill is mine, not yours. It is not in a bottle or a packet. It is not white or black or blue. It is mine alone to swallow, if I can. Mention it once more, Esther, and I shall smack you hard. Even harder. I wish not to hear you mention it.'

She spoke so quietly, so forcefully, that I instantly abandoned the still-mysterious bitter pill. I was accustomed, already, to my mother's shrieks and screams, and could detect an element of contrivance in them: her sudden rages often seemed as manufactured as her displays of charm. I was tempted, but only tempted, to laugh. I wasn't, now. I knew this rage was genuine. I was frightened, that was why.

She relented, seeing me afraid. 'Let us pop into the zoo, Esther. Would you like that?'

'Yes, please.'

'Your beloved tigers will not scare you nearly as much as your own mother.'

(My dream at that age was to live one day in the wild,

11

in Africa, among leopards, lions, tigers and elephants. The jungle of my choice contained neither snakes nor insects, and the river running gently through it was the home of harmless fish alone – it had no sharks; certainly no crocodiles or alligators.)

'Such grace they have,' said my mother, 'and such nobleness.' The two caged animals ignored our admiring gaze. 'Nature has cut them out with everything in the right place.'

I heard the catch in her throat, and saw that she was in tears.

'Don't cry, Mummy. It makes your face all ugly.'

'If I am ugly, you are to blame for it.'

I knew why I was to blame, and said I was sorry.

'You might have been me. The me I wasn't.'

I think I guessed the meaning of her strange admission, for I clutched at her skirt and pushed my head into it and repeated over and over that I was sorry. She threw her arms about my shoulders and we stood together, entwined, as close as we had ever been before and closer by far than we would ever be again.

'Hello there.'

He was standing by my car, which I had parked in a side-street near the hospital.

'Are you waiting for me, Stephen?'

'No. Why should I do that? I just saw you coming along, and I just stopped to say hello.'

'Hello, Stephen.'

'Hello.'

'Thank you for the book.'

'It's yours.'

'Where did you get it?' I pretended to ask the question casually, almost as an afterthought.

'Came my way. It came my way, that's all.'

'But where?'

'On the circuit.'

He had talked of the 'circuit' before – when he'd first come to St Lucy's in search of Tonio. 'Which circuit would that be, Stephen?'

'Just the circuit.'

'Oh, *that* one,' I said. 'How silly of me.'

My lumbering sarcasm went unappreciated. Perhaps he expected me to know which circuit was which. I waited for him to respond. Then, to end the silence, I offered him a lift. 'I'm going west, Stephen. Can I drop you somewhere?'

'No. I'm going south. I'll walk.'

'Good exercise,' I remarked, inanely.

'You've not noticed, have you?'

'Noticed? What haven't I noticed?'

'That I'm not dressed flash.'

'No, you're not. You're very – what shall I say? – very *sober*.'

'Sober's better than flash, is it?'

'No – no, not necessarily.'

'I could tell you hated me in blue. I made you blink, didn't I? I hurt your eyes.' He smiled, but only to himself. 'I put it on for him, for Tonio. I wore it to the church. Blue was Tonio's favourite colour.'

'Oh, Sammy, please write to me – ' There I was again, on my way to Chiswick that night, saying aloud what I've been saying aloud, involuntarily, for the last six years. The absurd request arrives on my tongue and makes itself heard whenever I'm distracted, and always – so far – when I'm alone.

How can Sammy write to me? He's dead. He's been cremated.

The first time the phrase came out, I was startled into laughter. The second time, I wept. *En route* to Gabriel, hearing myself say it for the hundredth time, I felt nothing more than irritation. 'Shut up, you fool, shut up, shut up, shut up,' I shouted, actually shouted, and banged my fist on the steering wheel.

The Sammy who still speaks to me, in dreams, is not the

charmer, the enchanter, who used to tease me with his 'golden sceptre' and call me Hadassah; who used to enquire after the health of my Uncle Mordecai, the son of Jair, the son of Shimei, the son of Kish; who used to make me glad to be alive. The Sammy I meet in sleep talks of pricks and cunts, and invites me to describe them for him, and curses me when I refuse.

There is a large oil painting in the main entrance hall of the hospital. It depicts the martyrdom – the imminent martyrdom – of the then unsainted Lucy at the hands of Diocletian's soldiers. She is wearing a virgin's white robe and a look of pert serenity as she awaits her death in front of the imposing column the Victorian artist, Sir Lawrence Cowell, has designed for her.

Few of the hospital's patients and visitors stop to admire Sir Lawrence's *Lucia Braves the Roman Foe at Syracuse*, though I once heard an elderly woman comment on the beauty of its gilt frame. The about-to-be-speared Lucy goes mostly unregarded by those in pain themselves. So I was mildly surprised to see that someone had stopped before the picture, and that the someone was Stephen.

I asked him what he thought of it.

'She's clean. She's like a nurse.'

'She's pure, Stephen.'

'She's stupid, really.'

'Why?'

'Because any minute now she'll be killed and she's near to smiling.'

'Her mind's on God, Stephen. Their swords and spears don't frighten her. She's a holy woman.'

'The Bishop said he was holy.'

'I beg your pardon?'

'The Bishop. The Bish. I said he said he was holy.'

'I'm afraid I can't follow you – '

'Just as well.'

'You're friends with a bishop, are you, Stephen?'

'Maybe.'

14

'How did you meet him?'

He turned from the painting and looked at me. 'That's not allowed,' he said. 'You're not allowed to ask me that.'

I refrained from reminding him that it was he who had mentioned the Bishop a minute earlier. 'I must go now. I have work to do.'

'Wait.' He brought something out of the pocket of the mustard-coloured cardigan he was wearing and handed it to me with the words, 'You can have this if you want it.'

'Another present, Stephen?'

'It's yours.'

His second gift was as bizarre as his first: a silver tea spoon, bearing a family crest on its handle.

I wondered to myself where it had come from. At some stop on the circuit, no doubt. 'Thank you. Thank you, Stephen.'

I put the spoon next to VOL. IX in the drawer of a filing cabinet in my office at the clinic. My loot, I thought; my booty.

'Ungainly as you are, Esther, you will kill your patients with your clumsiness.'

'How, Mummy?'

'Doctors are not awkward. They have hands that can be trusted. They must perform delicate operations with their knives.'

I was thirteen when I revealed my ambition to become a doctor. My mother scoffed, but my father advised me to delay making a firm decision until I was more mature: 'You might want to be a physicist or a lawyer or even an engineer when you're older.'

'Her ideas are already enough peculiar, Adam, without you giving her encouragement.'

'Her ideas are peculiar because they are her own.'

'She likes to forget that she is a girl child. This talk of doctors and engineers is bad for her. She will lose her female feelings.'

My mother slammed the living-room door behind her, to my father's obvious delight. 'That was a gem,' he said, taking his little notebook from the cigar box on his desk. 'We have heard one of your mother's finest tonight. "She will lose her female feelings." Sublime. There – it's recorded for posterity. Please promise me, Esther, that you won't lose your female feelings.'

'I promise, Daddy.'

He hugged and kissed me, and wished me the sweetest female dreams.

He was sitting on the steps leading up to the clinic at eight in the morning.

'Hello, Steve.'

'What did you call me?'

'Steve. It's a bit friendlier than Stephen.'

'I don't allow it. I'm Stephen to you and nothing else. What you just called me's common.'

'As you please, Stephen.'

(I was to learn that when Stephen was David, 'Dave' was not allowed; when he was Andrew, 'Andy' wasn't; and that when he became Richard, 'Dick' and 'Ricky' weren't allowed either.)

'You may think it's friendlier. Myself, I think it's – it's *forward*.'

'What about Tonio?'

'What about him?'

'Well, his name was Anthony, Stephen.'

'Not for me. It was Tonio for me. Understand?'

'I suppose so.'

'There's a difference.'

I did not ask him what that difference was.

'I've got something for you,' he announced. He stood up, and looked about him. Then he unzipped his green blouson, from which he produced, furtively, a small bust of Mozart.

'I don't know who he is, except he's old.'

'This is Mozart, Stephen. A famous composer. Austrian.'

'He's yours.'

But why? Why? 'Thanks again.'

'He'll keep you company.'

16

'Yes.'

'I'll leave you now.'

'Are you going to work?'

'Me? No. Work's done. I work nights. Days I'm free.'

'I work nights': once upon a time, in those far-off days before the awful acronym, I rarely had to work after six or seven in the evening. That was the beauty of venereology – you saw, and could treat, your patients in the mornings and afternoons. Except for the odd, extreme case, they took their diseases home with them. I never had to walk the wards, or sit at a bedside. My nights were my own, then.

And all courtesy of Alexander Fleming and his discovery of penicillin. 'You've been spared many nastier sights, thanks to him,' my teacher and mentor, Max Partridge, liked reminding me. 'The sores, the lesions, the missing noses. Thirty years ago, in my hot youth when George V was King, we were still treating some terrifying leftovers from the age of mercury.'

(How I miss you, Max: you and your 'happy hand'. I recall now, happily, the afternoon you made your 'shocking admission': 'Count yourself honoured, Esther. You're the first woman to hear my sorry tale.' I heard it over several glasses of Retsina, the wine I had temporarily forgotten I loathe, in a Greek restaurant you favoured for its waiters, two of whom – the swarthy Minos and the simian Petros – you had recruited for your 'Dionysian repertory company of the mind'. I should have been depressed by what you told me that day, should have felt downcast, for it was indeed the 'sorry tale' you'd promised. Yet when we left, I knew that my affection for you had deepened and broadened beyond measure.)

I might have cured Anthony Innocent of syphilis or gonorrhoea, once. In the golden age of penicillin.

*   *   *

17

On bright mornings, when there's no sign of rain, I sometimes walk to the hospital from Gabriel's house by the Thames. My route takes me through a little park, where I usually see at least one solitary magpie. I always salute it and wish it a loud and brisk 'Good morning', to fend off sorrow. This ridiculous custom was passed on to me by my mother. I find I cannot break myself of it, intelligent as I am.

It was on a magpie morning that I next met the boy whose name I was not allowed to abbreviate. He was on the steps of the clinic, again. He was wearing a dinner jacket with a velvet collar.

'Have you been enjoying a night on the town, Stephen?'

'Me? Why?'

'You're dressed for some grand party, or a ball.'

(Half-dressed, actually: an orange T-shirt, bleached jeans and suede boots completed his outfit.)

'Party? Ball? No, not me.'

'It must have cost you a lot of money.'

'What must have?'

'Your jacket. It's very smart. Very elegant.'

'It cost. Just say it cost.'

'Strange to see one so early in the day.' And stranger still, I said to myself, to see one on *you*, of all people.

'You don't think I look right in it, do you?'

'Yes,' I lied. 'Of course you look right.'

'Not my style, is it? Not my scene, really.'

'Yes, yes. I think you look – interesting, fetching.'

'What about different?'

'Definitely, Stephen.'

'I try to be different.'

'You succeed.'

'I mean, not just odd. Not just funny. I mean, different.'

'That's you.'

He stared at me. Then: 'I've got something you'll like.'

'Another of your presents?'

'Yes. Here.'

He had wrapped his gift this time, in pink tissue paper. I did not ask him where he'd acquired, or bought, a musical box that

18

played the opening bars of the waltz from *The Merry Widow*, since I could now anticipate his circuitous answer. I thanked him, and insisted that this must be the last of his presents.

'Why?'

'Well, Stephen, it's not as if we're close friends.'

'Doesn't matter. Doesn't apply. Right?'

(What was happening to me? What was I on the verge of saying?)

'Would you allow me to treat you to a meal one day?'

'If you want.'

'Are you free for lunch tomorrow?'

'Could be.'

'I'll meet you here then, Stephen, shortly before one o'clock. Try not to be late.'

It isn't often that love is mentioned in the clinic. Sores and chancres and pus seem unlikely manifestations of the affections. I write 'seem', for I am not to know what depths or shallows of feeling, what expressions of devotion or indifference, preceded their arrival. But today a patient spoke of love, in a voice marked by regret and bewilderment.

'She kept me waiting, Doctor. She said she wanted to put me to the test. She couldn't respect me, she said, while I was sighing and swooning around her in my silly love-sick way. I was to prove my seriousness, she said. She'd had enough, she said, of pretend-men. That was her phrase, Doctor: "pretend-men".'

'And you were one of them?'

'I was, I was. Until three weeks ago, I was. Then everything changed. She said I could stay the night with her. In the same bed, Doctor. After eleven months. That's almost a year.'

'Yes, I believe it is.'

'Even so, I wasn't to presume, she said, that she was inviting me in to take liberties. I needn't think I could go too far. I was to stop at – well, you know, Doctor, I don't have to explain. I told her I was content simply to lie with her, to hold her in my arms, to be naked with her for the first time. And I *was* content. I was.'

'What's her name?'

'Barbara.'

'Is Barbara the only girl you've had sex with?'

'Barbara is the only *woman* I have *loved*.' I started at the sudden vehemence of his response.

'I stand doubly corrected. There really has been no one else?'

'No, Doctor. Of course there hasn't.'

I believed him.

'She took my virginity, and gave me – ' He thought about what she had given him. 'She gave me *this*.'

'It's not so bad. It's curable.'

He shook his head. 'I know it is. You'll clean it up with penicillin. But you can't cure what she's done to me, Doctor. No one can.'

(I thought of my life with Sammy, and kept silent. That life was over, was done with. But was I 'cured' of it? Not totally. Not yet.)

'I'm afraid you're right,' I said at last.

'I never ever even began to think she would do *this* to me.'

'*This*, I have to say, usually comes as a surprise. Nobody anticipates catching gonorrhoea or syphilis, or any other similar disease.'

'I had such trust in her, such faith. I didn't even ever *begin* to doubt or distrust her.'

'Why should you have? Love's not to do with doubting people.'

'Barbara least of all, Doctor. She least of all. She made me want to better myself. To be worthy of her.'

(In a day or so, perhaps, I would be communing with this pedestalled creature; breathing Barbara's finer air. Perhaps.)

'When you next speak to Barbara – '

'Speak to her, Doctor?'

'I assume you'll be speaking to her. You love her, after all. She needs curing, too.'

He stared at me. I waited.

'I'm not sure I want to speak to her. Not now, anyway. I might call her terrible names.'

'She must be told she has gonorrhoea.' I added, gently, 'She could infect someone else.'

'Let her. Let her.'

'No, no. She might have something worse. It's a possibility.'

'I'll phone her, then.'

'Do.'

The young man left, and I remembered what Max said to me on the morning I became his doting assistant: 'If you hear the word "love" once in your working lifetime, you'll be lucky, Esther.'

Well, I was lucky, I suppose, today.

Stephen was punctual, as he was quick to remind me. 'You said *before* one, and not to be late. It's you who's late.'

'Yes, I'm sorry. I've had a hectic morning. Shall we be on our way?'

'I don't mind.'

'It isn't far. The restaurant's within walking distance. I ought to have asked you yesterday what kind of food you like.'

'Me? Bread, cheese – I don't care.'

'I can offer you something more exotic than bread and cheese, I hope.'

'I don't mind. I don't care. As I say.'

'I thought you might be honouring me with your dinner jacket.'

'My – ? The black coat, is it you mean?'

'Yes.'

'Didn't fancy it today. Doesn't go with my – ' He began to giggle. 'With my – '

'Why are you laughing, Stephen? With your – what were you going to tell me?'

'*En-sem-ble*. Doesn't go with my *ensemble*.' He was hooting now. 'Not black. Not with my *ensemble*.'

When his laughter had subsided, I invited him to share the joke with me.

'I can't allow that.'

'It's private, is it?'

21

'Yeah. Private.'

'It must be a very good joke.'

'Maybe.'

'You're still smiling.'

'Suppose I am.'

(As we walked on, in silence, I marvelled at the peculiar situation in which I found myself. Why was I befriending this boy? What did he want of me, and what could I do for him? I should have to wait, I decided, and discover.)

We resumed our conversation, if so it can be described, once we were seated at a table by the window in Les Deux Canards.

'I'm going to drink some wine, Stephen. I've finished work for today. Will you join me?'

'Wine? No.'

'Would you prefer beer?'

'No. I wouldn't. They lose their brains, not me.'

'Who are they, Stephen?'

'Wine drinkers. Beer drinkers. Drinkers.'

'Do you never touch alcohol?'

'No. Never. Just one time I did. Now it's not allowed.' He tapped his forehead with a finger. 'I look after my brain. I keep it clean.'

'Oh dear, Stephen, you're making me feel very wicked and very silly. But I do enjoy good wine, I must confess.'

'You enjoy what you want.'

'Even though my husband drank himself to death.'

(There: the unspeakable was being spoken – ordinarily, casually, as a matter of fact.)

'Why did he?'

'I've no idea. And I don't think he had.'

'He let himself lose his brain. Was that it?'

'It's one diagnosis. I suppose he did.'

'Stupid.'

The waiter came to take our order. Would Stephen care to try snails? No, no. What about smoked salmon, smoked eel? No. Pâté? No. An artichoke? No. Soup, then? Carrot soup?

22

'Just tomatoes.'

'Tomatoes, sir?'

'I think my friend would like a tomato salad. With basil, perhaps, and onions.'

'No onions,' said Stephen. 'Don't require onions.'

Veal and beef and lamb and chicken were not required either. A large bowl of tomatoes was all he wanted. And water.

'Do you always eat so frugally?'

'What's frugally?'

'Well, so little.'

'I asked him for a lot of tomatoes. That's not frugally.'

'You seem to be in a red mood today. Have you chosen tomatoes because they match your clothes?'

He looked at me and smiled briefly. 'Yes,' he replied after a pause. 'Yes. Because. Because I'm different.'

'What do you eat when you're wearing green?'

'Cabbages. Peas. Grapes.'

'And yellow?'

He thought for a minute. 'Squash.'

'Here's to you, Stephen,' I said, raising my glass of Sancerre. He responded with a nod. 'Your health.'

'My health's OK. My health's fine.'

'I'm sure it is.'

'Don't you worry about my health. I won't go where Tonio went.'

'No, Stephen. Of course you won't.'

'Tonio stumbled.'

'Stumbled?'

'Yes, and you're not allowed to ask me why. Understood?'

'Understood.'

'Just as well.'

'Since we're on the subject of Tonio, I've solved the mystery of his name. Or rather, one of my colleagues has. He was of Italian origin.'

'I know he was Italian.'

'Do you remember telling me he called himself "Daily Something"?'

'Maybe.'

23

'"Daily Something" is degl' Innocenti – I can't pronounce it perfectly – which means "of the Innocents". There's a hospital in Florence, in Italy, which used to be for foundlings – '

'What's foundlings?'

'Unwanted babies.'

'Bastards?'

'Some of them. Probably. Definitely. Anyway, Stephen, the unwanted babies who were brought to the hospital had to be given names – like Anthony degl' Innocenti, for instance. There were thousands of "of the Innocents", all named after the hospital. Anthony's family must have changed it to "Innocent" a long time ago, when they emigrated here. It was more convenient, and easier for English people to say.'

'I'm a bastard.'

'Are you, Stephen?'

'I said.'

'There's no stigma attached now.'

'What's stigma?'

'Stigma? It's when a person is made to feel ashamed, and looks as if he's bearing a mark. Oh, it's difficult to explain. Not a real mark. It's inside him.'

'I don't have a stigma. If that's what you say it is.'

'I'm glad to hear it.'

He finished eating his tomatoes, I my *poulet à l'estragon*. And then, at the end of the meal, he hooted again, almost uncontrollably, as he chose a ripe nectarine from the dish of fresh fruit the waiter set before us.

The nurse looked at me contemptuously. 'You're not married, Mrs Potocki? Is that sensible?'

'No, I'm not married. Not any more.'

'It isn't for me to say, but I think you ought to be.'

'It certainly isn't for you to say, even if you do think I ought to be.'

'I speak my mind, Mrs Potocki. I speak as a Christian.'

'I gathered.'

'I hope you know who the father is.'

'And I hope you're testing my blood pressure,' I said. 'That's what you're supposed to be doing.'

(Sometimes my calmness alarms me. '*Mrs* Potocki'; 'I hope you know who the father is': why didn't I respond – loudly, angrily – to the priggish nurse's determined insults? I could have snapped back at her that I had been her sensible woman once, married to an increasingly insensible husband, and had decided – not too late in life – never to be sensible again. I could have pulled rank, and made the smug bitch squirm. Instead, I chose to play at appearing indifferent, and to suppress my boiling rage.)

'A child needs a father as well as a mother.'

'Our child will have a father as well as a mother.'

'But not united in holy matrimony.'

'Correct.'

'Which is sinful, Mrs Potocki.'

'Which is fine by me, Nurse Sullivan.'

'The world didn't used to be like this,' declared my examiner, from the wisdom of her thirty, at most, years.

'You forgot to lock the car.' Stephen was in the driver's seat. 'I'm guarding it for you.'

'I can't believe it.'

'Here's your keys,' he said, handing them out to me. 'Now you can believe it.'

'I'll have to. This is the very, very first time it's happened.'

'I believe you.'

'Thanks. How long have you been sitting there?'

'Me? Hours, I'd say. Hours and hours and hours.'

'I'm sorry, Stephen. But grateful.'

'Twenty minutes. That's how long. Just twenty minutes.'

'Thanks, anyway.'

'Lucky for you I'm not a thief.' He smiled. 'Anybody else might have rode it away.'

'Yes, I *am* lucky you came to see me, and waited.'

'I didn't come to see you. I was just passing. I had my eyes open. I saw you'd lost your brain. So I waited.'

'Well, if I lost my brain, it was only for a moment. We're all forgetful when we're – ' I stopped, to light upon the apt false word. 'When we're confused.'

('Confused' – yes, 'confused' hinted at my state of forgetfulness; 'confused' would satisfy what little curiosity my unlikely new friend possessed. The truth was that I had been happy that morning, happy in the delirious sense that comes with sexual fulfilment. The confusion of happiness had caused me to forget to lock the car, to leave the key in the ignition.)

'Even you must feel confused every now and then, Stephen.'

'No. Not me. I have to be a step ahead.'

'A step ahead of what?'

'I'm not allowed to tell you.'

'So I'm not allowed to ask?'

'Right. You can give me a lift today. If you want to.'

'Of course I want to.' He shifted into the front seat as I got in. 'Where would you like me to drop you off?'

'Belgrave Square.'

'My word, that's an extremely smart address.'

'Too smart for me?'

'No, I didn't mean to imply that.'

'Doesn't worry me. I'm meeting a business contact. Money, money.' He rubbed his hands together, and laughed. 'Is my ensemble OK for Belgrave Square?'

'Your clothes?'

'Naturally. Do you think they – ' He paused. 'Pass muster?' He laughed again.

'Yes, I do.' He wore a brown tweed jacket, a white shirt open at the neck, fawn corduroy trousers. Only his two-toned shoes – part blue, part grey – looked incongruous. 'They'll pass muster.'

'Good enough for a room with a chandelier? In your opinion?'

'In my opinion, yes.'

'Am I fetching?'

'You do want a lot of compliments. Yes, Stephen, you're fetching.'

'I learned "fetching" from you. And "frugally", and "stigma", and "foundlings".'

26

'I hadn't realised I was your teacher.'

'I pick up things.' He sniggered. 'I store them up top.' He tapped his forehead with a finger. 'Things I hear about the place.'

'Call me Esther, Stephen,' I heard myself say.

'I can't allow any of that. Leastways, not for now.'

'One day soon, perhaps?'

'I said I can't allow it. Not yet. When I can, I will. Understand?'

'I understand.'

I dropped him at a corner of the square, in West Halkin Street. I promised to drive straight on, and not to notice the number of the house in which he was meeting his business contact.

After my father's death, my mother briefly relished her new role of Widow. Now that he was removed from her, she could declare herself Countess as often as she wished. So it was the Countess who mourned the Count, and the Countess who invited her few friends to the apartment after the Count's funeral, to share her, the Countess's, grief.

She was too distraught, far too distraught, to cope with merely practical matters. Her daughter, studying to become a certain kind of doctor, had her feet – which were not *cut out*, alas, for the ballet – firmly on the ground. Esther was the complete organiser, and almost a dreadful bully to her poor Mama, who was stricken, but stricken, by the Count's sudden, unexpected passing. 'Esther has arranged everything for me during these too horrible days. She has the strong shoulders for both of us. She is a deep well where her emotions are concerned.'

The deep well with the strong shoulders was asked one day if she would be a saint and look through her Tata's papers. 'I have not the heart or the strength or the energy, Esther. I have not the understanding, either, of all those old sums and figures of Adam's, all those old bills and legal documents. You will sort them out for me, won't you, please?'

I said I'd try, though I doubted that there would be much

27

sorting out to do, since Tata was meticulous in his dealings. Wouldn't Martin Lamb, his partner in the firm, be better suited to the task? 'No, Esther. There might be private stuff there, not for other eyes. I want no snoopers and snooping.'

I sat on the floor of my father's study with his box-files around me. Hours later, having examined the dull contents of six of them, I had almost decided not to bother with the remaining twelve when I opened an envelope containing several snapshots of a naked woman. She was not Maria Potocka, his wife, my mother – that much I could discern through the haze in which the inexpert photographer had captured her. With the aid of a magnifying glass, the stern or smiling face became recognisable, familiar to me. It was Wanda Stone, one of the few friends who constituted my mother's 'chosen circle', I was looking at – the same Wanda who had been the first to comfort her in her loss; who had suggested that they go on a Mediterranean cruise together, once the pain was no longer raw; who loved Maria 'like a sister'. Here was Wanda as I'd never expected to see her, and here was Wanda's vagina, which I'd never expected to see, either; certainly not in such detail.

'Daddy,' I said. 'Tata.'

In the seventh box there was another envelope and yet more photographs, but of another naked woman. It was Serena Johnson, one of my mother's former confidantes, I recognised now. My father had persuaded her to pose in the open air, in a field, against a tractor. In some of the snaps, she had a straw in her mouth. Her vagina, like Wanda Stone's, was shown in close-up.

'Oh, Daddy.'

A third friend of my mother, Eva Ashworth, whom I had always considered extremely frigid, was revealed as a cocotte in the series of photographic studies my father – I assumed it was my father – had made of her. Eva wore shiny black leather boots and nothing else as she straddled a motor bike (a motor bike! Whose?) for his delectation. What charm had he employed, what skill at cajoling, to get the prissy Eva to offer her breasts so provocatively?

'Tata.'

No, no, I thought: I shan't discover an uncovered Antoinette Hilton; not the grand, the imperious Antoinette. Truth to tell, Daddy had been intimidated by her, by the aloofness she wore with her pearls and gowns and furs. But now her 'ridiculous armour' was discarded – everything except her sneer and her jewellery – on the marble staircase of some palatial house. The setting was appropriate, at least.

'Oh, Tata, you dirty old man.'

Three other women, all known to me, had divested themselves for Daddy. I was surrounded by them now – by Wanda, by Serena, by Antoinette, by Helen Nash, by Caroline Forrest and Joanna Lamb; by my mother's entire 'chosen circle'. Their every vulva was mine to inspect. With the thought came laughter, my own liberating, shrieking laughter, which became, even as I enjoyed the strange sound of it, hysterical weeping.

'Esther, what is the matter with you?' my mother asked from the hall.

I knew panic then, and stopped howling. Had I locked the study door? I'd had no reason to. 'I'm all right,' I answered. 'Don't bother to come in. I shall be finished in five minutes.'

'Have you found something that's upset you?'

'Of course not. There's nothing upsetting. Only a lot of bills and invoices and dry old papers. Nothing upsetting, Mama.'

'But you were crying. You were more than crying, Esther.'

'I know. I was letting go of my feelings, Mama. Give me a moment or so by myself.'

In that moment or so, I gathered up the photographs and shoved them into my briefcase. I would burn them later, at the hospital.

A week passed before I saw Stephen again, on the steps outside the clinic, in the morning.

'I was getting worried about you,' I said.

'Me? Worried? Why?'

'I wondered if you'd met with an accident.'

'Me? Accident? Not possible. I have to be a step ahead. That's my rule.'

29

'I missed you. I missed our' – What had I missed? – 'our little chats.'

'I've been busy. On the move. Here and there.'

'On the circuit?' I asked, thinking I might learn at last what the circuit was.

He stared at me, and smiled. 'Yeah. On the circuit. On the good old circuit.'

'What exactly *is* the circuit, Stephen?'

'That's not allowed. I can't allow your question.'

'You make it sound very clandestine.'

'What's clandestine?'

'Oh, like a secret. Underhand.'

'Then it's clandestine, the circuit is. It's very clandestine. I'd say it's very, very clandestine, in my opinion.'

'You seem to enjoy mystery.'

'Me? Enjoy mystery? Yes and no. I've got to enjoy it. Haven't much choice, Doctor Lady.'

'Esther.'

'No, you're Doctor Lady. Till I feel different. Right?'

'Right, Stephen.'

'How's my ensemble today? Fetching?'

'As always.'

'Apart from the once, Doctor Lady.'

His ensemble, that Friday, was drab compared to his earlier ensembles. There was nothing incongruous or unusual to catch the eye.

'Am I sober enough?'

'Absolutely.'

'I've brought you something. It's yours, Doctor Lady, if you want it.'

'Stephen, don't you remember my saying that you must stop giving me presents?'

'I remember. And I remember telling you it doesn't apply. Remember? I haven't lost my brain.'

'No more after this. Please.'

'Put your hand out.'

I did so, and received a china strawberry. I thanked him, and said, truthfully, that it was the prettiest of his gifts.

'Don't try and eat it, Doctor Lady.'

'I shan't, I promise.'

'You can eat sausages.' He giggled. 'And nectarines.' By now he was overcome with laughter. 'But not both at once.'

Barbara, minus her pedestal, came to the clinic this afternoon. I wasn't aware that I was confronting a goddess until she handed me the contact slip I had written out for her doting lover. 'He told me he saw you last week,' she said, in a timid little voice. 'I hope it's nothing really serious.'

'I hope so, too.'

She's a mouse, I thought. His Aphrodite, his Helen of Troy's a mouse, a London mouse with nicotine-stained fingers. This, this is that very Barbara who loathes what she calls 'pretend-men'.

I learned later, after the diagnosis of gonorrhoea was confirmed, that it was the other man in her life who had infected her. It seems he possesses every quality her poor worshipper lacks – except, of course, complete faithfulness.

'He's in Spain at the moment. He goes there regularly. He tastes and buys Spanish wines. He's proud of his palate.'

(As, for a time, was Sammy: he was proud of his palate, too. He was discerning, then. I loved him for his pride, for his confidence, for his boundless knowledge of the Old Testament. I loved him for his dark beauty, above all; for those brown eyes that turned suddenly black. I would have said as much to strangers.)

'Please ask him to visit us when he returns.'

'Yes. He may have seen someone already, in Madrid. There's a place like this in Madrid, isn't there?'

'I'm sure there is.'

'There has to be, if you think about it. I mean to say, what I've got, what Jason's given me, isn't confined to England, is it?'

'That's right.'

'Having to come here, having to be looked at, having to – well, it's made me talk stupid, the experience.'

'I know.'

'I'm not the brazen type, Doctor.'

31

'I meet enough of the brazen ones, believe me.'

'Honest?'

'Honestly. Yes, honest.'

'I thought you were a night-worker, Stephen.'

'Me? I am.'

'But it's after eleven.'

'I know what the time is, Doctor Lady.'

'The car's locked, isn't it?'

'Seems to be.'

'I assume that you aren't waiting for me, that you were just passing by?'

'Yeah. Just passing by.'

'There's a coincidence,' I said. 'A chance in a million.'

'That's right, Doctor Lady. Coincidence. Funny, eh?'

'Now that you're here, may I act as your chauffeur?'

'You may. You can be. My chauffeur.'

He got in beside me.

'The chauffeur's usually alone in the front, while the rich man sits in comfort in the back.'

'This rich man's different.'

'Ah, yes. I'd forgotten.'

'Don't lose your brain, Doctor Lady.'

'A momentary lapse, Stephen. Where to? Belgrave Square again?'

'No. Done my business in Belgrave Square.' He laughed. 'Object achieved.'

'Where, then?'

'Wherever it is you're going, I'll come too, Doctor Lady.'

'I live in Bayswater, Stephen.'

'That's all right. Anywhere's all right.'

I invited him to give me his address and said I'd take him there, if it wasn't too far away, and he responded in his now oh so familiar manner, but with a variation: his address wasn't *allowable*.

'You do have a place to live, don't you?'

'Me? Yes.'

32

'But you'd prefer to keep its whereabouts a secret?'

'Correct, Doctor Lady. Clandestine's the word.'

'You're a good student.'

'Me? I used to be. Before.'

'Before?'

'Before, before, before – before I came down to London, Doctor Lady. Before things happened you are definitely not allowed to know about.'

'I have an imagination, Stephen. I can guess what things.'

'Oh, no, you can't, Doctor Lady. You couldn't guess the Bish, not in a million years you couldn't guess *him*.' He giggled. 'Him and his *ensemble*.'

I conceded defeat, I said, in the case of the Bish, whom I took to be the bishop he had referred to on the day we had met in front of the picture of Saint Lucy. Yes, he was right: I couldn't guess or imagine what role he had played in Stephen's life.

'Though I should love to know.'

'I bet you would.'

'Perhaps you'll tell me. In your own time.'

'Perhaps I will, and perhaps I won't.'

I was tempted, I remember, to ask him what he wanted of me, exactly; why he kept – coincidentally – waiting for the Doctor Lady who hadn't even treated him. Yes, I was tempted; and fearful, too, of his answer, which might not have been circuitous.

The temptation remained a temptation, as it still does. In the hundreds of words that poured out of him, later, there are only the faintest clues to what he wanted of me, or of Gabriel.

'I have a beautiful surprise for you, Esther. She is in the drawing-room, where she has already taken pride of place.'

'She' was Anna Pavlova, bought with a few of the many thousands of pounds my father had left my mother. She was made entirely of glass, and was almost life-size. The artist, a Venetian admirer, had worked in three colours: pale-blue for the dancer's head and body, pink for her tutu, and gold for her ballet shoes.

'Isn't she quite wonderful?'

'Yes, Mama.'

'She is the original, nothing less. The dealer told me there have been plenty of copies – much smaller, of course – but this is the very one the sculptor created.'

'I'm not sure that glass is sculpted. Isn't it shaped?'

'The man in the gallery called him a sculptor, not a shaper. I don't care, frankly, how she happened. She is quite wonderful and beautiful to me. To me, Esther.'

'Yes, Mama.'

'To me she seems to move. It's the way the sculptor, the person, has captured her. Look at her arms, look at her feet – she is as light as air itself.'

'Yes, Mama.'

'Is "Yes, Mama" all you can say, Esther? Are you blind to her beauty?'

I should have lied, but didn't. 'Yes, I suppose I am,' I answered.

She spoke again after a long silence. 'You are beyond me, Esther. I swear to God above, you are beyond me.'

Which is where I have stayed.

When Stephen and I met again, it was at our customary time. He was dressed sunnily – yellow T-shirt, orange trousers – for what promised to be a hot, sunny day.

'Did you get home safely the other night?'

'Me? Home? Yeah.'

'You could have slept in my spare bed.'

'That's not allowed, Doctor Lady. Not yet.'

'As you wish.'

'I do. I do wish.'

'You're looking happier than I've ever seen you.'

'Me? I'm in a good mood, Doctor Lady. On top of the world.'

'Why's that?'

'I just am. No reason.' He smiled at me – openly, warmly. 'I've brought you a present. A useful one.'

34

It was a china egg-cup, in the form of a broody hen.

'Thanks.'

'I must love you and leave you, Doctor Lady. I have important people to see.' He added, with a grin, 'On the circuit.'

I never told my mother that her husband was a secret photographer. I think I was protecting his reputation rather than her feelings. She had found enough cause to despise him.

'I can't understand why your beloved Tata was so ashamed of his title.'

'He wasn't ashamed, Mama. He considered it irrelevant and out of date.'

'Out of date? Is that what you heard from the old horse's mouth? Why should being noble be out of date?'

It wasn't being noble, it was being *a* noble, that offended him, I attempted to explain. Didn't she appreciate the distinction?

'No, Esther, I do not. Adam Potocki was a count because his father was a count, as was his father's father before him. He had centuries of noble blood in his veins, which he – which he turned his back upon.'

'Blood isn't noble, Mama. Blood is blood.'

'You speak as a doctor – I have to lie to my friends when they ask what kind of doctor you are – but I speak and know better than you.'

I said nothing.

'You are doing as he did, turning your back on your noble blood by working with lepers – '

'Not lepers, Mama.'

'With wicked people, then.'

'Not wicked, either.'

'With the scum of the earth, Esther, the scum of the earth.'

'Calm down, Mama, and listen. Kings and princes, lords and ladies, men and women with the noblest of noble blood, have caught the diseases I treat. I can give you names.'

'You can spare me your so-called names.'

'They exist.'

'There is a bad apple in every barrel, however noble,' she observed, leaving the room on an exit line my father, the lapsed count, would have committed to his little book, and cherished.

'Have your ears been burning, Stephen?'

'Me? Ears burning? You losing your brain, Doctor Lady?'

'It's an expression. It means that someone is talking about you. And someone *has* been talking about you. About us, as a matter of fact.'

'Us? Me and you?'

'That's us. One of the housemen here saw us lunching together and asked me if I'd become a cradle-snatcher.'

'You mean, like I'm the baby?'

'Yes, Stephen. He wanted to know what I was doing with a handsome young black.'

'That's not allowed,' he shouted. 'Black's not allowed. I don't, I *do not*, allow black.'

'But, Stephen, you are — '

'I'm not. Look at me, Doctor Lady. Just look at me — will you? Go on — stare. What colour am I?'

'Well — '

'What colour am I?'

'You're — I should say — brown. Yes, brown.'

'Yes, brown. Brown, yes. Make no mistake.'

'I'm sorry, but black seems to be the accepted word.'

'Accepted? I don't accept. When I talk to myself in the mirror in the morning, Doctor Lady, I'm talking to a brown face, not a black. Understand?'

'I understand, Stephen.'

'I am me, and what I am is brown.'

'Of course, Stephen.'

'Of course, of course. Just remember, Doctor Lady.'

'I shall.'

'I'm going to show you something.' He opened his shirt, which was blue that day. 'See this?' He pointed to a small circle of white skin on his chest. 'That's my white bit. That's the bit of me that tickled the Bish.'

Before we parted, he handed me my present — a marble paperweight, in the shape of a seashell.

No sooner had I decided to study venereology than I fell in love with a Jew. 'Esther, you will kill Maria with this second fall from grace,' said my father, holding me to him and kissing my forehead. 'The clap and the pox are bad enough, but the prospect of having a son of Zion in the family will surely induce a spasm, at the very least. We must tread warily. We must break the dire news to her by gentle degrees — a hint here, a hint there — until she realises that it isn't so dire after all.'

'Mother enjoys the taste of a bitter pill, Tata. She doesn't like it sugared.'

'Is that one of her sayings? It sounds as if it might be.'

'Yes, I think it is.'

'I will personally sugar this particular pill for her. I will sweeten Maria's tooth, I promise.'

He died before the sweetening was accomplished — of a heart attack, swiftly, in Fulham Road. Then, for a very short time, for the period of her immediate widowhood, my mother did not mention her daughter's interest in 'itches and spots' and the young man with the 'too pronounced nose'. The 'deep well' with 'strong shoulders' was useful to her, and while I was of use I was not to be offended — she recognised that much, in her grief.

Her terrible certainties — 'A girl of your blood and upbringing should not be trying to cure scum'; 'You will be marrying far beneath you if you marry this Mr Elkin' — received expression again with the arrival of Anna Pavlova. I visited my mother infrequently now, but whenever I did she geared the conversation towards my, or her husband's, failings. It was as if she had made the glass dancer her conspirator against us, with Pavlova representing all that was light and graceful in an otherwise dark and ugly world.

'It seems that I'm the bad apple in the barrel, Mama.'

'Late as it is, Esther, it is not too late for you to change. It is never too late in the Catholic faith. Your beloved Tata

37

has left you the money to be an independent woman. There is no need for you to work and no need for you to marry. Yet.'

'There is every need, Mama. Tata understood.'

'Then you have chosen the wrong work for you to do and the wrong man for you to wed.'

'I hope not.'

'I fear you have,' she sighed, stroking Anna Pavlova's outstretched arm. 'I so much fear you have.'

Stephen was curled up on a bench in the hospital's entrance hall. I shook him gently. He awoke and stared at me. He mouthed the two words 'Doctor Lady' and rubbed his eyes.

'You can't sleep here, Stephen. It's against the rules. You're not visiting a patient, are you?'

'Me? No.'

'I can offer you a spare bed.'

'Not allowed.'

'Tell me where your home is, and I'll take you there.'

'Not allowed.' He stood up, and yawned. 'My home's my business, Doctor Lady.'

'Good night, then. Or to be absolutely precise, good morning.'

He followed me into the street.

'I'll allow you to drive me, Doctor Lady.'

'That's kind of you.'

'To Bayswater. Like before.'

'Your chauffeur is at your service.'

'I was dreaming,' he said, as soon as we were in the car. 'About the Bish.'

'The mysterious bishop?'

'The very same, Doctor Lady. He was saying, in the dream, how he wasn't a suffragan.'

'A what?'

'Have I spoke a word you don't know, Doctor Lady?'

'I think you have. Say it again.'

'Suffragan. I can spell it, if you want. An "s", a "u", an "f"

38

and an "f", an "r", an "a", a "g", another "a" and an "n".
Suffragan.'

'I've heard it, of course. But I'm not exactly sure of its
meaning,' I lied.

'I'll put you wise, Doctor Lady. Listen carefully, and learn.
Take heed.' He giggled. 'A suffragan, for your information, is
a kind of assistant bish, not a proper one. The Bish I'm talking
about was a proper bishop, not a suffragan. Understand?'

'More or less.'

'He used to tell us he was the genuine article.'

'Us, Stephen?'

'Me and Tonio.'

'Anthony Innocent?'

'Yeah. Tonio. The Bish called Tonio his acolyte. "Where is
my precious acolyte?" he'd ask. "Up to his naughty tricks, I
suppose?" Oh, yes, Doctor Lady – acolyte. I learned a lot of
funny words from the Bish.'

'Unusual, certainly.'

'He'd let Tonio get away with almost anything.'

'I'm lost, Stephen. I'm totally confused.'

'Are you, Doctor Lady? All I said was that the Bish would
let Tonio get away with anything. Why? Because Tonio was his
favourite.'

I was still confused, I said, and would remain so unless he
told me of his and Tonio's friendship with this strange-sounding
bishop from the very beginning. A story has a beginning, a
middle, and an end – and it wasn't fair of him to start his
story in the middle, with no explanation of what had gone
before. That was why I was lost.

'How did you meet your bishop, Stephen?'

'Not allowed to tell you, Doctor Lady. Top secret.'

'Won't you allow yourself to reveal it to me?'

'Top secret. Which means I'm keeping it up top. Where no
one but yours truly can find it.'

He did not sleep in my spare bed that night. He didn't even
come into my flat, although he got as far as the front door,
which I had opened. His face, hitherto impassive, now registered
something like terror as he peered inside. 'I can't, Doctor Lady,'

he said, in a rush. 'Not yet. It's not allowed. Not yet. It really isn't allowed for me. I wish I could, but I can't. I honestly can't. Not yet.'

He backed away from me, turned, and darted down the stairs.

'It was I who chose Esther as our daughter's name, Mr Elkin. I had such a battle over it with my late husband, the Count. He wanted to call her something preposterous, like Beryl or Louise.'

'You chose well. "Esther" fits Esther to perfection.'

'I picked Esther because it was rare, it wasn't common. You were the only Esther at your Catholic school, I believe, Esther.'

'Yes, Mama, I was.'

'I'm not surprised, Countess Potocka.'

'Why are you not surprised, Mr Elkin?'

'You said Esther went to a Catholic school – '

'Naturally. A *Roman* Catholic school. She was raised a Catholic – more by me than by her father, the Count – even if she has decided to turn her back on the faith of her ancestors.'

'You remember who Esther was, Countess?'

'Esther? Which Esther do you mean?'

'Which Esther? You amaze me, Countess. There is only one Esther.'

'Is there? Who is she?'

'Tut, tut, Countess. You haven't forgotten *the* Esther, have you?'

'Mr Elkin, although the name is not common, there must have been hundreds of Esthers in history.'

'True, Countess. But only one of them has survived.'

'Survived? How survived?'

'In human memory, Countess. In literature. Along with Adam and Eve, and Moses, and Jezebel, and Salome, and King David, and King Solomon, and Noah. That's how she's survived.'

'She is a biblical woman, this Esther?'

'I'll say she is. She has a book all to herself. Not a very long one, but a book nonetheless. She comes between Nehemiah and Job.'

'She is Jewish?'

'Oh, yes. She is the great liberator of my people. It was Esther who foiled the plans of the wicked Haman to slaughter the Jews in Persia. We honour her every year at Purim.'

'Where is that, Mr Elkin? In Israel, perhaps?'

'Purim isn't a place, Countess. It's a festival, a holiday.'

'Well, thank you very much for the lesson in old religion. I was brought up, and so was my daughter, with the New Testament. Do I hear the kettle whistling? Would you be an angel and make the tea, Esther?'

'Yes, Mama.'

Sammy joined me in the kitchen.

'My golden sceptre's raring to go, Hadassah. Shall we fuck ourselves senseless tonight, sweetheart?'

'Let's.'

I was convinced that I had seen the last of him. I looked for Stephen each morning on the steps of the clinic, and waited for him each evening before driving off to Chiswick or Bayswater. His terror-stricken face came to me one night in a dream, from which I awoke in a state much like terror.

'Hello there, Doctor Lady.'

I stared at him, as if he were an apparition.

'It's the fetching foundling. Remember? The fetching, *frugal* foundling.'

'Hello, Stephen.'

'How's the world treating you, Doctor Lady?'

'As the world usually does. And you?'

'I'm on top of it. That's where I am.'

'It's good to see you,' I said. 'I approve of your ensemble.'

(He was all of an elegant piece, I remember, in his pale-grey suit, white shirt, green silk tie and dark-brown shoes. This was a prosperous Stephen, in appearance: a young, suave man of means.)

He bowed at me.

'Have you been away, Stephen?'

'Me? Away?'

'It's two weeks since you ran off into the night.'

'Me? Ran off? Not possible, Doctor Lady. That wasn't myself. That was someone else.'

'But, Stephen – '

'Someone else entirely. Someone you thought was myself and wasn't. Someone who lost his brain for a minute. Understand?'

I returned his stare. 'I understand.'

'You're one clever lady, Doctor Lady. Now you can close your eyes and put your hand out.'

'Another present, Stephen?'

'Do as I – ' He hesitated, then smiled. 'Do as I command.'

I did as he commanded.

'Open sesame. That is an order.'

I saw that he had given me opera glasses made of ivory.

'Thank you, Stephen.'

'My pleasure.'

'You've bombarded me with gifts. I really have enough now, Stephen. More than enough.'

'I'll decide when enough's enough. Goodbye, Doctor Lady.'

'Goodbye, Stephen.'

The matron at the nursing home rang me this morning to say that my mother, whom she calls Mrs Potocka, is ill. 'She isn't eating. She is actually refusing food.'

'Is she talking, then, Miss Lavelle?'

'No, no. She shakes her head. She wrinkles her nose up in disgust when the nurses bring her meals. She has gone without lunch, supper and breakfast. We thought you would want to know.'

'Thank you. Has a doctor looked at her?'

'He's with her at this very moment.'

I sat beside her for an unprecedented six hours, playing the faithful, the dutiful daughter. I heard her every tiny cough, and wiped away the sweat as it accumulated on her brow. I watched her in her lively sleep and in her deadly wakefulness.

I was there, showing a concern that others could see. I was by her bed when it mattered. Mine is not one of those mothers – the Matron assures me she has at least four of them in her charge – who has been disposed of, cast conveniently out of sight. 'The only reminders that they have children are the cheques that come once a year to pay for their upkeep. It's guilt money, and it's always on time.'

I sat beside her, wondering yet again if she knew it was me she glanced at and if my presence pleased her. Why should I care if it didn't? I had brought her nothing but disappointment from the day she learned that I was not cut out for the ballet, so it hardly seemed possible for me to please her now. I had turned my back on my noble blood and my female feelings; I had married a Jew who drank too much, and I had worked on behalf of the scum of the earth instead of the pure and decent, dirtying my life through my involvement with the dirtiest parts of their dirty bodies. And I had broken, one terrible Sunday afternoon, her most treasured possession: that solitary emblem of light and grace in a world grown dark and ugly.

Even my schoolfriends displeased her. They weren't pretty. They ought to have been. 'It is a crime to be as plain as Alice is, Esther. And her poor parents have given poor Jane the name she so much deserves, for no one could be plainer.' Alice and Jane were bookish, like me. We were swots. Clothes and make-up interested us, but not to the detriment of our studies. We had ambitions. 'Alice is going to be an archaeologist, is she? She will be happy among old pots and fossils. And what has the so plain Jane decided to do with herself?' Well, Mama – I have often wanted to say to her – Jane became a brilliant actress, whose Juliet – yes, Mama, her Juliet – is already a legend. The critics who wrote of her radiant, youthful beauty were aware that Jane was in her thirties and that she was not, they had to admit respectfully, particularly beautiful. They were all astonished by what she had done to herself, since it amounted to a complete transformation. I wish my mother had witnessed it, as I did: the incredible metamorphosis that was Jane's Juliet.

These were the thoughts that came to me this afternoon, at the start of my vigil. From Alice and Jane, and my mother's silly scorn for them, they turned on the instant to the momentous event of my fourteenth year, when I was ordered to stop using the 'so childish' word 'Mummy' and address her as 'Mama' instead. Did that order signify the end of a certain remaining warmth between us, a warmth my use of 'Mummy' was alone able to convey? I think it did. I know I found 'Mama' restrictive. 'Mama', as I said and heard it, was a verbal straitjacket from which no affection, however slight, could escape.

('Let Maria persist in her Mama nonsense if she must, but you are not to call me Papa, Esther. It belongs in a bygone world, and it sounds stuffy. I shall still be your Tata, which is a nice Polish term of endearment, as well as your Daddy.')

'Mama,' I whispered, seeing her awake. 'Mummy.'

How absurd, how ridiculous it was to be disobeying her. And how daring of me; how brave. With what bitter pleasure I spoke the forbidden word, now that she was beyond chiding me.

'I'm here, Mummy.'

There was no response. I would have been surprised, startled, if she had responded. The tiniest flicker of light in her eyes would have sent a chill through me; would have shattered our dreadful peace of the last decade.

'I'm with you, Mummy.'

In the flesh, at any rate, I told myself, guiltily: in the flesh that contains another life, the life I have made with Gabriel Harvey, whose own Mummy walked out one Wednesday morning and never came back. The gentle man I love waited nearly twenty-eight years for her return – and discovered, when he was forty, that she had killed herself in a seedy hotel in Marylebone, seven weeks after leaving home. She had swallowed bleach. 'I shall pretend it's gin,' she wrote to the husband who was to keep her death a secret, out of misplaced fondness for the son he lectured and bullied and affected to despise.

There were countless occasions during my childhood, and later, when I wanted my mother to disappear – to slam that much-slammed door with one final, resounding slam – and leave Daddy and me to our happy ways. Although he would be deprived of those exit lines he recorded so gleefully in his special little book, we would both be better off without her, I reasoned. She was an obstacle to the pair of us, but particularly to me, whose interest in the human body she deemed morbid. 'The horrible squiggly bits and pieces inside people are not for young girls to know about. You have most peculiar ideas, Esther.'

'I've still got them, Mummy.'

An obstacle, yes; a hindrance: I sat by her bedside today and remembered thinking once that the setting-up of barriers was her keenest diversion. As soon as one was on the verge of collapsing, another would be put in its place, on the inspired spur of the moment. When I dared to ask her why she seldom (my euphemism for 'never') encouraged me, she deflected me from my impertinent course by responding, 'It is not a parent's duty to encourage bad habits. Especially in a daughter. A daughter who is going to walk with a stoop if she refuses to correct her so sloppy deportment.' Two more of her barriers were thus set in position, thanks to my naivety. I ought to have been satisfied with my father's support and approval, which were constant. I should have realised they were enough.

'Oh, Mummy.'

It occurred to me, then, that for all my supposed bad habits I had been in some respects a model child. I was always polite to her, deferential even, and continued to be polite well into the Mama era, when the urge to demolish the Potocka blockade was frequently overwhelming. I kept myself in check. My protest against her values was there in my school work, in the unladylike books I had started to read (the Greek philosophers, Hume and Gibbon, my beloved George Eliot) and the career I had decided upon. There was no reason to be rude to her. That would have been an additional luxury.

'I used to stick up for you, Mummy.'

A girl in my class had the gift of mimicry. She had met my mother at a prizegiving and had 'caught' her on the spot – the stance, the voice, the sweeping gestures. I surprised Monica one day in mid-performance, playing the 'batty snob' in the playground to a group of friends who recognised the object

45

of her derision. I heard Monica say, "'I had dreams of Esther becoming a dancer, but alas she is not *cut out* for the ballet,'" and slapped her face. 'She's my mother,' I screamed. 'That's my mother you're making fun of. She's my mummy and I love her.' I ran off, aware that I had shocked them into silence with my heartfelt outburst.

I smiled, recalling the accuracy of Monica's impersonation.

My mother's voice, which amused and delighted the clever Monica, had an unusual effect on Sammy. 'Are you sure she's your mother, Hadassah?' I asked him, in turn, what on earth he meant by such a question. 'It's her voice,' he answered. 'It sounds unfucked.' I laughed, and invited him to elaborate. 'Her timbre has an unfucked sound. I know what I mean, but it's difficult to explain. There are several kinds of fucked voices, and they vary according to character. I'm thinking of the "let's get it over quickly" fucked voice, very brisk and businesslike, or the "Don't come for at least an hour" fucked voice, which is slow and lazy and lies deep in the throat, or the "I'm such a happy fucker, I'll fuck anywhere and anyhow you care to fuck me" fucked voice, which I have to confess is the kind of fucked voice I appreciate most. But your mother sounds as if she's never done it in her life, and never likely to, and it makes me horny, just the sheer fucking unfucked sound of it – horny for you, Hadassah, the daughter she must have had by remote control or in a previous existence or on another planet or, or . . . I've run out of conceivable possibilities. I warn you, Hadassah, it's dangerous for me to visit Mama. Five minutes of her no-can-belto and the golden sceptre is soaring up, up and away into the sexual stratosphere.' I said I'd heed the warning.

'Mummy.'

I did not reveal to Sammy that my mother had almost admitted to being frigid. I say 'almost' because she didn't allow herself to make a clear confession. That was not the behaviour of a lady. She spoke, rather, of men and women in general, not of Adam and Maria in particular. I listened, and neither challenged nor refuted her pronouncements. The male of the species, I learned, is the hunter. In olden days, in the so ancient mists of time, he killed the wild beasts that roamed in the forests, and skinned them, and brought home the carcasses for his wife to prepare for dinner. (His wife? Dinner? In prehistory? I stayed silent. What was this rigmarole in aid of, and where would it lead her?) 'He is still the hunter, but a so much more civilized one. Money is the beast he chases. The bigger money he catches, Esther, the better his wife and family live.' (I pictured my father stalking bank notes with a bow and arrow, and made no comment.) 'It is hard, tiring work he has to do. But it is necessary work. It is the work God in His Wisdom has allotted for him.' (And the female of the species, she of the feelings – what had the wise God allotted for her? I was soon to find out.) 'We women, Esther, have been put here for quite a different purpose. We leave the men, our husbands, to deal with the unpleasant things. We are here to offer them comfort, if we can.' I said nothing. 'The comfort men require – and God has designed us to give – is not always easy to provide. For some women, Esther, it is not so easy.' She stopped, embarrassed perhaps by the idea of what she had nearly admitted to. 'Oh, I *am* a chatterbox today.'

It was then that I asked the question of questions, for the one and only time. 'If I had been cut out for the ballet, Mama, and had succeeded in becoming a ballerina – a famous ballerina – would you have expected me to marry and start a family?'

'No' was her immediate answer.

'Why?'

'Because a ballerina's life is one of total dedication to beauty.'

I refrained from saying that other than ballerinas have dedicated themselves to beauty: poets, composers, painters. My father came into the room, and his arrival seemed to add to my mother's embarrassment.

'Why, Adam, you're back early.'

'No, I'm not. I'm half an hour later than usual, as a matter of fact.'

He kissed and embraced me. 'Dinner at eight-thirty, please, Maria. Half an hour later than usual.' He went through to his study, to relax in his favourite chair with a mild Havana.

'Or to look at his photos, Mummy,' I said as she stirred, opened an eye and closed it.

His photographs: one spring afternoon, a few months after Tata's death, I visited my mother on an impulse, to find out how she was faring. I let myself into the flat and heard women's voices. She was entertaining her 'chosen circle' to tea. I was on the point of escaping when Antoinette Hilton appeared in the hall. She said it was lovely to see me, and that I simply must join their little party, which was just progressing from the Earl Grey to the Moët et Chandon stage. 'We've decided to put some sparkle in Maria,' she confided. 'She's been down in the dumps of late. Understandably.'

'Esther, what a nice surprise,' said my mother. 'Have you brought Mr Elkin with you?'

'No, Mama. He's working on his film script.'

'Esther's Mr Elkin is in films,' she informed her friends. 'He is swarthy – I think "swarthy" best describes him – with a slightly too pronounced nose.'

(That 'slightly', I remembered thinking, marked an improvement of sorts.)

'Doesn't Esther's Mr Elkin have a Christian name?' asked Eva Ashworth.

'He has a name,' I replied. 'Samuel. Sammy.'

'We're going to toast Maria, Esther. We're going to wish her a merrier widowhood than the one she's been having,' said Wanda Stone. 'You will raise a glass with us?'

'Of course I will.'

'You are wicked girls to bring me so much champagne. A whole case, Esther, these so wicked girls have bought.'

My mother's innocent use of the word 'wicked' suddenly reminded me that the 'girls' – in their sixties; one, Antoinette, already past seventy – were indeed 'wicked'. They had posed in the nude for Adam Potocki. Each of them had thrown her own peculiar, personal caution to the winds. I marvelled once more at their recklessness as they sat around me, nibbling at the cream cakes – 'Oh, hips, hips, will you never be slender again?' Helen Nash enquired of the ceiling – my mother had provided. Was Eva aware that Antoinette had capered on a marble staircase in nothing but her pearls and earrings? Did Antoinette know about Eva's leather boots? Had Tata told Joanna that Helen shared with Caroline and Mama's ex-confidante Serena a liking for the great outdoors? These unasked, and probably unanswerable, questions preoccupied me while the champagne was being poured into 'so inappropriate' glasses.

'Esther, why are you staring at Eva? You are embarrassing her.'

'I'm sorry. I didn't intend to be rude. I was day-dreaming, I suppose.' We toasted my mother; wished her happiness.

'I am determined that we shall take our Mediterranean cruise, Maria,' said Wanda. 'We shall be two jolly old birds of passage together.'

Everyone laughed, and then I heard myself laughing too, but louder; laughing as I'd laughed when I was surrounded by the photographs – vulva upon vulva – on the floor of Tata's study. The smiling faces of his unlikely models made my laughter the more intense. I realised that I was shrieking. I realised that I was having hysterics.

'She is hysterical,' Helen Nash remarked. 'Is she prone to fits, Maria?'

'Esther, Esther, control yourself, please. What is the matter with you? You are worse than a hyena.'

I tried to apologise, but was incapable of speech. I signalled that I had to leave the room, and fled. I ran down to the street, spluttering.

'I kept seeing Eva on her bike, and Joanna with her spade, Mummy,' I said, and giggled. I wiped the sweat from her forehead, which I kissed. I told her that I would return soon, to be with her at the end.

When I got home, I played back the messages on my answering machine. The last was from Miss Lavelle, who was delighted to tell me that Mrs Potocka had eaten a hearty supper and, Oliver Twist-like, had asked for more. Not in words, it went without saying. She had banged on her plate with a spoon.

Wanting to laugh, to have hysterics even, I wept instead.

* * *

According to my diary, the next time I saw Stephen was on the day the Egyptian patient refused to let me examine him. He called me, through his equally vociferous interpreter, an unclean Englishwoman. My services had been rejected before – by an Irishman, who was too embarrassed to drop his trousers in my presence ('I couldn't, not in front of a lovely lady'); by a nervous youth, who grew ever more alarmed as I assured him that I was only doing a job like anyone else; by an impossibly tall man with an impossibly high opinion of himself who asked to see my superior, the better to ascertain that I was efficient enough to treat him. I accounted these my three failures. I had reasoned with the dozens of others who had attempted to slip away, and had won them over, eventually.

But this man was not to be persuaded of my ability or skill. He shouted at me in Arabic, and then his friend translated what he had said, at much the same volume. I was engaged in an unclean activity, I could not help hearing, and I ought to be ashamed to be where I was, in a men's clinic. When the second, repeated outburst had subsided, I remarked, calmly, 'Tell him that if he has caught a disease from a woman, he should not be upset at the prospect of being cured of that disease by another one. I may be a woman, but I am also a specialist.' The message was duly relayed, semi-thunderously. It was answered with spit: a generous, thick globule that landed in my hair.

'My colleague, Dr Gatenby, will look at you,' I said. I walked slowly out of the office. I went to the washroom, where I had the longest shower I can remember having.

'Good evening, Doctor Lady.' Stephen was waiting by my car. 'You look grimmer than grim and sadder than sad.'

'Yes, I am.'

I waited for his response. 'Aren't you going to ask me why?'

He hesitated. 'If you want, then. Just this once I'll allow. Why?'

'Because of a man who humiliated me. Who denied me the right to treat him. Who spat on me.'

'Spat? With spit?'

'Of course with spit. A bloody great dollop of it.'

'I've been spat on. With spit.'

'By whom?'

'Not allowed to say.'

'Well, I'm allowed to tell you who spat on me with spit. An Arab, Stephen. An Arab who believes that it's unclean of me to be doing what I'm doing. A man who has discovered that an unclean woman in Mayfair, a prostitute, has given him more than value for his money. She is to blame, and so am I, since he obviously believes that covering his blessed penis with a piece of rubber is unclean, too. That's why I'm how I am.'

'Cool down, Doctor Lady. I wouldn't lose your brain over him, if I was you.'

'You're right. I must keep my brain intact.'

'What's intact?'

'In one bit.'

'That's the word, then. Keep your brain intact – *intact* – is my advice.'

'I'll try and take it.'

'There's something else you can take.' He produced from the pocket of his raincoat, with a mock-flourish, a glass candlestick. I took it from him. 'Wait a minute.' From his other pocket, he produced another. 'Two of them,' he said. 'A perfect pair.'

'Thank you, Stephen. Thank you.'

We got into the car.

'I wasn't planning to go to Bayswater tonight,' I said. 'Chiswick's my destination. Where my lover lives.'

'OK.'

'Shall I drop you there?'

'Fulham'll do.'

'The Fulham route it is.'

'Listen, Doctor Lady. Listen hard. I'm a – '

'You're a – ?'

'I'm a – '

'What are you, Stephen?'

'I'm a – '

'Yes?'

'No, I'm not. I'm not allowed to say. Not yet.'

We shared an uneasy silence for the rest of the journey.

'You must have a curious view of life': that single phrase, with slight variations, has been addressed to me a hundred or so times in the course of my career. When it offends me, as it does occasionally, it's because of the tone of voice in which it's cast – a sniggering tone; a tone that seems to invite a conspiracy of prurience. 'Mine's no odder than anyone else's,' I reply. 'No more curious than a plumber's or a dentist's or a nun's.' It is then that I'm told to come off it, to stop pretending: 'They don't have to look at private parts.'

'Why is an attractive woman like you doing a job like that?': oh, that hateful 'attractive'. I countered the unctuous man's question with one of my own. 'Should I be better qualified if I were unattractive?' He accused me of deliberately clouding the issue. 'You know perfectly well what I mean,' he snapped. 'One doesn't expect to find a good-looking girl working in a clap clinic.' I smiled at him. 'Doesn't one? Why ever not?' I went on smiling. 'I refuse to be brow-beaten,' he answered, and turned to make easier conversation with the dinner guest on his other side. 'Now what do you do for a living?' he asked her. 'Something nice and normal, I hope.'

I remembered Sir Unctuousness this morning, when the student I am treating for that old puzzler, non-specific urethritis, suddenly enquired why, out of all the medical disciplines, I had chosen venereology.

'I had a road-to-Damascus experience,' I said. 'I was converted. From paediatrics.'

I explained how. A famous doctor, Angus Sinclair, had come to the university where I was studying to deliver a lecture on the subject of which he was acknowledged an authority, venereal diseases. The auditorium was packed. He spoke, mesmerisingly, for an hour and a half. 'It was a history lesson, ranging over five centuries. Had he contented himself with historical matters, I might never have seen the light.'

'What happened?'

'Dr Sinclair removed his glasses and abandoned his notes. He began to shout. He seemed to change in an instant from a doctor to a preacher – one of those hell-fire-and-damnation types, like his compatriot John Knox. The men and women who contracted syphilis – it was only syphilis he mentioned, not gonorrhoea – deserved what they got, he ranted. They were immoral. They had committed sins of the flesh. The treponema stayed in their blood until their dying day, the lasting evidence of their wickedness . . . As you can imagine, I was horrified by what I heard.'

'You didn't agree with him?'

'I wouldn't be sitting here if I'd agreed with him. There was worse to follow. He went on to say that although he despised his patients he was inclined to feel some sympathy – not much – for the ones who expressed shame for what they had brought on themselves. The rest, the unashamed, were beyond any redemption.'

I left the lecture hall in a daze, I said. I was mystified by the doctor's outburst. I believed then, and believe still, that the business of healing has to be disinterested. I could not begin to understand why Angus Sinclair had decided to spend such a large part of his long life among those very human beings he affected to despise. He made no mention that day of the thousands – millions – of innocents who had suffered the ravages of syphilis. His hatred contained them, too. And I hated his hatred.

'I'm sorry. I've been most unethical, talking about myself. I'm not paid to indulge in autobiography. I hope I've answered your polite question.'

'Yes, you have. Thank you.'

'You seem genuinely curious.'

'I am.'

'Would you be quite so curious if I were a man?'

'No. I suppose not.'

'You're honest as well. Now let me be inquisitive. What are you studying?'

'Something pretty useless. Medieval literature.'

'That's not useless. Chaucer's pretty useful.'

'You've read Chaucer?'

'You look shocked. Is it more shocking to have read Chaucer than to practise venereology?'

He smiled. 'Perhaps it is.'

'I've shocked a lot of people,' I said, 'but never with my love of Chaucer.'

One by one by one, my mother's chosen circle was disbanded. Antoinette Hilton had the impertinence to die, and Helen Nash went off to live in southern Spain ('She says the climate is good for her arthritis, but I happen to know there is a man – a so much younger man – at the bottom of it'), and Eva Ashworth put herself, and her money, into a religious retreat. The others were cast aside.

'Wanda has written to me, Mama. She is very distressed. She wants to find out if she has offended you. Has she?'

'That is entirely my concern.'

'But has she?'

'She knows herself whether she has or she hasn't.'

'She is your dearest friend.'

'Oh? My dearest friend, is she? I am grateful for the information, Esther.'

'She loves you like a sister, Mama. You've often said so.'

'I say so no longer.'

'Mama – '

'I wish not to speak of her. Or any of them.' She pointed at Anna Pavlova, who was now lit from above as if she were on a stage. 'I keep the company I want.'

'You happier, Doctor Lady?'

'Yes. Yes, I am.'

'No more spit spat on you?'

'No, Stephen. I don't get spat on every day, thank the Lord.'

'You thank Him, do you? The Lord?'

'I was brought up to, by my mother. "Thank the Lord" is just another expression for me now.'

'The Bish thanked the Lord.'

54

'I should hope he did. A bishop would be a very funny bishop indeed if he didn't thank the Lord.'

'The Bish made us thank Him, too.'

'Us?'

'You won't catch me, Doctor Lady. I'm a step ahead, remember. I haven't lost my brain. "Us" is me and Tonio.'

'And you both knew a bishop?'

'Yeah. We knew a bishop all right. We knew the big bad Bish himself.'

'Is he bad, Stephen?'

'The Bish? There's worse than him.'

'Who?'

'I'm not allowed to say.'

'What a surprise.'

He ignored, or did not notice, the sarcasm. 'I could name worse than the Bish, if I was allowed to.'

I told him, truthfully, that I was too tired for riddles, and that I was also rather hungry. I had planned to drop in at a local bistro on my way home.

'A bistro, eh? A *bistro*. I'll come with you, Doctor Lady. I'll pay for your food. I'm flush tonight.'

'I couldn't – '

'Why couldn't you?'

'I was going to say I couldn't accept, but I can. Are you sure, though, Stephen?'

'Me? Sure I'm sure. I'm even surer. Are *you* sure my *ensemble* is sober enough for your *bistro*?'

'Of course it is.'

(He wore a green tartan jacket, a turquoise shirt with frills down the front, jeans with discreet holes at the knees, moccasins.)

'The frugal foundling strikes again!'

'He certainly does.'

'Is the chauffeur ready?'

'She is.'

As soon as we were shown to a table at Mathieu et Michel, Stephen insisted that I choose the most expensive things on the menu: 'Have the best, Doctor Lady. I'm flush.'

'The most expensive doesn't necessarily mean the best.'

'It does sometimes.'

'Give me an example.'

'Houses to live in. Cashmere wool.'

'You like cashmere?'

'Me? Yeah.'

'I haven't seen you wearing it.'

'You will.'

'What is it you own? A sweater? A coat?'

'All sorts. You'll see.'

'I can't wait.'

'I'm *fetching* in cashmere.'

'I bet you are.'

I had assumed that Stephen was vegetarian, but now learned differently. 'I require a steak,' he said to the bemused waiter. 'And I require it medium-rare, if you please.'

'And Madame Potocki – she requires?'

'*Carré d'agneau*. Pinkish, as usual.'

'Are there any further requirements?'

'I – '

'Don't you want to lose your brain a little bit?' Stephen interjected.

'Yes, perhaps I do. I'll have a glass of the house red. And what about you, Stephen?'

'I fancy' – he paused, and grinned – 'the juice of the passion fruit myself.'

'We can provide passion-fruit juice, monsieur. That will be no problem.'

'Well, mercy upon you, and thanks.'

'*Merci* to you, monsieur.'

The waiter left, and Stephen and I looked at each other. Then I broke the silence by remarking on the fact that a medium-rare steak didn't match anything he was wearing.

'Match? What you on about?'

'The tomatoes, Stephen. The last time we ate together – the only time we ate together – you were dressed in red.'

'Me? In red? It was a joke. It was your daft idea.'

'I was half-expecting you to order a plate of cabbage.'

'I wouldn't half-expect anything from me, Doctor Lady.' He shook his head, slowly. 'I wouldn't, not if I was you.'

'Really?'

'Really and truly. Understand?'

'No, to be honest. I don't understand what you're trying to say to me.'

'I'm trying to say – I'm not allowed to say what I'm trying to say – just don't half-expect, that's all.'

The waiter put our drinks on the table.

'You've never asked me, Doctor Lady, where I come from.'

'It's obvious. Yorkshire.'

'Yorkshire's big. There's a lot of Yorkshire.'

'Where in Yorkshire, then?'

'Halifax. You heard of it?'

'Oh, I seem to think so. It's famous for its textiles. Why did you leave?'

'Reasons.'

'Which reasons?'

'Reasons I am not allowed to – to *divulge*.'

'Naturally.'

'Top-secret reasons.'

'Concerning your family?'

'*My* family? No. Not *my* family.'

'Someone else's?'

'Yeah. You're one clever lady, Doctor Lady. Someone else's family.'

'Whose?'

'Not mine.' He grinned at me. 'Not Stephen's.'

'I've told you already this evening – I'm tired of riddles.'

The fastidious Stephen, who had picked at the bowl of tomatoes, was not in the least fastidious with the steak. Large as it was, it soon vanished.

'My word, you polished that off quickly.'

'Me? I was hungry.'

'You've blood on your chin.'

'Mucky pup.' He wiped the blood away with a paper napkin, which he screwed into a ball. 'Spick and span, am I?'

'Yes.'

I became conscious, then, that someone who wasn't the waiter had stopped at our table. Looking up, I saw a middle-aged man looking down at Stephen.

'Hello, Andrew,' he said. 'Forgive me interrupting your dinner. How are you?'

'Fine,' replied Stephen.

'Aren't you going to introduce me to your friend?'

'No.'

'I'm Esther Potocki. Not the easiest name to remember.'

'And I'm – let's say I'm an acquaintance of young Andrew here.'

'Pleased to meet you.'

'Charmed.' He clearly wasn't. 'Eat your salad, Andrew. It's good for the complexion.'

Stephen, or Andrew, grunted.

'Laconic as ever. Goodbye, Miss – '

'Potocki.'

'Miss Potocki. And goodbye to you, Andrew. Keep your promise of – what was it? a year ago? – and phone me. My number's in the directory, in case you've lost it.'

We were silent after the man had gone. The waiter reappeared and we chose our desserts – *crème brulée* for me, and a slice of chocolate cake for my unlikely host, who did not allow the entire world to call him Stephen, I knew now.

'Staring at people's rude, Doctor Lady.'

'He called you Andrew, Stephen.'

'Me? I heard him.'

'Is Andrew your real name?'

'For him it is.'

'Why should he know you as Andrew, and I know you as Stephen?'

'Because, because. Because that's how it happened.'

'Do you have other names?'

'Me? Plenty.'

'What for?'

'Fun, Doctor Lady. Fun, fun, fun.'

'That's a strange kind of fun, Stephen. Or is it Andrew?'

'No, it isn't Andrew. I'm Stephen. With a "p" and an "h", not a "v". I'm Stephen for you, Doctor Lady.'

'I'm Esther to everyone,' I said. 'Stephen.'

'Esther, this is Gabriel. Esther Potocki, Gabriel Harvey.'

'Hello.'

'Hello.'

'Gabriel and I went to school together. Centuries ago,' said Peter Fisher. 'We nicknamed him the Starch-angel Gabriel because his shirts were always whiter and stiffer than ours.'

'For a time, they were. Then they became scruffy, like the shirts of the other boys.'

'Esther's at St Lucy's, too, Gabriel.'

'I'm a venereologist, Mr Harvey. I'm not in the respectable part of the hospital, as Peter is.'

'Are some illnesses more respectable than others?'

Peter and I answered yes simultaneously.

'There's a hierarchy of diseases, I'm afraid, and I work with the ones on the lowest rung of the social ladder.'

Peter had to leave his own dinner party early that evening, because of an emergency operation. For an hour or so after his typically frantic departure, Gabriel and I talked with Peter's wife, Hannah, about other-than-medical matters. And it was while we were talking, and laughing, that I looked across the table and thought: I must not hurt you. Sammy's eyes were bright once, as yours are now. I can't destroy you, too, Gabriel Harvey.

Hurt? Destroy? What was I thinking of? There seemed no possibility of my ever being involved with Peter and Hannah's friend, so why was I giving myself such insane instructions? A shiver ran quickly through me, I remember, and Hannah saw me clutch my shoulders and asked if the room was draughty.

'No, of course it isn't. Someone just walked over my grave, Hannah. I don't know who.'

It was ten-past midnight when I got up to go. Peter hadn't returned, and Hannah was silly with sleep. 'I'm on duty tomorrow, alas. I enjoyed meeting you, Gabriel.'

'Likewise.'

'Perhaps we'll run into each other again.'

'Let's be more certain than that. Shall we? Let's ignore "perhaps" and make a definite date.'

'I don't have my diary with me.'

'Would a Sunday be convenient? The last Sunday in the month?'

'Yes,' I said. 'Yes, that would be convenient.'

'I live on the river. *By* the river, I should say. In a house I bought with ill-gotten gains.'

'It's a beautiful house, Esther,' Hannah managed to say. 'Eighteenth century. Designed by – designed by – a painter who isn't Gainsborough.'

'Zoffany, Hannah darling. Johann Zoffany.'

'That's him. Sophie kept me up all last night with her crying. That's why I've forgotten your painter.'

In bed, later, I assured myself that I did not find Gabriel Harvey physically attractive. There was his height, or rather the lack of it, to consider – he was scarcely more than five feet tall. I towered above him. He looked boyish, despite his years, despite his greying hair. He was amiable, and self-deprecating, and quietly witty, but I could sense no danger in his nature – the danger I had loved, then feared, in Sammy. No, he was no match for Sammy, the young and vital Sammy, with his 'golden sceptre'.

Yet why had I thought of not hurting him, not destroying him, and why had I shivered? Where had this ludicrous notion come from? It had no basis in reality, none whatsoever: if I were to fall in love a second time, God help me, it would not be with a man like the nice, the gentle Gabriel.

'And I didn't destroy you, Sammy. You know I didn't,' I sobbed into the pillow. 'You know bloody well I didn't.'

'Which way tonight, Doctor Lady?'

'Hello, Stephen. What do you mean – which way?'

'Who's lost her brain already? I mean, is the Doctor Lady going home, or is she going to her lover?'

'She's going home.'

'Isn't she in the mood for him?'

'She, Stephen, is always in the mood for him. She needs a break, though. She could do with a rest. She often enjoys being alone, at the end of a working day.'

'What's he like – your *lover*?'

'Kind. In a word.'

'Is he young?'

'My age.'

'Old. What's he call himself?'

'By a name. Gabriel.'

'Gabriel, eh? Never met a Gabriel.'

'Thinking of using it?'

'I might.'

When we were in the car, I had to remind him, twice, to put on the safety belt.

'The Bishop, the Bish – does he have a name, Stephen?'

'That would be telling. And I'm not allowed to.'

'Top secret, I suppose.'

'Yeah. Very *clan-des-tine*.'

'Why is that? Is there something wrong with him? Has your Bish been up to no good?'

'You and your questions.'

'Is he Anglican or Roman Catholic?'

'The Bish? He talks funny. Funnier than you. Says a lot of foreign words.'

'Latin ones?'

'Is "Dominus" Latin? Is "vobiscum"?'

'Yes.'

'He sort of sang them. In a wobbly voice. Made Tonio laugh, he did. And me.'

'I don't think they are meant to be laughed at.'

'Oh, but you had to laugh at him. You couldn't help yourself, the way he wobbled. There he stood, in his *ensemble*, wobbling and wobbling, and Tonio and me had to cover our mouths with our hands to stop the laughter from coming out. Him and his *"Dominus"*! Him and his *"vobiscum"*!'

'Churches aren't places to laugh in.'

61

'We weren't in a church, Doctor Lady. We were nowhere near a church. We were in the Bish's palace. In his special, private chapel, in his palace.'

'Curiouser and curiouser.'

'It wasn't a proper palace, the Bish's. Not like Buckingham. Not big and grand like Buckingham.'

'You say "wasn't". Has it gone, then? Has it been pulled down?'

'Who knows? I don't.'

'Was it – is it – in London?'

'Questions, questions. In London, yes.'

'I shan't ask you where.'

'I wouldn't be allowed to tell you.'

'I assumed as much.'

After parking the car, I walked along the street with Stephen and stopped outside the large Edwardian house that contains my flat. I wished him good night.

'You can invite me inside. If you want to.'

'Really? You ran off when I invited you in before.'

'I won't this time.'

'It will have to be a brief visit, Stephen. I can't allow you more than half an hour.' I realised that I had used Stephen's word, and smiled. 'That's all I can allow you.'

He followed me up the stairs to the third floor.

'I never take the lift. Lifts give me claustrophobia.'

'Me too.'

'And anyway, the exercise is good for me.'

'I hate lifts. I hate it when you're closed in. When you're breathing other people's breath. I hate the tube as well, the famous London underground. I hate it. I do my best to avoid it, Doctor Lady. I hate it, knowing there's earth on top of you, over your head, waiting to fall. It's only animals ought to move about underground, in my opinion. I screamed on a tube train once, I'm here to tell you.'

'Screamed? Out loud?'

'Very out loud. The train had stopped and wasn't moving. We were between stations. The heat was horrible. I was stuck close to this fat woman, I was stuck so close I could see every single spot on her face, like as if they were under a magnifying glass, and the train stayed stopped and wouldn't budge, absolutely wouldn't budge, and I hated it, Doctor Lady, I hated it. That's when I screamed out loud, *very* out loud, and I had to be controlled. No, I had to be *restrained* – that's what the fat woman said. "He has to be restrained." Well, I didn't have to be *restrained* for long, because I think the driver must've heard my screaming, or someone did, because the train went hiccup, hiccup, hiccup and started to start – not fast, but starting. And when it stopped again, it stopped in a proper place, a station. Baker Street, it was. Beautiful, beautiful Baker Street.'

'Here we are, Stephen. Are you sure you want to come in?'

'Me? Yeah. Why not?'

'The ghost you saw last time is probably still around.'

'Which ghost?'

'I opened the front door, as I'm doing now,' I said, 'and you peered inside, and then you looked frightened. I thought you'd seen a ghost. You know that expression, don't you?'

'Me? Yeah. Course I know it.'

'Is he still there?'

'No.'

He hesitated on the threshold.

'Enter.'

He remained in the doorway.

'Feel free to run off.'

'No.' He stepped into the hall, tentatively. 'No.'

'Go through to the sitting-room.' I closed the front door. 'Relax, Stephen. Relax.'

'I *am* relaxed.'

'You seem very tense to me.'

'I am not. I'm relaxed. Understand?'

'If you say so.'

'I do say so, Doctor Lady.'

I turned on the lamps and advised him to sit on the sofa, as it was more comfortable, more spacious, than the chairs.

Again he hesitated.

'What are you afraid of?'

'Me? Nothing.'

'Honestly?'

'Yes, honestly. I'm not lying. I am not telling you a lie, Doctor Lady.'

'Sit down, then.'

He held my gaze while he sat down. 'Happy?'

'I feel like losing my brain – part of it, at any rate – with a whisky. Can I offer you a drink?'

'Me? Milk. I fancy milk.'

'Milk might be a problem. In fact, it *is* a problem. I don't have any.'

'I'll do without.'

'There's orange juice.'

'I'll do without.'

I poured myself a generous measure of Scotch and joined him on the sofa. Although I was some distance from him, he edged away.

'Where've you put them?'

'Put? Them?'

'The presents I've given you. I can't see them.'

'They're in my office at the clinic.'

'They shouldn't be. They oughtn't to be. I won't allow you to keep them in the clinic.'

'Please explain.'

'It isn't fit. It isn't right, to keep the presents I've given you in that place.'

'Tell me why.'

'It's not your home.'

'True.'

'It isn't where you *live*.'

'Obviously.'

'And it's where you live my presents ought to be. In here. On the tables.'

'I'm sorry.'

'And that book, that old book, ought to be here with all those other books you've got.'

(Ah, yes – poor sad VOL. IX, separated from VOLS. I to VIII, and VOLS. X, XI and XII.)

'I'll bring them back, Stephen, I promise.'

'I mean, they're gifts. Gifts don't belong in a clinic. Not with germs and even worse.'

'I suppose they don't.'

'I didn't – I didn't *find* them for you so as to let anybody look at them.'

'Anybody? Are you referring to my patients?'

'Could be.'

'What's wrong with the patients seeing your gifts?'

'I can't allow it. That's what.'

I was on the point of revealing that all the presents, with the exception of the bust of Mozart, were out of sight, locked in a filing cabinet. I observed, instead, that the men and women who came to me had far too much on their minds to be bothered with ornaments, however interesting or attractive.

'I'd rather you kept them here. The gifts.'

'I will. In future.'

'I've another one for you.'

He brought from his pocket an alabaster egg.

'I presume you're not allowed to tell me where you – *found* this.'

'Correct, Doctor Lady.'

He stood up and stared about the room, as if he were trying to memorise it.

'I must be off,' he said. 'On my rounds.'

'Are you going to work?'

'Me? Work? You never know.'

'It wasn't such an ordeal, was it, sitting in my flat?'

He looked at me. 'A bit *claus-tro-pho-bic.* Only a bit. Not like in the train.'

'I should hope not.'

'My joke, Doctor Lady.'

'You're welcome to pay a return visit.' I accompanied him into the hall. 'Whenever you wish.'

He nodded, to acknowledge the offer. 'You read all those books in there?'

'Most of them, yes. Quite a few were left to me by my father. He was a great reader, in several languages.'

'What about your husband?'

'What about him?'

'Did he leave you any books?'

'No. Not really.'

'Not the reading type, was he?'

'He read when he wanted to. He wasn't a book-worm.'

'What did you say his name was?'

'I didn't. Sammy.'

'Sammy, eh? Is that common for *Sam-u-el*?'

'Yes. I'm afraid it is. He preferred to be called Sammy.'

'Me, I prefer Gabriel to Samuel. Sounds better, Gabriel.'

'I'll pass on the message.'

I opened the door for him. He walked out to the landing.

'I forgot to compliment you on your ensemble tonight, Stephen. It's fetching. I love the floral tie.'

'Floral? Oh, the flowers. Tulips.'

'Very colourful.'

'Makes a splash. Goodbye, then. See you soon, Doctor Lady.'

'Yes, Stephen. Probably. Yes.'

I listened as he descended the stairs. Reaching the second flight, he began to run.

Gabriel Harvey was standing outside his house, glass in hand, gazing at the Thames.

'I was admiring the swans. They're honouring me with a visit today. As you are,' he added, smiling. 'Come into my museum. I must warn you that the rooms are surprisingly small. And do beware of the floorboards. My cleaner, Mrs Thwaites, went berserk with the wax polish on Friday morning. You will be able to see your terrified face approaching you as you trip up.'

'I'm not the only guest, am I?'

'You are, indeed. Is that all right?'

'Yes,' I lied.

The truth was that I was fearful. I wanted company at that moment, chattering company. As he led me into his study on the first floor, with its view over the river, I was possessed, once again, by the ridiculous idea that I must not hurt him. I would have welcomed distraction.

We sat on a bench by the window and drank champagne.

'I'm glad you're here, Esther. You looked distinctly apprehensive when I invited you.'

'I'd no reason to. It was late at night. I was tired and tipsy.'

'You had every reason, actually. I rather threw myself at you, didn't I?'

'Did you? I can't say I noticed.'

'I thought, you see, it might be possible for us to become friends.' He went on, in a rush: 'Have some olives. They're flavoured with garlic and herbs from the garden. The spare bowl's for the stones.'

'Thank you.' I ate an olive, and told him it was delicious. 'Yes, it might well be possible. Let's hope so.'

We were silent.

'Who is the man in the hat in the picture?' I asked.

'George Fox. The founder of the Quakers. I bought him in an Islington junk shop years ago. He's one of my heroes.'

'You're a believer?'

'I'm an agnostic, Esther, with an occasional leaning towards the mystical. Yes, that's near enough. I admire George for refusing to take off his famous hat on the insistence of a mere human magistrate. He only took it off for his God, who spoke to him in the strangest places – in the fields near Lichfield, for example.' He picked up the champagne bottle. 'What a disastrous host. Your glass is empty, and I've been gabbling on about George Fox. My apologies.'

'Accepted.'

There was another, longer silence.

'Someone like you – someone so practical, so down to earth – must consider me very odd.'

'How do you know I'm practical and down to earth?'

'You have to be, Esther. It's your work.'

'Syphilis keeps me down to earth, certainly. But I do have my airy side. I may be just as odd as you, if not odder. Who says you're odd, anyway?'

'Almost everyone, I should imagine.'

'I've often wondered – and I'm sure I shall go to my grave wondering – by what curious yardstick of sanity we who call ourselves sane arrive at the logical conclusion that other people are odd, or even mad. I don't mean the really mentally deranged, of course – I mean other people. Almost everyone's wrong, I think, Gabriel. You're no odder than the next man, whoever he is.'

It was then that I noticed a school desk, of the kind I recognised from my days at Dame Muriel's, set against the wall in a corner of the room.

'Yes, your eyes aren't deceiving you – it *is* a school desk, also acquired in Islington. I have to confess that I use it. Because I'm so small and so thin, I can still get inside it without too much discomfort. It's where I wrote my book *Lords of Light*, and where I'm attempting to write a second – about swindlers. From preachers to crooks. Very odd, yes?'

'Do they have anything in common?'

'Quite a lot, as it transpires. I'll give you a detailed answer as soon as the book's completed.'

We ate lunch – sorrel soup; salmon *en croûte* with ginger; a chocolate mousse flavoured, and decorated, with rosemary – in Gabriel's kitchen. Above the table, in a gilt frame, was the neatly inscribed message 'DO NOT SPIT. MATRON'. 'It's a souvenir of a place I once worked in – a home for elderly women called the Jerusalem – and it dates from the time many years earlier when there were male incumbents.'

('Matron's warning might have come in useful today,' I was to remark to Gabriel, when the irate Egyptian deemed me unclean. 'Though I can't believe it would have deterred him.')

'The old ladies weren't given to spitting, were they?'

'A couple of them foamed at the mouth occasionally. No, they weren't given to spitting, on reflection. Now please try and enjoy your meal, Esther.'

At some point during the afternoon – while I was eating, and delighting in, the salmon, perhaps – it occurred to me that my host could be homosexual. If he were, then my ridiculous fear of hurting him was totally unfounded.

'Are you gay?' I asked, in a tone that struck me instantly as being far too studiedly bright and breezy.

'I'm nothing. As yet. You're looking across at a virgin.'

'Am I? Are you?'

'I'm afraid so. The pleasures of the flesh have passed me by. I was in love with my mother, you see.'

'How in love with her? In a physical sense?'

'No, no. A thousand times no.' He smiled at me. 'I didn't have *that* problem. I had plenty of problems, but not that particular one. She went missing, Esther, when I was a boy. I had to put something in the terrible empty space that was left in my life after she vanished, and what I put there was this sweet and perfect woman, this ideal mother, who had walked out on her husband but not her son. I put her there on a pedestal, and if you'll pardon two clichés in the same sentence, I held a torch for her. It burned from the 1st of February, 1950 until the 4th of June, 1977, when I learned the truth my father had kept from me. My mother had killed herself, with a bottle of bleach, in a hotel, on the 20th of March, 1950. She'd been alive for just seven weeks of our long, long separation – seven weeks, Esther, out of twenty-seven, coming on twenty-eight, years. Oh, I'm sorry. All these dates, these numbers: they must be boring to you.'

'What stopped you falling for a person of your own age?'

'She did. She stopped me. She wouldn't let me go. I worshipped her. I had not thought of loving anyone else. The possibility didn't exist. I dreamed only of her return – craved it, prayed for it. I knew that I would never be complete unless that empty space was filled by my living, breathing mother. A ghost's there now.'

'Poor Gabriel.'

'It's all over. Over and done with. Take some salad.'

'Thanks.'

'You've had enough of my revelations.'

'I haven't.'

'Well, I've had enough of them. It's not everyone who admits to being a virgin on such a slight acquaintance.'

'May I ask you one more presumptuous question?'

69

'You may.'

'It's this. Do you want to lose your virginity?'

'I do want to. I think it's my ambition, Esther. I do want to. That's my honest answer.'

'I hope you succeed. In your ambition.'

'I'm tired of my life as a nothing.' He got up from the table and began to clear the dishes. He had his back to me as he said, 'I'll have to meet a person, a woman, who doesn't mind about my – my innocence. Perhaps I will, sooner or later.'

'You will,' I encouraged him. He had already met her, but I wasn't going to tell him so – not for a week or two, at least. 'I'm sure you will.'

'I wish I had your confidence.'

'Are they still in there, Doctor Lady? The presents? Where they don't belong?'

'I took them home, as I promised.'

'Really? Truly?'

'Yes, Stephen.'

'Word of honour?'

'Come in and see for yourself if you doubt me.'

'You won't catch your friend Stephen in there, Doctor Lady. Not in there with them.'

'I'm your friend, am I?'

'No, my enemy. That's why I bring you gifts. That's why I wait for you, morning and night. Because you're my enemy. It strikes me, Doctor Lady, that your brain's fast becoming lost property. You'll be needing a ticket to reclaim it.'

'Forgive me, Stephen. We're friends.'

'Are we?'

'Yes, of course.'

'What sort of friends are we?'

'It's difficult to say.'

'I bet it is. We're not like me and Tonio, you and me. We're sort of *politer*.'

'That sounds all right.'

'Suppose it does. Politeness is a virtue.'

'Definitely.'

'The Bish used to go on and on sometimes about politeness, specially when we was – *we were* – playing him up. "Remember, lads, that manners maketh man," he'd go. "There's no excuse for *uncouth* behaviour." You don't consider me uncouth, do you, Doctor Lady?'

'No, I don't.'

'The Bish said I could do with a bit of fine tuning. That was at the start. I couldn't expect to be a *Strad-i-vari-us* like Tonio, but with a bit of fine tuning, he said, I could pass muster in the orchestra. "Anthony," he said, meaning Tonio, "will raise you to concert pitch. Won't you, Anthony?" "Have I ever failed Your Grace?" Tonio gave him back. "I'll tune him up for you." And the Bish laughed his funny laugh, and took a swig from his *goblet*.'

I told Stephen I was lost and puzzled. The Stradivarius, the orchestra, the tuning up, the concert pitch – I was all at sea with this talk of music.

'Who isn't the clever Doctor Lady this morning? You aren't. Listen and take heed. We agree that I'm not *uncouth* – '

'Yes.'

'Good. The reason I'm not uncouth is the fine tuning I got from the Bish and Tonio. They made me *presentable*.'

'Now I understand. They taught you manners.'

'And *etiquette*. And *decorum*.'

Polite as he was to me, he hadn't shown much courtesy to the man in the bistro, the man who had addressed him as Andrew, I remarked.

'Me? Him? He doesn't deserve my etiquette and my decorum, Doctor Lady. Not him.'

'Why?'

'I'm not allowed to say. Not yet.'

'Was he rude to you?'

'Me? Might have been.'

'He seemed rather cynical.'

'What's cynical?'

'You are quite extraordinary, Stephen. You know so many strange words – "etiquette", "decorum", even "suffragan" –

71

and yet you haven't heard of "cynical", which is pretty common.'

'Yeah. Well. That's it.'

'I found the man sarcastic. Does that make sense to you?'

'Me? Yes. He is sarcastic.'

'And sarcastic is like cynical.'

'OK.' He tapped his forehead with a finger. 'Cynical's up there now. In cold storage.' He grinned at me. 'Ready for use when required.'

He invited me to touch, to feel, his jacket.

'It's very soft material.'

'Cashmere wool. The softest.'

'And the most elegant. And the most expensive.'

'Money no object. Am I fetching in it?'

'As always.'

'Flattery will get you a present, Doctor Lady. An ornament. For your home, understand.'

It was a china shepherdess.

'My collection is mounting. Thank you, Stephen.'

'There's something you can give me in return, if you can. I have a question for you. Makes a change, eh? You're the one with the questions as a rule.'

'Ask me, then. Fire away.'

'When I came down here from Halifax and met the Bish, the Bish said I was a *heath-cliff*. "He is a *heath-cliff*, Anthony," he said. "A *heath-cliff* to the life." But Tonio said, "I'm not on your wavelength, Your Grace. How can a boy look like a cliff on a heath?" The Bish thought this was funny, and laughed till he choked, and that was the end of it. So my question is: what was he on about, the Bish?'

What the Bish – the Bishop – was on about, I tried to explain, was that he, Stephen, bore a resemblance to a character, a wild character, in a famous book, *Wuthering Heights*. 'By Emily Brontë,' I added, while he stared at me, astonished.

'Which word heights?'

'Wuthering. *Wuthering Heights* is the name of a house. In Yorkshire, where you come from. "*Wuthering*" has to do with the strong wind that blows across the moors, I think.'

72

'He's wild, is he?'

'He has a temper.'

'Is he a bastard? Excuse me – a foundling?'

'I haven't read it since my teens. Yes, he probably is a foundling.'

'Is he handsome as well as wild?'

'In a rough kind of way. Actually, Stephen, I can't see the likeness myself. He certainly doesn't have your taste in clothes. Heathcliff isn't the dandy you are.'

I saw my first patient of the day approaching, and said goodbye to Stephen, who was still smiling with pleasure at the compliment I had paid him.

'We have burrowed our way up to the sunlight,' I told the group of medical students I was showing round the clinic. 'Twenty years ago, many of us worked underground, in dark and dingy rooms, with penitential seating for the shameful patients. I don't exaggerate. I did my training in one of those subterranean places. To reach it, you had to locate – if you could – an undemonstrative door at the side of the hospital, descend two flights of stairs and walk several hundred yards along a corridor. A Via Dolorosa, indeed, and at the end of it was another door, on which the words "Special Clinic" had been painted, in yellow. Inside, the walls were brown and the floor was covered with ancient, cracked linoleum. It was in such special – not to say, choice – surroundings that we went about our specialised business.'

We often had to work with staff whose attitude of mind perfectly matched the décor, I continued. For every excellent, impartial nurse, there was invariably another who signalled disapproval or contempt towards the man or woman who had trudged the length of the Via Dolorosa for treatment. ('"The VD that leads to VD," as my superior, Dr Partridge, used to joke.') These sour individuals were specialists in the frosty look that had to be deployed instead of words, performing little miracles of revulsion with the eyes, the nose, the lips.

'I've lived too long with that superimposed "special" –

"special" in the sense of "set apart from". We're not set apart here, as you can see. We haven't been hidden away in a shed somewhere behind the main building, and we're not down in the bowels of the earth, next to the boiler room. Those irises in that vase on the table may be just flowers to you, but to me they're evidence of a small, slow revolution that has brought us from the murky depths beneath Lambeth General to the first floor of the Osler Wing at St Lucy's.'

After the students had gone, I thought of Max, the other male virgin in my life. Being celibate had not precluded him from loving Graham, a much-married charmer whose appeal eluded me ('He's so obvious, Max,' I complained. 'He actually times his smiles'), or from assembling what he called his 'Dionysian repertory company of the mind', which consisted of the two Greek waiters, Minos and Petros, and certain film stars, and innumerable young men he had treated with sympathetic skill. 'They have a riotous time in my head, while my happy hand demonstrates intense appreciation.'

A stranger, overhearing Max in exuberant flow, might have accounted him frivolous. That stranger, in common with most people who judge others on the basis of a few overheard remarks, would have been wrong. 'It's apropos of the fact that your solitary vice is the solitary vice itself,' I said to him on that long-past day of his 'shocking admission'. He raised his glass of Retsina, and thanked me. 'But then, I don't regard masturbation as a vice,' I added. 'If I were crippled or desperately ugly, I'd be abusing myself round the clock.'

'It's a sin, Esther, and it's one I have to practise. "The usual, is it?" asks my priest when I go to confession. "Yes, Father. The usual." I often feel like apologising to him for being so lustful with such limited resources, though I do try to vary the monotony in subtle ways. Last Wednesday, for instance, I admitted to my insane desire for an actor called Troy Donahue. "Troy? Troy?" the old man interrupted. "What sort of a Christian name is Troy, and he an Irishman, too?" "He's American, Father." "Ah, well, yes, I suppose he would be. This Mr Troy no doubt rides a horse?" He wheezed at his witticism and I returned to my catalogue of misdemeanours.'

(What would Stephen's multi-denominational bishop – the once-flamboyant Bish – have made of Max's catalogue? Would he have advised the tortured soul to forsake his rack and let his hands roam freely? 'My own hands have not been idle,' I can hear him saying, 'but they have not been constrained either.' I picture Max in the Bish's palace, at the Bish's confessional, and smile at the incongruity of his ever being there.)

Max never spoke of sins and misdemeanours to his patients. He listened if they wished, or needed, to talk, and it was the quality of his listening the more astute among them respected. 'My teacher was the great Angus Sinclair, a man of immense intellect who was blessed with only a modest amount of compassion for his fellow creatures. His was one bedside manner I quickly decided not to emulate.' I understood why, I said, having heard him lecture once, in Newcastle. 'He was getting on then, Esther, and going a wee bit gaga. I was heartbroken when he blew his brains out. I was bloody wretched, I can tell you. Strange as it may seem, I was deeply fond of the irascible so-and-so. He showed me his fatherly side, what there was of it, cautiously.'

Max maintained that a streak of illogicality runs in everybody. 'Mine's a God-streak, the most illogical and incomprehensible of the lot.' A faith had to be totally adhered to or not at all, he argued, and he adhered to his hook, line and – happy hand apart – sinker. He was content to love Graham from afar, if his being godfather to the six children of Graham's three turbulent marriages could be regarded as sufficiently distant. The chaste kisses he shared with Graham were the closest he had come to a physical manifestation of his feelings, and they had to be enough for him. Graham was even barred from joining the Dionysian repertory company: 'He's strictly *persona non grata*. I wouldn't dream of having fun with him – not the Minos and Petros kind of fun.'

Why, I wondered, had he not become a monk? 'You don't get to treat too many cases of gonorrhoea in a monastery. Because I need to function in our wicked world, Esther. My immortal soul is all very well, but I think I'd go mad if I had to contemplate it from sunrise to sunset. And as for self-denial, no one could

75

deny himself more than I deny myself already. The way things are, I am monkishly useful, and thus I intend to remain, God willing.'

I left the clinic that evening determined to tell Gabriel that I was the woman who could – what was the appropriate expression? – cope with his innocence. Yes, I'd cope with it. With any luck, I'd release him from it, too.

But how? That was a delicious, an exciting prospect. I should soon know how, I hoped.

'You're not like me, are you, Doctor Lady?'

'I am a woman. That does make a difference of sorts.'

'No, no. In your clothes is what I'm talking about. As regards your *attire*. Your *gear*. You don't go to the trouble I go to. You don't go to *any* trouble, in my opinion.'

'I couldn't begin to rival you.'

'Me? Correct. You could not. The fetching frugal foundling is out on his own, he is. In a class by himself.'

'He can give me the benefit of his expert advice, then. I'm always happy to learn.'

'You said I was flash in the blue suit I put on for Tonio. It wasn't sober for you, you said. I made you blink, didn't I?'

'Yes, you did.'

'That was my only mistake, wasn't it, with *attire*?'

'In my opinion. Yes, Stephen, it was.'

'But everything else, my other ensembles – they weren't mistakes, eh?'

'Definitely not.'

'So there you are, Doctor Lady.'

'Where am I, exactly, Stephen?'

'Well, you aren't like me, as I say. There's no colour to your clothes. I've never seen them, really – your clothes.'

'With some people, you don't.'

'I want mine seen.'

'Why?'

'Because, because.'

'Because?'

76

'Because, Doctor Lady, I go to the trouble. Understand?'

'Of course I understand.'

I went on to explain that clothes weren't important to me, and never had been. My wardrobe was neither large nor varied. I had driven my mother to despair when I was a girl, through my lack of interest in dresses and hats and jewellery and make-up.

'She thought I was unnatural. She said I was unfeminine.'

(That wasn't completely accurate: Mother's word was 'unfemale'. 'You are a so unfemale child to me, Esther. You cannot be a male, however much you try. Your head is a woman's head and should have only a woman's ideas inside it.')

'Don't you ever dress up, then, Doctor Lady?'

'Not for work, Stephen. I can't imagine that my patients would trust me more if I came to the clinic in my glad-rags.'

'What glad-rags have you got?'

'Precious few. Just a ball gown and a couple of things I throw myself into for smart occasions.'

'I know what that means. It means I won't see you in them.'

'Do you want to?'

'Me? Perhaps.'

'I'm a frightful sight, dolled up. You'd laugh, Stephen, I promise you. I wasn't born with the natural graces.'

He shrugged. 'If you say so, Doctor Lady. I had a present for you, but I've left it – at home.'

'I don't expect you to give me a present every time we meet.'

'This one's special.'

'Home is still a secret, I assume.'

'Home?'

'Where you live, Stephen.'

'That home. Yeah. It's still a secret, where it is.'

'It's in London, obviously.'

'Who says?'

'It must be.'

'Suppose it is? Listen hard, Doctor Lady, and take heed: I can't let you into the secret. I'm not allowed to. Not yet.'

'What a mysterious creature you are.'

'I'm not a creature. I'm a man.'

'Yes, yes. I wasn't being rude. The word can be used in a flattering way. For instance – you are a very fetching creature in today's ensemble, Stephen.'

'Me? A fetching creature, am I?'

'Definitely. That wouldn't be a silk shirt you're wearing, would it?'

'It would. It would, Doctor Lady, it would.' He started down the steps. 'It would, it would, it would.' He turned when he reached the street, and waved. 'It would,' he shouted. 'It would.'

'It wasn't a success the first time with Sammy,' I lied. 'We were clumsy as hell. We threw ourselves at each other and collided.'

I kissed Gabriel's forehead; ruffled his already ruffled hair.

'I'm sorry.'

'You've no reason to be. None whatsoever. I shan't storm out of the house in high dudgeon.'

'I'd love to see what high dudgeon looks like.'

'You won't be getting the chance.'

I didn't storm out of the house when we failed a third, a fourth, a fifth time. 'I'm beginning to think I'm fated not to lose it,' Gabriel murmured. 'It's kind of you to persevere.' Before our sixth attempt, he said he had a suggestion to make that I might find alarming or distasteful, or both.

'It sounds intriguing, anyway.'

'It has to do, I'm afraid, with my mother. Oh, Esther, it's ridiculous.'

'What is?'

'This – this thing I have to ask of you.'

He was silent.

'I'm waiting, Gabriel.'

'While my mother was away – while I thought she was away, on a long holiday, somewhere – I often used to put on, when it was very late at night and I was feeling most alone, an item of clothing, Esther, a certain item of clothing that helped to bring her nearer to me.'

'The item of clothing – was it a woman's?'

He nodded. 'A frock. A blue frock. It was like one she – my mother – was wearing on a beautiful spring afternoon, when I was little. I bought my copy of it from a stall in the market at Petticoat Lane. It made me strangely warm, that frock; it made me glow, especially on her birthday.'

'Have you still got it?'

'No. I tore it into shreds, after the truth came out. I saw, in a flash, that the warmth it had given me was no warmth at all. I had a bit of a breakdown then.'

'And now?'

'And now I have another dress, or rather dresses. I buy them for my twin sister, whose measurements are – miraculously – the same as mine. I've three, to be precise.'

He looked at me, and blushed.

'I think you are on the verge of proposing something alarming, Gabriel.' I spoke softly. 'Aren't you?'

'I warned you that I'm odd, and here is the proof.' He cleared his throat. 'Here is the proof,' he repeated, and stopped.

'The proof, please,' I said. 'Let me have the proof.'

'I can't.'

'You must. You really must, now.'

'Oh, Esther, what am I doing? What am I going to say to you?'

'I have no idea, but I wish you would hurry up and say it.'

'Well, the proof of my oddness lies in the fact, the undeniable fact that – ' He hesitated. 'I want you to see me in one of them.'

'The dresses?'

He nodded.

'Why not, then?'

'Are you sure?'

'Probably.'

'Because if you aren't, we could simply forget this, and – '

'Not succeed again?'

'That seems to be the alternative.'

'We've no choice, have we?'

'I should warn you, Esther – there aren't any accessories. I mean that I don't have a wig, or a handbag, or even the right shoes. It's just me, as I am, in a dress.'

'Show me. You as you are, in a dress.'

'All right.'

He didn't move from his chair.

'What's the matter?'

'Oh, God, Esther, there's another complication.'

'Is there?'

'I want you to see me in the dress, but I don't want you to see me getting into it.'

I said I was happy with the complication, which didn't sound too complicated.

He stood up. 'Shall I go and get into it? Or shall we call it a day?'

'The answer to your first question is yes, and I'm afraid I can't be bothered with the second.'

Gabriel left the room, and I filled my glass to the brim with white wine, and drank most of it in a single gulp. I caught myself telling Sammy that I'd finally gone mad, and hoped that my lover, my unusual lover, hadn't heard me. 'It was never like this with you, Sammy,' I whispered. 'Never at all like this.'

'Come up,' Gabriel called from the top of the stairs. 'I'm ready.'

Yes, but am I? I thought, and drained the glass. I'd been broad-minded and understanding about the idea of his wearing a dress, but how would the reality affect me? Would I be tempted to laugh? Would I do now what I most feared doing – draw back, instinctively, in disgust? I halted outside the room in which we had tried to make love with no imaginative embellishments, and realised that I was apprehensive about my own part in his fantasy. What role was I intended to play?

'If you can't face me, Esther, don't come in.'

I went in, and faced him. He stared at me in terror, in sheer terror. It was his fear, and only his fear, I registered first. His body and whatever was covering it were blurred before me.

'Gabriel,' I said. 'There's nothing to be frightened of. Really there isn't.'

'Do I look ridiculous?'

'No.' The blur vanished, and I saw him as he needed me to see him. 'No, you don't.' I dared to make light of the situation, and ventured, 'You could have shaved the hairs off your chest.'

'I'm not that serious. I'm only a mild case.'

'Shall I undress you?'

'Please.'

It was a simple cotton dress, with a zip at the back, which I loosened.

He stood naked now, smiling sheepishly at the prominent evidence of his desire for me.

'That's a lovely surprise, Gabriel. And so welcoming.'

'Guess who I was last night, Doctor Lady. If you can.'

'Stephen, it's far too early in the day for your riddles.'

'I'll meet you later, then.'

'Why not? I shall be free for a while at lunchtime.'

He was waiting on the steps when I came out of the clinic shortly after one o'clock.

'I've brought some sandwiches, Stephen. I thought we might have a little picnic, in the park.'

'You and me?'

'Us. Together.'

'I'm not sitting on the grass, not in these trousers I'm not. Grass stains green. And there's bound to be dog's mess, too.'

'You *are* fussy. We'll find a bench instead.'

'I had a pair of white trousers once went green from the grass. I'm not having these ones stained the same.'

'They're rather swish.'

'Swish? Did you say swish?'

'Yes. It means smart.'

'The Bish used to say it – swish – whenever he lost his brain. "I am the swish bishop," he'd say, and laugh his funny laugh.'

'I don't suppose it would be possible, Stephen – I don't

81

suppose it would be allowed – for you to introduce me to your bishop some day? You've made him sound so interesting.'

'Me? Introduce you to the Bish? You're dead right, Doctor Lady, it would not be possible, it would not be allowed. What do you want with him, anyway?'

'He doesn't sound – the way you describe him – like an ordinary bishop.'

'Him? He isn't ordinary. That's true. He's out on a limb, is the Bish.'

'Where is he now? In his palace?'

'You and your questions. He's – where he is. You and him'd make a couple, and that's true, too. You're both funny with your words and your voices.'

'Are we?'

'I said. But the Bish is funnier than you, Doctor Lady, specially with his "*Dominus*" stuff and his "*vobiscum*". You never talk that funny.'

'I'm glad to hear it.'

We came to the park, and walked until we found an unoccupied bench. There was an offending green leaf on it, which Stephen picked up and dropped on the grass.

'Are you hungry?'

'Me? I can eat.'

'There's chicken, and there's beef, or there's salad.'

He shrugged. 'The beef'll do.'

'I think I'm just about ready for your latest riddle now,' I said. 'If you can remember what you were trying to tell me early this morning.'

'Me? Of course I can remember. My brain doesn't go missing. No chance.'

'Tell me, then.'

'It's last night. It's who I was.'

'Tell me more.'

'Guess who I was.'

'Stephen, I assume. Or Andrew, perhaps.'

'No and no. I was wilder than them.'

'I don't understand.'

82

'You ought to. I was a wild foundling last night.' He sniggered. 'Wild as the wind.'

'I'm none the wiser.'

'When I met this man last night, on the circuit, I was all set to be a Robert. I haven't been a Robert for over a year. I keep track, you see. This man, he asked me my name, as they do sometimes, and it was on the tip of my tongue to say it was Robert, when I thought to myself: Robert's dull, and I don't feel like being dull; Robert's anybody; a Robert's a Robert. So I told him I was – I took a deep breath first – I told him I was Heathcliff.'

'You didn't.'

'I did. I certainly did. "You're joking," he said. "I am not joking," I said. "Nobody's called Heathcliff," he said. "I am," I said. "It's out of a film," he said. "It's out of a famous film." Well, him saying that gave me an inspiration, on the spot, so I said, "My mum saw that film, and that's why she called me Heathcliff. Stranger things," I said, "have happened." And that was it. That clinched it. He believed me, Doctor Lady, he believed me.'

'Incredible.'

'Different, eh? It was Heathcliff this, then, and Heathcliff that, and I have to say it made a change from – ' He paused. 'It made a change.'

'From?'

'From David, from Richard. From the usual.'

'Ah yes, your many names.'

'I'd have thought, me being Heathcliff, that he couldn't do what you did to me with Stephen – turn it into "Steve". It's common, in my opinion, and forward, people doing that. I won't allow "Dick" or "Ricky" or "Andy" or "Bob" or "Mike" or "Mick" or "Ted" or any of those. You'd have thought, wouldn't you, with Heathcliff, that he couldn't be forward, not in that way. He was, though. He called me "Heath". He said to me, bold as brass, "You're a nice boy, Heath", and I told him I didn't allow "Heath", not ever: I was Heathcliff to him and nothing else.'

'Are you a prostitute, Stephen?'

He bit into his sandwich. He finished eating. He wiped his mouth with the back of his hand.

'Me? Yeah. Yes, I am.'

'You could have lied, but I'm pleased you decided not to.'

'I've got other secrets, Doctor Lady. Real ones. I've got plenty more, don't worry.'

'I'm sure you have. Everybody's got them.'

'Not as good as mine. Not as clandestine as mine.'

He accompanied me back to the clinic. As we were parting, I suggested that he might like to come in and have some tests done. His job put him at terrible risk.

'You're wrong, Doctor Lady. My job doesn't. I've always been careful. I'm not going to stumble, like Tonio stumbled. I wouldn't allow myself.'

It is April now, and Sammy died in April, seven years ago, on the 26th, at twelve minutes past four in the morning. As each successive anniversary has come round, I have willed myself to treat the day like any other, but my will has usually failed me. The time, the day, the month all signify something that displaces logic.

This particular morning of the 26th has differed from its five grisly predecessors. To begin with, I didn't wake up shortly before four, in sorrowful anticipation of the moment of his going. I slept on. I slept until six, in fact, when I was woken by a kick inside me – the assertive kick of my unborn child. I advised the kicker to be patient, and drowsed contentedly.

'Sammy, Sammy, I haven't forgotten you.' Out came the guilty words as I waited for the kettle to boil a whole hour later. 'Of course I haven't,' I insisted, almost as if I were trying to appease his ghost. 'Of course I bloody haven't.'

While the tea was brewing, I heard him say, 'That's about your limit in the kitchen, isn't it? Pouring hot water on a few leaves?' It was his favourite taunt. 'Yes, Sammy, that's about my limit,' I answered. 'Thank you for reminding me.'

The young Sammy, who called me his Hadassah, would have laughed such an accusation to scorn had someone made it. So:

his wife couldn't cook. She admitted she couldn't. She deserved to be lauded for her honesty. There was an abundance, a superabundance, of women with no talent for cooking who were either too stupid or too complacent to come clean. They cooked, and what they cooked was dire, and yet they persisted in their folly, those agents of dyspepsia, because they lacked Esther Elkin's visionary courage. 'Esther avoids the stove out of love for her husband, whose sensitive appetite she has no wish to ruin. She's a paragon of all the virtues.'

He drank, then: beer and wine and whisky and gin, whatever appealed. He drank among friends and admirers, of whom there were many. There was no design to his drinking, no pattern. I could not begin to imagine that there ever would be.

His mother was alive and, seemingly, well. Maureen had been a 'squawker and a hoofer', as distinct from a singer and dancer, for most of her life. 'I wasn't stage-struck, Esther, no, not me,' she said. 'I never would have squawked and hoofed if Sammy's dad hadn't gone and died young. I had a voice and a nice pair of legs and no brains to speak of, so what else could I do to earn a crust and feed and clothe His Nibs here? Nothing, that's what.'

Maureen was unaware that her struggle to raise him was the subject of the film Sammy was working on when he met me. 'I hope it's a comedy, Esther, with plenty of laughs for everyone to enjoy,' she confided. 'But I rather fancy it won't be. There's a deal of gloom in my son hasn't come up to the surface yet.'

Her prediction was right. *A Song, A Dance* is not a comedy, with plenty of laughs. It has a soundtrack, but no dialogue. The mother's feelings for her son, the son's for her, are conveyed with looks and gestures. The mother sings and dances – at home; at a party; in several dingy rehearsal rooms; on a stage in a chorus line – while the son watches and listens. That's all.

'He's clever, isn't he, my Sammy? Not using any words, and me such a gasbag. She *was* meant to be me, that poor woman, wasn't she, Esther?'

'Yes, Maureen.'

'Bless him. Whisper it not in Gath, dear, but he's shown me more miserable than I really am. I never would have scowled at a producer the way she did, or glared at the pianist either. I needed the jobs too much, I needed the lovely money come Saturday night, I couldn't afford to be churlish. That poor woman didn't smile nearly half enough for my liking. If she had just cracked her face once or twice, I'd have been far happier with her. Still, bless him, though.'

Maureen was always blessing Sammy, I reflected as I sat at the kitchen table, drinking tea. She moderated every mild criticism of his character with her ritual 'Bless him'. Any honour or glory taken away from Sammy was given back with that cheery benediction.

She read the reviews of *A Song, A Dance*. 'This one says it's a "bleak work of art".' She looked up from the paper. 'I'm not bleak am I, Esther? I mean, if the film's bleak, the mother has to be bleak, too. I've been called many things, but not bleak.' I assured her she wasn't. 'It's praise, is it, that "bleak"?' I nodded. 'Strange kind of praise, to my way of thinking. I mean, imagine, Esther, if someone came up to you in the street and said, "You're very bleak today, Mrs Elkin. How *do* you do it?", you wouldn't be best pleased, would you?' I shook my head. She picked up another paper, and was soon snorting. 'No bleaks in this one, Esther. "Sam Elkin's *A Song, A Dance* has a gritty integrity." I know what integrity is, and I know my Sammy's got it, but why "gritty"?' I suggested that the reviewer was using 'gritty' in the sense of 'tough', perhaps. 'Well, I can't agree with him, in that case.' She went back to the article. 'He's laid "gritty" to rest.' she revealed. 'Now he's saying it's sad and poignant, and now he's nearer the mark. That's my trouble with it, really.'

'Trouble, Maureen?'

'Its being so sad and so poignant. What *I* see and what these writers in the papers can't is Sammy's deal of gloom rising up and blotting out the fun we had. I never would have survived if I'd been like that poor woman, moping and moping the way she did. Utter it not in the streets of Askelon, dear, but he might have given her a bit more sparkle, a bit more of the old *joie de vivre*. She ought to have smiled when she sang. That's another trouble for me – her voice. I was a squawker, not a *chanteuse*. People rushed to cover up their precious glassware the moment they saw me parting my lips. They never would have done that with her. They'd have unrolled the red carpet, opened the champagne and told her to cheer up because she had a fortune in her throat if she only but knew.' She stopped, and gave herself a slight slap on the cheek. 'I'm finding fault and I shouldn't. Bless him, anyway.'

'You did like the film, didn't you, Maureen?'

'I loved it, Esther. I adored it. You saw the state of my hanky afterwards. I never would have cried else. No, dear, my troubles over it come from it being my story and its not showing me with my warts and my failings – and for its blotting out the fun the two of us had. Otherwise, it's beautiful. Except that he does show her as being a martyr, and I never was a martyr, bless him.'

It was then – I remembered – she gave her son the benefit of her many doubts. She said, tentatively, 'I rather fancy what he was after capturing in his film, Esther, was – dare I say it? – my soul. He was after catching the hidden Maureen inside the real one, which is why I didn't recognise myself. Trust my Sammy to go and choose something really difficult to put across. That's his nature – turning his back on what's plain for all to see, and coming up with his deal of gloom where you'd least expect it.'

I was happy with Maureen's company this anniversary morning, and went with her again in memory to my mother's flat, a few weeks before the 'so ignominious' wedding took place at a registrar's office in Kensington.

'How do you behave in front of a countess, Esther? Sammy said I must curtsey.'

'Sammy's a devil, Maureen. Ignore his advice. He's making mischief.'

'Why would he want to do that?'

'You'll understand why when you've met her.'

'Will I? You could be wrong. The workings of my son's mind aren't always easy to follow.'

'Is that you, Esther?' my mother called out as I opened the front door.

'Yes, Mama, it's me.'

'Mama!' Maureen exclaimed, under her breath. 'Mama yet!'

'Yes, I'm afraid so.'

I almost had to push Maureen into the drawing-room. 'Mama, let me introduce you to Sammy's mother.'

'Maureen Elkin. Pleased to make your acquaintance.'

'Good afternoon, Mrs Elkin.' My mother held out her hand. 'Forgive me for not rising to greet you, as is my custom. I am inconvenienced today by a so irritating pain in the left leg.'

Maureen's nervousness vanished immediately. My mother's hand remained in the air, untouched. 'Don't mention pains in the legs to me, dear,' said Maureen, seating herself opposite the surprised invalid. 'I've had pains in my legs from the day I started as a hoofer. Pains are part and parcel of a dancer's life.'

My mother's hand slowly descended. 'You are a dancer?'

'Was, dear. Was for ages. I'm nearly sixty now, and a high kick'd do me in, if I had the nerve to try one. It's the same with the splits, which used to be a speciality of mine – I can still just about get down there, though I creak like the door in the haunted house on the way, but it's coming back up again that causes the trouble. You feel such a fool, stranded.'

'You were not, I gather, a ballet dancer?'

'You gather right, you don't gather wrong. I've worn many a tutu in my time – a tutu or two too many, some would say – but a ballerina I never was. I didn't have the ambition, dear. I went into dancing for a living out of dire necessity, at an age when most ballet dancers are planning their retirement. I was a neat little tapper, you see, and I had a strong pair of lungs, and there was this vacancy, in the chorus at the Victoria Palace and I got the job straight off, which was a miracle, really, because the show ran for ever, and do I mean for ever, I mean for ever, dear – three lovely long years.'

'You were a chorus girl, Mrs Elkin?'

'I was. Up until last January, I was. My career's been nothing if not cosmopolitan, I can tell you. I've been a cowgirl in the Midwest, a woman of easy virtue in an opium den in Hong Kong, a lady-in-waiting in Ruritania, a pajama-factory worker in North America, a member of the Salvation Army in the Bronx

88

and a nun – would you believe? – in the Austrian Tyrol. And all Jewish.' Maureen laughed. 'All of them bagel eaters.'

'How fascinating for you, Mrs Elkin.'

'Do excuse me, dear, for gabbling on and forgetting your poor leg, which is what got me going in the first place. Whereabouts is it, the pain – calf or thigh?'

'Oh, it's – it's – in the knee.'

'I sympathise, dear. I've known anguish with my knees, I really have. Describe the pain for me. Does it jab at you or does it throb? Does it come and go or is it constant? I'm a bit of an expert on painful knees. I might be able to help you.'

'It's nothing serious, Mrs Elkin – '

'Maureen, dear. I'm Maureen.'

'It isn't serious at all. It is kind of you to offer help, but it will not be necessary. Esther, would you be an angel and make the tea?'

'Yes, Mama.'

'Does Mrs Elkin favour Indian or China?'

'She's easy, dear,' said Maureen. 'She'll drink whatever's in the cup.'

'Let us have Lapsang, then, Esther. It is so much more refreshing in muggy weather.'

Maureen was admiring Anna Pavlova when I returned.

'Did you see her dance, dear?'

'Yes. I was very, very young.'

'You must have been.'

'In Paris. At the Opéra.'

'And you can remember her, can you?'

'Vividly.'

'That's wonderful.'

'I wanted Esther to become a ballerina. My late husband, the Count, paid for her to have lessons with a Madame Vera, who was said to be the finest teacher of the Petipa method. Alas, things did not happen as we desired. It was this Madame Vera's view that Esther was not *cut out* for the ballet. Her heart was not in it and her feet were not inspiring.'

'Esther's feet look perfectly OK to me.'

'They were not OK, as you remark, for this Madame

Vera. They were not OK at all. That was the nub of the matter.'

'I think she was well spared, dear. For every Pavlova there's a hundred nobodies, and you wouldn't have wanted her to be one of them, would you? Wasting her *fouettés* on the desert air, so to speak? No, Esther's fine as she is, with her feet on the ground.'

My mother announced that she had a headache.

'You *are* in the wars today, dear.'

'The wars? Which wars?'

'With your pains. First your leg, and now your poor head.'

'I shall survive.'

'That's the spirit.'

'I only need a little peace and quiet, Mrs Elkin. The simple remedies are the best.'

'I quite agree.'

'I shall lie down with the curtains drawn.'

'I often do that myself, when the world seems to be on top of me.'

'You do? How sensible. I shall probably lie down shortly. In my room. In the quiet.'

My mother's unsubtle repetition of her unsubtle hint achieved its aim: we went soon after.

'I didn't call her Countess once. I couldn't let myself, Esther, I don't know why. Was she offended?'

'Perhaps.'

'Perhaps? Was she or wasn't she?'

'I can't give you a definite answer, Maureen. Her behaviour mystifies me. The one thing I'm certain of is the pain in her leg. It's non-existent.'

'She wasn't forthcoming with the symptoms, that's true. I tried too hard to be friendly, I suppose. I had to break the ice somehow.'

Maureen's second attempt at friendliness was to be her last. My mother had decided that she would endure the 'so ignominious' marriage ceremony for the dreadful reason that her daughter was involved in it, but I must understand that there were limits to her endurance: 'I shall be polite to your

Mr Elkin and the woman who "dears" me. I cannot promise that I shall be charming into the bargain. May I bring Antoinette and Wanda for moral support?'

'I should like them to be there anyway, Mama.'

'At least it will be over quickly. That is a consolation.'

'Yes, Mama. It will be over quickly.'

The ceremony, when it came, was brief, as she had anticipated. It had been scheduled for two-thirty but was delayed until three because the registrar was suddenly taken ill. 'A bilious attack,' explained the usher. 'He's partial to French food. Snails and such.'

We waited in the corridor outside the office.

'There isn't even a chair to sit on. And the smell of disinfectant is cruel to the nose.'

'The smell it's covering up is probably nastier, dear,' said Maureen. 'You're very smartly turned out for the day of days, if I may say so.'

'This – ' My mother indicated Maureen with a flick of her glove. 'This – Wanda, Antoinette – is Mrs Elkin. Mrs Elkin is Esther's Mr Elkin's mother. The bridegroom is her son.'

'Pleased to make both your acquaintances.'

'Mrs Elkin used to be a performer in the musical theatre. She was a chorus girl.'

'I was, indeed. I had a smile fixed on my face for thirty-odd years.'

Maureen mentioned some of the shows she had squawked and hoofed in.

'Then I've seen you on the stage, Mrs Elkin,' said Antoinette Hilton. 'Many times. But I'm afraid I don't remember you.'

'Don't be afraid to be afraid, dear. I wasn't meant to be remembered. That's a chorus girl's unhappy fate.' She chuckled. 'I was one of a team, always.'

'If that so wretched man doesn't arrive to marry Esther and her Mr Elkin, I fear we shall have to listen to Mrs Elkin's entire history. Where can he be?'

I glanced at Maureen, who was clearly hurt by my mother's rudeness. She responded, in a quiet voice, 'Where can he be? I'll tell you where he is. He's in the lavatory, shitting through the eye

91

of a needle. That's where he is, Your Majesty.' Then, turning to me, she said, 'I'm sorry, Esther. I hope I haven't upset you. I'll watch my manners from now on.'

My mother excused herself from the reception – 'I shall leave you and your husband to celebrate as you wish' – and was never to meet Maureen again. She was already dead-in-life by the time, six years later, the growth appeared on Maureen's tongue.

'I thought I'd just bitten it while I was gabbling and caused a pimple to sprout. It's happened before. But no, it's not a pimple, Esther love. It's something much worse.'

I was to keep her cancer to myself, she insisted. It would be easier for everyone's peace of mind, including her own, if Gath, Askelon and Sammy remained in a state of ignorance on the subject. Sammy must go off to Venice unawares and bask in the fame his film was bringing him. He'd have to stare her illness in the face soon enough, but not for the moment, not while he was prospering. 'He's not strong like you, Esther. He has his deal of gloom, bless him. Let's pretend for as long as we can.'

We sustained our pretence for a few weeks only. Maureen refused to be 'chemotherapied' – the thought of being bald was too much for her. 'I shall die with my hair on,' she joked. 'Nicely rinsed and set.'

Maureen died with her hair on, and Sammy – slowly, at first; then, gradually; then, steadily – drank to console himself. Then I ceased to be his Hadassah. Then I lost my love to gin.

'I bet you didn't expect to see me again so soon, did you, Doctor Lady?'

'Of course I did.'

'Even after me allowing you to know what I do for a living?'

'Yes, Stephen. Even after.'

'You're not shocked?'

'Should I be?'

'Yeah. You're a woman.'

'I'm pleased to hear it. That was the conclusion I came to

when I last looked. Thousands of women do what you do for a living. It *is* the world's oldest profession, Stephen.'

'Is it?'

'So they say.'

'No, what I meant was, Doctor Lady, is that you're a decent woman, like a doctor.'

'You do realise, don't you, what I'm a doctor *of*?'

'Me? Yeah. I'm not stupid.'

'Well, because of my work, Stephen, I've had to examine lots of prostitutes, of both sexes. I haven't time to be shocked.'

'You're not disgusted?'

'No, not really.'

'By me, I mean?'

He watched me hesitate. 'No, Stephen.'

'Are you sure?'

'Yes, I am. I would feel happier if you'd chosen another career, but there it is.'

'Chosen, Doctor Lady? Me? The fetching frugal foundling? I just wonder. I just wonder what you'd *recommend*.'

'There must be plenty of jobs you could do.'

'Yeah. Plenty.'

'When you were younger, at school, didn't you have an ambition to be something or someone when you were grown-up?'

'Me? No.'

'A film star, perhaps? A footballer?'

'You're losing your brain, Doctor Lady. I hate football – hate it, hate it, hate it. And before you ask, I'm not allowed to tell you why.'

'I shan't, in that case.' I went on, desperately, 'You could be a model, Stephen, with your dress sense.'

'Me? Like in photographs?'

'Yes, exactly.'

'I wouldn't enjoy that – posing. Jack on the circuit did a bit of it, modelling, and said it was dopey. Jack said you had no say in what clothes you wore, and had to look as if you had a stink under your nose. Posing's dopey, in Jack's opinion.'

'Is Jack a friend of the Bishop, too?'

'You never give up, do you, Doctor Lady? Jack's met the Bish, yes. Jack is familiar with the good old Bish.'

'Jack's one of his acolytes, is he?'

'Jack? The acolyte? No, Tonio was the acolyte, nobody else. Only Tonio was chosen.'

'Why was that?'

'Because, because. Because the Bish liked him best, that's why. The Bish thought Tonio was the bee's knees. "Where is my precious acolyte?" he'd ask. "Up to his naughty tricks, I suppose?" Which Tonio usually was. He let him get away with anything.'

'But not you, not Jack?'

'Me? Jack? No. We were his sheep, the Bish used to say. We were in his faithful flock. Tonio was above me and him on account of his superior intelligence. "Anthony is my second-in-command," the Bish told us. "You will take orders from him whenever I am summoned forth on my urgent clerical rounds." Which is what we did, except that Tonio's orders weren't really orders.'

'Did the Bishop always call him Anthony?'

'Tonio. Yeah. It was only me was allowed to call him Tonio.'

'Why, Stephen?'

'You and your "whys", Doctor Lady. Because I was privileged, that's why.'

I remembered that the dying Anthony Innocent had greeted him as Sugar Cane. 'And what name did he have for you?' was my next, calculatedly ingenuous, question.

'You can't catch me out. I keep a step ahead. The name he had for me is top secret and totally clandestine. Understood?'

'Yes, Stephen,' I confirmed, yet again, and added that I had to see my first patient.

'I want to meet your lover, Doctor Lady. Your Mr Gabriel. I want to see what he looks like. I want to see what kind of man you go for.'

'I think he'd be curious to meet you, too.'

'Have you been talking to him about me, then?'

'I've mentioned you, yes, Stephen.'

'Did you tell him *all* about me? About what I do?'

'No, not all about you.'

'So when will you be – ' He stopped, and grinned. '*Effecting an introduction?*'

'On Sunday, if you're free,' I heard myself answer.

'I'll be free. I'll make myself free. Free as the air and the birds flying in it.'

'Twelve o'clock, on the bottom step,' I said, and entered the clinic.

'Try not to be late, Doctor Lady.'

'There's someone in the waiting-room who will appeal to you, Esther,' said my colleague, Gerry Gatenby. 'Knowing your love of painting and literature.'

'What are you up to, you rogue?'

'He's a walking work of art. He might have been made for you. Shall I send him in?'

'Gerry, what are you playing at?'

'He's one in a million, I swear, Esther. You'll thank me for passing him on to you. He's a startling apparition.'

Gerry left, and a moment later the startling apparition walked in. I was duly startled at the sight of him.

'No need to be frightened,' he said. 'I'm quite harmless.'

'I'm reassured. Please sit down.'

'It's only decoration, after all.'

'Yes,' I replied, too stunned for other words.

'My head is the Garden of Eden.' He had lost his hair at sixteen, he explained, from alopecia, and the family doctor had told him he would stay bald for good. 'I wasn't happy at the prospect. I was miserable, to tell the truth. I went inside myself and had no wish to come out. I glowered at anyone who so much as looked at me. Then, one summer evening, I saw this amazing man in Hyde Park – at Speakers' Corner, to be precise. He was demonstrating to the crowd how he had escaped from prison – not just one prison, but several: Sing Sing, the Santé in Paris, Devil's Island and Wormwood Scrubs. He was an international criminal, he boasted, wanted for something or other in three continents. But what was really amazing about him – for me, at least – was the fact that he was tattooed from top to toe. He was like a living, breathing picture. When he'd freed himself from the chains he was tied in, I strolled across and spoke to him. I asked for the name of his tattooist, and he laughed at me and said there had been a dozen of them over the years and they were probably dead and buried by now. Well, one of them was still alive, and it was he who did my garden for me: Freddy Phillips, known as the Rembrandt of the Tattoo.'

'He did a remarkable job. Is that the Serpent sliding out of your ear?'

'The very same. When I first went to Freddy P's, it was only my horrible scalp I wanted done. But then I thought: Why not go the whole hog and have my ugly mug painted too? So I gave him more room for manoeuvre, and the Garden of Eden spread, or ran wild, depending on your point of view. The roses are particularly authentic, aren't they?'

'Yes. Yes, they are.'

'Have you ever travelled to Curaçao?'

'No, I can't say that I have.'

'Let me take you on a day trip, then. It will entail me undoing my shirt and exposing my chest, but that shouldn't trouble you. A person in your position must be accustomed to naked flesh.'

I nodded.

'Not *so* naked, in my case.' He stood up, and removed his jacket. 'Curaçao is an island in the Caribbean. It's the largest in the Netherlands Antilles. According to the 1972 census, the estimated population is one hundred and fifty thousand and eight. That isn't a vast amount of people, you'll agree. What other information can I provide? Oh, yes. The area of the island is four hundred and forty-four square kilometres, which is a hundred and seventy-three square miles. Curaçao's the perfect paradise, by the sound of it.'

'You haven't been there yourself?'

'No, not to date. Hope springs eternal, though. Meanwhile, I have the map. *Et voilà!*' He threw his shirt on to the chair and stood before me with his map of Curaçao revealed. 'Freddy P said it was the greatest challenge of his tattooing life. Look how he's managed to fit everything in – every little town, every little port, just as they're marked in the atlas. There's Noord Punt – I believe that means "North Point" in Dutch – under my throat, and there's the capital, Willemstad, to the right of my belly-button, and Punt Kanon, which is similar to our Land's End, is hidden inside my trousers for the present. And those blue squiggles surrounding the island are the Caribbean Sea, in all its oceanic glory. They carry on over on my back.' He turned to show me. 'That shark lurking in the water was Freddy P's last-minute inspiration.'

'Very menacing,' I remarked.

'These are birds on my arms. Still, I didn't really come here to give you a display, much as you seem to appreciate it. I do have a problem, I'm afraid. You'll know where it is.'

'In the penis, I assume.'

'Precisely.'

I was seized in that instant by a ludicrous thought. 'Your penis – it's not tattooed, is it?'

'The answer's yes. I must apologise for it in advance. I had it done as a joke – not serious, like Curaçao.'

There were letters, I saw, forming the word 'loop'.

'What's the significance of "loop"?'

'You've got me blushing behind my garden now. I'm totally embarrassed. When it – when it grows bigger, if you follow me, it spells – oh, Christ, I'm really and truly embarrassed – '

'It spells?'

'It spells, when it's bigger, "lollipop". As I say, I had it done for a joke, after several pints of beer.'

'But wasn't it terribly painful – being tattooed while you were erect?'

'I honestly can't remember. What with the beer and the anaesthetic, it couldn't have been too bad. This isn't Freddy P's work, by the way. A run-of-the-mill tattooist's responsible – the sort who'll shove any old muck on a person so long as he pays for it.'

I asked him to pull back his foreskin, which he did.

'Freddy Phillips has standards,' he continued. 'He's a pacifist.

97

He'll do you a fiery dragon with a bit of coaxing, but not a knife or a sword. And as for swastikas – never, never. He had such a demand for them once, he was forced to put up a notice in his studio with the message "Strictly No Swastikas". He lost tons of clients as a result. He wasn't worried, because he was obeying his conscience, not thinking of his profits. He's rare, Freddy P.'

I was curious to know why he had left his hands free of tattoos, since he appeared to have had every other part of his body decorated.

'To please my parents,' he responded. 'They begged me to keep my hands in the state God intended. It was the least I could do for them.'

The man with the lollipop – or Mr Lollipop, as we here shall no doubt soon be calling him – screwed his eyes up tightly and winced when the nurse took a sample of his blood, I heard later. 'He was scared of the needle, Doctor. Of the needle! Can you credit it?'

'Did you manage to find a suitable vein in the aviary?'

'I did. Just about. Under a parrot.'

There is, it transpires, a Mrs Lollipop, who is not to be blamed for her husband's gonorrhoeal infection. She is devoted to him, and he to her, he asserted. It was he who had strayed from the nest for that single wild night, with his man's lust spurred on by lethal Swedish vodka, and it was his fault entirely for letting a complete stranger – a woman, a woman – lure him into an upstairs bedroom, while the party went on down below. He would never drink Absolut again – certainly not in such a gigantic quantity – and he would try to trace the stranger who had given him his first, and last, dose of clap. He wanted nothing more than that his life return to normal and slip into its steady, comfortable rhythm.

I suspect that Mr Lollipop will stay lodged in my memory for ever: impossible, now, to displace from it the map, the shark, the host of blue and red birds, the Caribbean Sea 'in all its oceanic glory'. His loop, too, his embryo lollipop, will become a permanent fixture. That decorative individual has joined Horace in the special recess of my mind which has been, until today, Horace's alone. What a strange and intriguing pair they make for me – iconic, almost, of the physically repellent.

Horace was in a decidedly un-Horace-like condition when I encountered him twelve years ago. He was clean and smelled only of the strong carbolic soap he had been scrubbed with during the enforced washing of the previous day. He had had to be cut out of his clothes, which were heavy with the accumulated dirt of decades. He had been picked up, foaming at the mouth, from a gutter in Charlotte Street, and brought into the casualty department of the Middlesex Hospital, where six orderlies, no less, had held him down, the better to facilitate his release from the foul-smelling rags. 'It was like trying to land a stinking whale,' observed one of them, with a theatrical sniff for emphasis.

The doctor who examined the scoured and shining Horace found that the ancient tramp had syphilis. I was completing my training at the hospital, and was invited by my superior to assist him in his dealings with Horace, who raged and grunted and snorted in captivity. We were alarmed by the fact, the irrefutable fact, that Horace had caught the disease recently – at the very peak of his filthiness; in the same putrid clothing someone had subsequently stashed, at arm's length, into the incinerator.

Our attempts at discovering the identity of Horace's extra-ordinary partner were met with leers and smirks. 'She's a saint,' was all he said of her. We were left wondering if there was, indeed, a saintly quality in her character, for how else could she have borne the sheer stench of him? Or was it, simply, that she was his equivalent in female form, as happily unaware of her own putrescence?

Horace and Mr Lollipop are extreme cases, perhaps, yet each of them prompts me to marvel at the inexplicable nature of sexual attraction. Does Mrs Lollipop delight in the map of Curaçao adorning her husband's copious chest? Do her fingers move gently from Westpunt to Tafelberg on their way to Punt Kanon? Is the regular transformation of 'loop' into 'lollipop' the cause of her keenest ecstasy?

I smile at the notion, and then I imagine myself as Mrs Lollipop, who has somehow learned that Esther Potocki enjoys

– enjoys? she positively revels in it – the silent moment when she has to remove her lover from his imprisoning dress. Mrs Lollipop can hardly contain her laughter as she pictures the scene: a man, a grown man, wearing nothing but a pretty frock, waits nervously while the peculiar Esther Potocki decides whether she will or she won't help him out of it. What a performance! What a rigmarole! Never such goings-on in the Lollipop residence, thank you very much. Oh dear, oh dear – it's the next bit that strikes Mrs Lollipop as perverted, for Esther Potocki is delirious with excitement now as she lifts the dress and sees – this is no laughing matter for Mrs L – an unlollipopped cock. This is more than Mrs L can tolerate.

The tolerant Esther Potocki – the senior consultant physician in genito-urinary medicine at St Lucy's – has realised lately that her darling Tata might have inspired a measure of intolerance in her had she known of his photographic activities while he lived. She has started to ask herself if he was, in some deeply sly and circuitous way, taking revenge on the wife he had come to despise. It was no accident, surely, that the women he persuaded to pose for him were Maria Potocka's few honoured acquaintances, her 'chosen circle'. His loving daughter has begun to wonder when it was that the abstruse idea of capturing Antoinette and Eva and Wanda and Helen in those absurd attitudes first occurred to Adam Potocki. And, once possessed of that idea, how did he manage to cajole each of Maria's 'girls' into bringing it to fulfilment? Was there no resistance to his odd, his preposterous, demands? Did none of them accuse him of voyeurism? Did no one slap his face, or threaten to tell his innocent, trusting Maria? Did no one enquire, in the most genteel manner, what he wanted the photographs *for*?

The tolerant, successful daughter of Adam Potocki catches her father now as he looks at his wife with bemused contempt, in anticipation of the exit line – another gem – he will record in his special book. Esther Potocki catches him now in the light of the knowledge she gained on the afternoon she went through his papers and found herself staring at Wanda Stone's vagina, and it's a knowledge, she understands now, she has needed to discard, in order to preserve the Tata who died her absolute hero. He would be that still, she knows, if she hadn't done her mother's bidding and gone into his study. He would have remained her own dear Tata – her Tata *in toto* – if Maria Potocka had opened the boxes instead. The grief-stricken countess, seeing that intimidating mass of old bills and legal documents, would never have persevered with the so boring task, and the hidden evidence of his esoteric vengeance would not have been uncovered.

So I thought as I cleared the desk I shall not be using for seven months. A different doctor – Gerry, or my temporary replacement – will be attending to Mr Lollipop when he returns next week.

In the meantime, I was late for the breathing lesson I take alongside Gabriel, the father of the child we conceived in the ecstasy that followed the removal of his polka dot dress.

'I wasn't going to come, Doctor Lady,' Stephen said when he was seated beside me. 'But I allowed myself to change my mind.'

'Why and why, Stephen? Why weren't you going to come, and why have you changed your mind?'

'You'll die asking why, Doctor Lady. Well, I wasn't going to come today because I didn't want to. And then I decided I did want to. That's the why of it.'

'I see.'

'Is Mr Gabriel – your lover – expecting Stephen?'

'He's expecting you, yes.'

'Me? I'm Stephen where you're concerned. And him. What's he got for himself – a house or a flat?'

'A house. It's over two hundred years old.'

'Am I wearing the right clothes, do you think? Is my ensemble good enough for your lover's house?'

'Perfectly good enough. He doesn't live in a palace.'

'I'm used to a palace, Doctor Lady. The Bish had a palace.'

'I remember you saying.'

'It wasn't big and grand like Buckingham. Not half so palatial. No chandeliers, for instance.'

'I don't immediately associate chandeliers with bishops.'

'He'd have had one, the Bish, if he could've. That was the only item missing, he said. A chandelier would have provided the final flourish.'

'What did he mean?'

'The Bish? Search me. Even Tonio had to guess what he was on about sometimes, "With due respect, Your Grace," he'd say. "Your acolyte isn't on Your Grace's wavelength." No, I think the Bish wanted a chandelier just like he wanted screens and statues and the other daft and dopey things he had in his chapel.'

'You must mention the Bishop to Gabriel.'

'Me? I might.'

'He's fascinated by preachers. I assume the Bishop preached occasionally.'

'Sermons?'

'Exactly.'

'Sermons from the *pulpit*? Oh yes, the Bish gave us plenty of those. We knew we were in for a sermon from the pulpit whenever we saw him putting on his ensemble. "Round up my silly sheep," he'd say to Tonio. "I have words of wisdom for them." And did he have words, Doctor Lady. You never heard so many. It was hard not to drop off, I can tell you. I'd have to nudge Jack Saul to stop him from snoring.'

'Is he the Jack who did some modelling? On the circuit?'

'I suppose you think you're one clever lady, Doctor Lady. Yeah, he's the Jack. He's the same *ne'er-do-well* Jack Saul.'

'The same what?'

'Ne'er-do-well. "Master Jack, you are a ne'er-do-well," the Bish'd say to him. "A devilish young ne'er-do-well", he'd call him.'

'How very old-fashioned of the Bishop.'

'He was old-fashioned all right. He was right out of this world, the Bish. He was the funniest of the funniest, specially when he was in his pulpit.'

I parked the car in the tree-lined street that runs behind Gabriel's house.

'You look scared, Stephen.'

'Me? You're losing your brain. I'm not scared.'

'He's rather gentle and shy.'

'Your lover?'

'Yes.' There was a solitary black swan on the Thames. 'I wonder if he's flown here from Australia.'

'Mr Gabriel?'

'No, Stephen, that swan. It's far more likely that he's been bred in this country. Perhaps somebody's set him free, or perhaps he's escaped.'

'He killed it,' Stephen almost shouted. 'In his fist.'

Then he stopped, and seemed to go into a trance.

'Who, Stephen? Who killed what in his fist?'

He opened his mouth, but said nothing. He stared at the bird on the water.

'Who?' I asked again.

He turned to me and shook his head briskly, as if he were ridding himself of the last vestiges of sleep.

'Nobody. I'm not allowed to say his name.'

'Are you sure?'

'Sure I'm sure I'm sure. Let's go and see your lover, Doctor Lady. He's expecting us.'

Gabriel's front door was open.

'Come in,' I said to Stephen, who hesitated on the threshold. 'Come in.'

'Where is he?'

'In the kitchen, probably. Or in his study upstairs. Does it matter where he is?'

'I want to see him first. Before I go in there.'

'Why?'

'I just do.'

I called out to Gabriel, 'We're here, sweetheart.'

Stephen sniggered. '"Sweetheart",' he said, disdainfully. '"Sweetheart"!'

Gabriel appeared, wearing an apron. We kissed. Stephen waited, apprehensive, on the doorstep.

'This is the friend I was telling you about, darling.' (Stephen mouthed the word 'darling' twice.) 'Gabriel, meet Stephen.'

'Do please come in, Stephen.' Gabriel went to him and offered his hand. Stephen fixed his attention on it for a long moment and then decided to offer his own. 'You seem to be frightened of something.'

'Me? No. I'm not frightened. Why should I be frightened?'

'I've no idea, Stephen.'

'What's Doctor Lady been telling you?'

'I can't give you a short answer, so please do come in. We can sit in the garden while the weather lasts.'

Stephen was still hesitant. 'Who else is in there?'

'No one.'

'I'm not fond of lots of strangers.'

'Neither am I, Stephen. I hate walking into a room filled with people I've never met.'

'Are you rich, Mr Gabriel?'

'I'm not poor. Why do you ask?'

'This place you've got here. It must've cost you.'

'It did. I bought it with money that came my way by accident. A few years ago, I wrote a book about preachers. A Hollywood producer read it, and paid me thousands of pounds so that he could make a film based on the life of one of them – Roger Kemp of Liverpool. It's called *Mersey Messiah*. You may have seen it.'

'Me? No. I haven't seen your film.'

(Oh, Sammy, I thought, you directed a little masterpiece, a classic of the cinema, and what did it bring you? Modest fame, perhaps; a certain prestige. Nothing more. It didn't bring you a house by the Thames.)

'You haven't missed anything. It's trash.'

'Is it, Mr Gabriel? I wouldn't know.'

'Stephen, this is ridiculous,' I interrupted. 'Are you coming in or aren't you?'

'Me? I suppose.'

The telephone rang, and Gabriel excused himself, and with his disappearance Stephen seemed to relax. He smiled at me and entered.

104

'Here I am, Doctor Lady. Safe inside.'

I led him through to the garden.

'I couldn't live in this place,' he confided, in a whisper. 'Not if you paid me.'

'Why is that?'

'You and your "whys". Because, because. It's *claust-ro-pho-bic*, that's why. The ceilings are too near my head. They're all right for him – your sweetheart, Doctor Lady, your darling – being so small. But not for me.'

'Men and women were smaller when this house was built in 1789. The ceilings wouldn't have been too near for them.'

'They are for me. I'd feel trapped in this place.'

'Don't you like anything about it?'

'Me? If I got given thousands of pounds for a film, Doctor Lady, I'd buy a big, big house with big windows.'

'Would you?'

'Me? No, I wouldn't. Actually. I don't want houses. No, if I got given thousands of pounds for a film I'd buy thousands and thousands of ensembles. Cashmere wool and sea-island cotton and silk, that's what I'd buy.'

'Where would you store them? You'd need an enormous wardrobe.'

'I'd have one put up special, Doctor Lady. A proper deposi-tory, with my name on the outside.'

'Which name would that be, Stephen?'

'I am not – repeat not – allowed to tell you.'

'Of course you aren't.'

Gabriel came out of the kitchen, carrying a tray on which were a bottle of champagne and three glasses.

'Stephen doesn't drink, Gabriel. He's a teetotaller. He has to keep a step ahead. He never loses his brain.'

'Sensible man. Would you prefer orange juice? Or fizzy water, perhaps?'

'Me? I'd prefer a drop of what you're having, Mr Gabriel. That's what I'd prefer.'

'But, Stephen – ' I began.

'But, Doctor Lady, I know what I prefer. Understand? I have arrived at that conclusion.'

'I see.'

'I shall – ' He broke off, and laughed. 'What I shall do is *imbibe* a *modicum* of bubbly.'

'To Stephen,' said Gabriel.

'To Stephen.'

'To me, myself and I,' said Stephen, taking his first sip.

There were to be other surprises on that final day in Stephen's company. From champagne he went on to white wine, from white to red, and after lunch he had an anisette. He spurned nothing that was put before him – the spicy prawns, the roast lamb with asparagus, the cheeses, the lemon tart. He cleaned his every plate. When Gabriel enquired if he had enjoyed the meal, Stephen replied, 'Me? It's all gone, isn't it? I wouldn't have ate it if I hadn't.'

He talked. He talked, at Gabriel's invitation, about the Bishop, the Bish, and the more he talked, the more Gabriel was riveted. Stephen kept reminding us that the wine hadn't made him lose his brain, and that he was still a step ahead, and that he knew what he wasn't allowed to say, which meant that he wasn't going to say it. He talked of Anthony, the Bish's acolyte, and of Jack Saul, who was now on the circuit, and of the Bish's funny words – his '*Dominus*', his '*vobiscum*', his 'suffragan' – and of his, the Bish's, palace in London, the precise location of which he was not allowed to divulge. He talked for minutes on end, without interruption.

'When did you last see the Bishop, Stephen?'

'Me? A while ago.'

'Years? Months?'

'Years, actually, Mr Gabriel. But I'm not allowed to tell you how many.'

'I think I know who your bishop is. You've given us such a vivid description of him, I think I've guessed his identity.'

'You have, have you? Who is he then, Mr Gabriel?'

'I think he's the Bishop of Wandle, Stephen.'

There was a silence.

'You're one clever Mr Gabriel, aren't you? You're even cleverer than the Doctor Lady. In my opinion.'

'Am I right?'

Stephen nodded. He drained his coffee cup and rose from the table. 'Listen hard, you two, and take heed.'

'We're listening.'

'You'll be getting a present from me in a few days' time. A precious gift. It's a present for both of you. Understand?'

We said we understood.

'I can't stay longer. I'll walk back, Doctor Lady. I must love you and leave you.' He sniggered. 'I must be off.'

'Don't go yet.'

'I have to go, Mr Gabriel. I can't stay longer.'

We went to the opera yesterday evening, to *Wozzeck*. So moved were we by the performance that neither of us could speak afterwards. Outside the theatre, Gabriel took my arm. Then we set off in a daze, in the surprisingly warm September air.

I awoke during the night from a dream as absurd as it was harrowing. I was back in the restaurant where we had eaten supper, sitting at the same table, looking across at the same famous actress, who was wearing the same turban. I was bewildered, yet again, by the half-smile that refused to move from her face, giving her the appearance of a glamorous ghoul. 'Surgery, Esther?' asked Gabriel once more, and, 'Surgery,' I rereplied. 'She has definitely been under the knife.'

The actress vanished, but her half-smile remained, briefly, like the Cheshire Cat's. 'I am lovely, lovely, lovely,' it said. 'I am immovably lovely,' it shouted, before it faded away. I was alone now, among the tables covered with snow-white cloths. A tiny fleck of dirt suddenly settled on the pristine tablecloth nearest to me, and when I tried to brush it off my hand froze. A sigh, not mine, came from somewhere. I watched as another fleck descended, and another, and another, until there was a heap of them. I heard a second sigh, and knew that it was coming from the rapidly mounting dust. My hand ached to demolish it, but found itself powerless. It grew and grew in front of me. I saw, then, that the hundreds of flecks were forming into a human shape, and that the human shape was Sammy.

'The miracle of the ashes, Hadassah!'

107

He was calling me by my Hebrew name, so I knew he was happy. He was King Ahasuerus, holding out his golden sceptre toward his young bride: 'It's yours, my love, and yours alone.'

'Oh, Sammy, you sweet, sweet idiot.'

'That's me.'

I laughed, but he was not amused. I was the Polish bitch now, the Polish prig; I was the inadequate woman he viewed through gin.

'Sammy, be reasonable.'

In a world of cancerous tongues, he hissed, what was the use of reason?

'Sammy, what's become of you?'

'You can see what's become of me. I was ash, thanks to you, but now I'm flesh and blood. I have gallons of blood to spill for you, Mrs Elkin – to spill for you over again. You remember how it gushed out of my mouth? I can give you a repeat performance. My oesophageal varices are ready to pop, pop, pop for you, just as they popped, popped, popped in those pre-ash days.'

'I can't bear it, Sammy. Please be dead. Please be dead.'

I was amazed, on waking, to find Gabriel sleeping soundly beside me. Hadn't I screamed at my resurrected husband? Hadn't I cried out to him? Obviously not.

I sat by the window in Gabriel's study in the faint early light. Our baby stirred inside me. I thought of the happiness awaiting us, the happiness its arrival would bring, and glowed. The prospect of joy is always this luminous, I realised, always this simple and immediate.

I had forgotten, in my complacency, what had moved us so deeply only hours before. At the very end of Berg's opera, the unnamed son of the desperate Wozzeck and his mistress, Marie, is left all by himself. His little friends have run off to the forest in expectation of seeing Marie's corpse. Her murderer, Wozzeck, is dead, too, drowned in the water that seemed like her enveloping blood to him. The boy is pretending that he's riding a hobby-horse. 'Hop, hop!' he sings. 'Hop, hop! Hop, hop!'

I have not allowed myself, yet, to reveal to Gabriel why the sight of the fragile boy on the deserted stage caused me such anguish. It was Sugar Cane I saw there, in pale disguise. It was none other than Sugar Cane.

TWO

My mother always insisted that we lived in an apartment. It was her belief that apartments were superior to flats, for reasons not entirely concerned with size and spaciousness. Apartment people were people like us – people of means; people of a certain standing in the world – whereas flat people, if you would pardon the so silly sounding expression, were the men and women who served in shops and waited in restaurants and delivered one's letters.

'What do you think of our apartment?' she asked my friends Alice and Jane the first, and last, time they came for tea.

'It's lovely,' said Jane.

'And very large,' said Alice.

'We chose it, my husband and myself, for its – what is the word? – roominess. I have to tell you, though, that large as it is, it is less large than the *appartement* in Paris in which I spent the happiest years of my young life.'

'Did you really grow up in Paris?'

'Yes – Jane, is it? – I really did. From the age of nine – or perhaps it was ten – I did. After my family had fled from Cracow. Cracow is in Poland.'

To my mother's astonishment, both Alice and Jane were more interested to hear about Cracow than Paris. She had very few memories of the place, she snapped, and all of those were personal to her. When she thought of Cracow, she saw only chimneys and smoke making the blue sky black, and nothing else. No, she did not wish to talk of Cracow, which she would anyway never see again, now that it was behind the so terrible Iron Curtain.

'Was Mr Potocki born in Cracow, too?'

'My husband? No. He is from Warsaw originally, of a once noble family. I have to tell you – Alice, is it? – that I was not born in Cracow exactly, but in Proszowici, on my father's country estate. You have many crumbs in your skirt.'

'That's because I'm mucky by nature,' replied Alice. 'I can't seem to help it.'

'Then you must try not to. You are a girl. You will be a woman one day. A woman who eats untidily is not an attractive sight to a man.'

My mother proceeded to give the three of us one of her lessons in etiquette. We were privileged children, she reminded us, and ought to be aware that we had standards to keep up. Jane, for example, should not be sitting slumped in her chair the way she was, and Alice was definitely too old at thirteen to be scattering her cake around her, and Esther was disgracing her Mama at this very moment by pulling childish faces. We made a sorry trio.

Alice let out a nervous laugh, and was immediately mortified. She stared at my mother, then slowly began to cough. 'There's a frog in my throat, I'm afraid,' she explained, before launching into an unconvincing coughing fit.

'Fetch your friend some water from the kitchen, Esther. I fear she will choke to death otherwise.'

After Alice and Jane had gone, I stood alone in my room and wondered how I could consider myself privileged with such a mother as Maria Potocka. 'You are a girl. You will be a woman one day' – hearing her deliver that familiar truism for Alice's benefit, I had felt my flesh prickle with embarrassment. I'd wanted to vanish, but elected to pull those 'childish faces' instead. They were the semaphore by which I conveyed to Jane and Alice that I did not share my mother's stupid views. I was too polite, and too cowardly, to tell her to shut up, for her own sake as much as ours.

(Neither Jane nor Alice was to refer to that afternoon visit again: not while we were at Dame Muriel's, at least. Their tact exceeded in quality anything my mother accounted good manners.)

A week or so later, I remember, I was accosted by the madwoman. That's what I conveniently called her.

'I've been watching you,' she said. 'They say a cat can look at a king. Well, this cat's had her eye on you, little Princess.'

'What do you want?'

'What *do* I want? Where shall I start? What does Princess suggest?'

'I'm not a princess.'

'Yes, you are. You're a princess if I say so, and I do say so, so there. What do you want to give me?'

I had two shillings and some pennies in my purse, which I offered her.

'Charity, is it, Princess? Poor as I am, I've never accepted charity. It's against my jolly old principles. You can shove your money. You can eat your bleeding money.'

She seized my arm, and held it in a firm grip. With her free hand, she stroked the lapel of my blazer.

'A lovely piece of cloth, Princess. The finest Shetland wool, if I'm not mistaken. Dame Muriel likes her girls to have the best. How is dear Dame Muriel these days?'

It was then I decided the woman was not merely strange, but probably raving mad. Dame Muriel, the school's founder, had died in 1797, in a nearby Benedictine convent.

'Dame Muriel's dead. She's been dead a long time.'

'No, she hasn't. She's alive. I saw her only the other morning. She was using a walking stick – hobble, hobble – but she was alive all right.'

I begged the woman to let me go.

'Not just yet, Princess. Not until I've finished what I have to finish.'

I shall kick her in a moment, I thought. I shall struggle free of her, and run as fast as I can. I'll hit her with my satchel, if needs must.

'It's not often I get to touch royalty,' she said, tightening her grip.

115

'I'm not a princess. I'm really not a princess. My father's a solicitor.'

'I don't believe you. You're lying to me.'

'I'm not. I swear I'm not.'

'Yes, you are. You're a pampered little liar.'

Desperate now to placate her, I conceded that I was.

'There's a change of tune! Well, missy, you don't expect me to believe you're a princess, do you?'

I told her, truthfully, that she had confused me; that I wasn't sure how to answer her.

'You're a rich little pampered missy who thinks she's better than she is because she's at Dame Muriel's – that's who you are. I smell, don't I?'

'No.'

'I do, missy. I stink. Don't I stink?'

'Yes.'

'And my breath – it's foul. Let me breathe on you, missy.'

She breathed directly into my face. The promised foulness was composed of onion and something oddly scented, which Sammy would one day make familiar to me. I reeled back from the blast.

'Not the breath of a lady, is it? Not like your lovely mummy's, is it?'

'No,' I said. 'No.'

'Has prinked and pampered and protected little missy seen enough of me? Eh? Heard enough of me? Smelt enough of me? Eh?'

'Yes.'

'That's not very polite. A well-brought up girl would reply, "No, madam, I haven't seen enough of you, thank you for asking," but not you. You're a rude little bitch, aren't you?'

Yes, I said: I am, I am, I am, I am.

'This is what I want from you, little missy. This is all I ever want from any of you. It's only your tears I'm after. Not your charity, not your filthy bleeding money – just your tears. Squeeze out a few more for me, missy, and I'll be happy as they come.'

I had no difficulty complying with her request.

'More, more, missy. Don't stop. Blub, blub, blub.'

She released me, then, and walked away. 'Goodbye,' she shouted, without turning back. 'Goodbye and good riddance, little bitch, little missy.'

The 'little bitch' – who was, in fact, the tallest girl in the class – said nothing to her mother about the madwoman who had humiliated her in a smart London street. She was late getting home because of the heavy traffic, and for no other reason.

I knocked on the door of my father's study. He was at his desk when I entered, smoking his usual mild Havana.

'Is it already time for dinner, Esther? Is your mother in a state?'

'No, Tata.'

'No to both questions?'

'Yes, Tata.'

'You look upset.'

'I am.'

'Come over here and tell me why.'

I went and sat by him. He kissed my forehead.

'I met someone today. A woman.'

'Who is she?'

'I don't know.'

'She preferred to remain anonymous?'

'Tata, she grabbed hold of me in Albany Street.'

'The devil she did.'

'She was suddenly there in front of me. She called me a princess to start with.'

'Your mother would have approved. My joke, dearest.'

'She was being sarcastic, Tata.'

'Obviously. What else did she have to say to you?'

That I was pampered and protected, I told him; that I was a rude little bitch; that I was a liar. She'd also said that she wouldn't accept my charity (I'd offered her the two shillings I had in my purse) because charity was against her principles, and that she had seen Dame Muriel out walking with the aid of a stick.

'How resourceful of her. Did she frighten you?'

'Yes, she did. She twisted my arm and breathed in my face. She swore at me as well.'

'You didn't scream? You didn't shout for help?'

'No, Tata.'

'And nobody saw you?'

'There was nobody about.'

He asked me to describe the woman – her voice, her face, her clothes – in close detail. I was to imagine that I was in a court of law, in the witness box, supplying a jury with vital evidence. 'Try to be calm and clear-headed, dearest. And truthful.'

The woman's hair was black, I said, with bits of grey in it; her cheeks were very red; two or three of her teeth were missing; her voice was rough-sounding and common –

'What do you mean by common?'

Harsh, I answered, vulgar, not in the least soft or gentle; and her clothes were shabby and worn, particularly her old raincoat, with its frayed sleeves; and her fingernails were long, like talons, and black with dirt . . .

'I have her picture, Esther.'

And then I revealed that the woman had made me cry, and that my tears had made her happy: 'It's only your tears I'm after,' she'd hissed. 'Don't stop. Blub, blub, blub.'

My father nodded, and relit his cigar.

'She's mad, Tata.'

'Envious, certainly.'

'Of what?'

'Of your being educated at Dame Muriel's. Of your pampered and protected life, my dearest.' He smiled at me. 'For you have been protected, and rightly so. I'd be philosophical about that poor woman, if I were you. I can't think she's done you any lasting harm. She's offered you a glimpse of the great big horrible world beyond our comfortable flat – or should I say apartment? Yes, "apartment" is the accepted term – and you may end up feeling grateful to her.'

'Grateful, Tata?'

'Perhaps, perhaps.' He rose from his desk. 'You'd better go and help your mother in the kitchen.'

He gave me another kiss on my forehead.

'If she bothers you again, Esther, we shall have to take action of some sort. Bring her to justice.'

While I waited for sleep that night, I assured myself that the next time I met the envious woman I would show her no fear. I would talk to her, reason with her, invite her to confide in me. I would put out my hand to her in friendship.

But there wasn't to be a second time, and so I never had the chance to display my new-found fearlessness. I looked for her often, and even lingered in Albany Street in the late afternoon in the hope, as it came to be, of seeing her.

Almost a year has gone by since Stephen vanished.

The precious gift he had promised us at the lunch was delivered to the clinic some days later by courier. The box, which was tied with red ribbon, was addressed to 'Doctor Lady Potocki, Osler Wing, Saint Lucy'. It contained two cassette tapes, each labelled HIS STORY BY STEPHEN and numbered. On the plain postcard that accompanied the present Stephen had written, 'Dear Doctor Lady and Mr Gabriel. You can play these tapes if you want to. It is up to you. You may learn something from them. Stephen.'

This, I remember thinking, was the most unexpected gift of all. I had assumed that everything else he had given me – VOL.1X, the marble paperweight, the candlesticks – was stolen property, nimbly filched while his clients were out of the room or otherwise occupied. I had not anticipated receiving an autobiography from my strange, elusive friend.

'I never could say what I'm going to say to you face to face,' it begins. 'I'd die before I could. You have to understand from the start. I can only say what I'm going to say to you because there's nobody here.'

A long silence follows.

'There's only me here alone with the machine. I'm in Jack's place, which is in London somewhere, but nowhere near you, Doctor Lady and Mr Gabriel. It's miles away, actually.'

'Do you think he's teasing us?' I asked Gabriel as we listened to a second long silence. We were playing the tapes for the first of many times. 'He's more than capable.'

'We'll soon find out.'

I was on the point of laughing at Stephen's cheekiness – sending us the precious gift of his silent life story, recorded on tape – when his voice enquired if we were still with him:

Because if you are, you must listen hard and take heed. I've already said to the clever Doctor Lady that I come from Halifax, which is a city in Yorkshire. It's famous for its textiles, such as cotton. Doctor Lady knows how I enjoy wearing cotton next to my skin – my *brown* skin. I had to wear nylon once when I was a boy, but it brought me out in spots, it gave me a nasty rash. Anyhow, I wouldn't be seen dead in nylon today. I wouldn't put it on if you paid me. I actually consider nylon common.

Have I ever told you my mother's white? Well, I'm telling you now. She's as white as you are, Doctor Lady, and her hair's fair like yours. She's not a natural blonde, though. She's been a blonde out of a bottle for ages, she says, ever since life took against her and made her go grey while she wasn't looking. That was a while back, before she met *him* – him who I can't allow myself to talk about. Leastways, not yet.

I'm a bastard. I would prefer to say I'm a foundling, but I've been informed on the best authority that a foundling's not the same as a bastard. That's a pity, because I fell for *foundling* as soon as the Doctor Lady spoke it in that funny voice of hers. 'The fetching frugal foundling' – it sounded neat to me. And talking of frugal, I wasn't exactly frugal at Mr Gabriel's house, was I? What with all that food and all that wine – which I shan't be drinking again in a hurry, thank you very much. I shouldn't have been drinking it then, except that the devil got into me, as he can if you let him, and I did let him in that day, and I'm still stuck to work out why. I came close to losing my brain in your palatial residence, Mr Gabriel. I came very close indeed.

I've never seen my father, my dad, and chances are I never

shall. It's years since he passed through Halifax and set my mum's heart in a flutter and broke it by leaving her. It's as many years as I've been alive, and a few months extra. Some of those years she spent waiting for him, carrying what she called her torch. She could have had her pick of plenty of men, but she always gave them the good old heave-ho, alias the brush-off. Then the time came she stopped waiting and carrying her torch, and the one man in the world she should have given the brush-off, she didn't.

I'm not ready for *him*. I would prefer not to mention him at all. That's what I would prefer, Doctor Lady and Mr Gabriel, but I don't see how I can. I'll allow myself to mention him if I have to when I have to, but I won't enjoy doing it. He's worse than ever the Bish was, and he's not in prison, which he ought to be, in my book.

I'm wearing a cashmere wool jumper today, in case you're interested. That means you, Doctor Lady. It's lovely and soft against my brown skin. You'll be interested to hear that your friend Stephen – me – has got rid of the suit you thought he was so flash in: the suit that made you blink and hurt your eyes. If you could see me this minute, in my ensemble, you would say I was dressed sober. And sober-dressed is better than flash-dressed, isn't it?

Dear Doctor Lady and Mr Gabriel, I'm not sure I should be doing this. I don't even know that I should allow it.

He was to speak hundreds of words into his friend's recorder – the words, he kept reminding us, he was unable to speak in our presence – as soon as he became confident in his lonely undertaking. At the beginning of his story, though, there are several periods of silence, varying in duration, expressive of his doubt and anxiety:

My brain, which I haven't lost, tells me I can go on talking. My brain says to me: Stephen, you can talk a stream because the tapes are yours, and yours to do what you want with.

You could easily give the clever Doctor Lady and her darling Mr Gabriel a different precious gift. They'd be none the wiser.

All true, isn't it? You may never get to hear any of this. It's up to me whether you do or not. It's entirely up to me.

I played the tapes again today, in their entirety, while Gabriel was at the British Museum, researching into the lives of long-dead forgers and swindlers. Two nights ago, at the end of the performance of *Wozzeck*, I had seen Stephen in my mind's eye, pretending to ride a hobby-horse like the real little boy on stage. His childish apparition had come to me in the terrible quiet of the opera's last moments, picked out by a spotlight from the descending darkness. And the imagined sight of him had brought me an inexplicable anguish.

Inexplicable, yes, because Stephen – or whatever his name is – was only a peripheral friend, an insinuating presence on the very edge of my life. So I try to convince myself, as I sit here in Gabriel's study, looking out at the unruffled Thames, waiting for the contractions to begin.

I try, in a half-hearted fashion, and fail. The truth is that I have been obsessed with Stephen these past few weeks. It's the *idea* of him more than anything else – the idea of who he has chosen to be, and who he might have been instead.

Perhaps, if I saw him now, I would ask him what he wanted of me. Had he intended me to be his rescuer? His precious gift, revealing as it is, does not reveal that particular intention.

You'll have guessed one thing, you clever pair of people. My dad's not white. My mum told me he's darker than I am, which means he'd likely allow the Doctor Lady to call him black. He's from Jamaica, in the West Indies. How he got to Halifax my mum wasn't sure, or if she was she never let on. He was passing through, she said, on his way up to Glasgow. He had a job there, with prospects. She could join him, my mum, once he'd found a place to live in. Well, you'll have guessed another thing: she didn't join him. Not ever. He forgot to send for her, she said. He clean forgot. Just imagine – I might have grown up in Glasgow, and lived a different life from the life I'm living.

I might be talking funnier as well, like they talk up in bonny Scotland. There was a Scotch boy on the circuit for a time, and Jack Saul and me and the rest of us wondered how on God's earth he ever did business because most of his words were trapped down his throat. He sort of gurgled. At least you can make out what I'm saying, Doctor Lady, even if it is in riddles.

Oh yes, those riddles; those clockwork 'Not allowed's. It was Gabriel who ventured an explanation for Stephen's recourse to teasing, and that after a single afternoon in his company. 'He needs to bewilder you. He has to make himself as opaque as he possibly can, in order to keep you interested in him. He wants to merit your respect and this is the only way he knows. He's scared of your finding him ordinary. He wants you to consider him unique.'

'He *is* unique,' I said. 'But not quite as unique as you, my darling.'

The day of what we have come to call the 'final lunch' was nearly at an end, but I was in no mood for sleep.

'Let's forget about him. Go and put on your dress. I fancy you in the polka dot tonight.'

'Come up,' I heard Gabriel say, minutes later. 'I'm ready.'

I had a granny, but I never met her. Actually, she wouldn't meet me. My mum took me along to her funeral when I was nine, as it was the right and proper thing to do. 'Your gran couldn't understand a white woman loving a black man,' she said, when we were walking home to our flat from the graveyard. My grandad, who was dead before I was born, would have understood, though, she told me. He was broad-minded. He was a fireman who died in a fire – one of

123

the biggest blazes in the history of Halifax, in case you're interested.

Anyway, anyhow, it was a bit later on that my mum decided she was tired of waiting. For him, my dad. 'I'm getting myself a husband while I'm still short in the tooth.' That's my mum. 'He popped the question last evening, and I closed my eyes and sent up a quick prayer and opened them and said yes. Love isn't in it.' Those were her words.

She'd grown tired of waiting, but she was really marrying him for my sake. 'A boy of your age needs a father. It's not natural for a boy of your age not to have a father.' And I said I didn't need a father, and I didn't care about natural, I was happy as I was. 'Is he white, Mum?' I asked her, and instead of saying yes, I remember, she said, 'Of course he is,' without noticing. 'If he's white, he *can't* be my father. Not if he's white.'

And as for white, she had a white wedding. She went down the aisle dressed in white. I wondered to myself at the time why some of the people in the *congregation* were laughing, and when I mentioned it to the Bish he said in that funny voice of his, 'The reason is simple, my son. The bride who wears white is proclaiming that she is a virgin. Your dear mother should not have done so. *Ergo* the mockery of the assembled *throng*. Thoughtless, I know – but the presence of your delightful self at the ceremony was more than sufficient proof that she was not as she wished to be regarded.'

He had a funny way of speaking, had the Bish.

Stephen is something of a mimic, as Gabriel is. He is most alive on the tapes when he is impersonating the Bishop of Wandle, or his hated stepfather, or the Honourable Grenville, or the horrible Nick, or any of his varied clients. The best of these assumptions is that of his friend Tonio – the Anthony Innocent who died at St Lucy's – because it is marked by affection and admiration. He seems to be acting the others, but in an almost eerie way he often becomes his quick-witted mentor.

Gabriel has only one subject for his mimicry: his father,

Oswald Harvey, who hid from him the fact of his mother's death for a quarter of a century. Gabriel loses himself completely as he brings the strutting martinet back to life – calling his son 'Piss-a-Bed' and lecturing him on the evils of the suede shoe ('You would be wise to steer clear of suede, that's my firm opinion, young man') and the dangers awaiting boys with a talent for cookery, and the virtues of the English aristocracy – *the cream de la cream*. 'I can't shake him off, Esther. I love to hear people laugh at him. My late revenge, I suppose.'

I learned years ago, in the playground at Dame Muriel's, that my mother used to be the kind of character impersonators relish. Remembering how the otherwise-forgotten Monica appropriated Mama's 'I had dreams of Esther becoming a dancer, but alas she is not *cut out* for the ballet', I realise that the laughter her take-off inspired has gone on echoing for me. I find I cannot mock the Countess Potocka any more, not even for Gabriel, and much as I conspired with Sammy whenever he referred to her as 'the Clytemnestra of Regent Mansions' – and besides, I don't have the knack, the necessary skill.

I know I've already told you, but just in case you didn't listen hard and take heed, I'll tell you again. I never could say this if I was in front of you. I mean, I couldn't look you straight in the eye, Doctor Lady and Mr Gabriel.

Well, we moved, my mum and myself, to *his* place, after they were married. Love wasn't in it, she'd said, but that didn't stop her having two of them at one go. Twins! Twin boys. It was *him* who chose their names. Jason, he chose, and Kirk. I'd sooner die than call myself Jason or Kirk. Or *his* name. When I'm working, I mean.

Even when they were tiny babies, he was gibbering to everybody that they were born footballers, while he twiddled their toes.

Football, football – it's football day and night for him. The first thing he said to me was, 'Are you a footballer, young Stephen?' and I said, 'No, I am not,' and he wasn't happy with that. He wouldn't leave it alone. 'If it's coaching you require, I'm your man.' I told him no thanks, but on he went, like he does. 'I'd have been a footballer myself, but it was just my rotten luck to get knocked off my bike by an idiot in a lorry. My left leg hasn't been right since.' That's his joke, Doctor Lady and Mr Gabriel, and he says it to everybody, and it creases him up every time. 'Here it comes,' says my mum nowadays, under her breath, as soon as he starts in with his 'I'd have been a footballer myself, but – ' stuff.

His name's Stanley. I've never been, and never will be Stanley for anyone, let alone Stan. I even hate saying it. I said it – Stanley – for Tonio, but not for the Bish. For the Bish it was *him*, that's all.

He said to my mum, 'We only need another nine to make a team.' Boys, he meant, of course: more Jasons and Kirks. He put her in pod again and she swelled, but it wasn't twins came out. It was a girl. Donna, her name is. My mum had to have a funny-sounding operation so as to have her. 'You can whistle for your other nine now,' she told him.

It was after the twins had come, his words started. He was careful, at the start, my mum couldn't hear him. *Hottentot* was his first. 'Come here, Hottentot,' he'd order me. Or, 'Hottentot, fetch me my slippers.' Or, 'See how white your little brothers are, Hottentot.' And in the mornings, when he came into my room to wake me up, he'd pull off the blanket with, 'Down in the jungle something stirred. The drums are calling you to school.'

Next it was *piccaninny*. Then it was *coon*, then it was *Sambo*. And I'll tell you this, Doctor Lady and Mr Gabriel, I never told on him to my mum. My pride wouldn't allow me. No, it was Jason bawling 'Coon!' at me gave his game away. 'Where did you learn to say that?' she asked him. She soon found out where, and the words stopped for a bit.

I'll tell you something else. He swears. He swears worst of all when he's drunk and lost his brain. Listen hard and take heed, Doctor Lady, and you too, Mr Gabriel – what I'm going to say now is *him* speaking, not me. Right? Understood? I don't use *fuck* and *shit* and *cunt* and the rest, but he does, and because he does, I don't. I wouldn't anyway, actually. I see no point. I actually consider swearing common. And stupid.

'What a very *refined* young sheep you are,' said the Bish, when I told him I consider swearing's common. 'If only the other strays in my flock would follow your example.'

And that went for his beloved acolyte, Anthony, he said . . . Yes, Tonio swore, but not like *he* swears, not ugly-like, not every word in three. He's like a machine-gun with his brain lost: fuck-fuck-fuck, he goes; shit-shit-shit; cunt-cunt-cunt.

That fuck-fuck-fuck stuff is his, not mine. I hope you've understood.

My mum had said to me, 'Love isn't in it, Stephen. I'm marrying him for security.' Security! Three more kids and a husband fuck-fuck-fucking his head off, that was her security. 'You'll have a nice home with your own room, I promise.'

Which she didn't break, because I did have my own room in his nice home. Except, except. Except, Doctor Lady, if all I'd wanted was my own room it'd have been enough. But it wasn't all I'd wanted. Not by a long chalk.

'This room of yours is a fucking monk's cell,' he said once, barging in after I'd forgotten to lock the door. 'What's fucking wrong with you? Where's the photos of pop singers? Where's the photos of film stars? What makes you think you're so different, piccaninny?'

'Because I am,' I told him. 'Because I am.'

That set him off. 'You've no fucking right to be. That's what I think. A boy of thirteen coming on fourteen with no photos on his bedroom walls is some kind of fucking freak, that's what I think.'

I'm going to stop talking his talk now, Doctor Lady and Mr Gabriel. I hate myself talking the way he does. It really gets me down.

I've only been doing it for you.

'Are you sure she's your mother, Hadassah?'

We had spent the afternoon in the 'icy wastes' of the apartment in Regent Mansions, and were back now in our cosy flat in Kennington. We had only a few hours left together, since I had to return to Newcastle in the morning, on the earliest train, to prepare for my final exams.

'What on earth do you mean by such a question?'

'It's her voice,' he answered. 'It sounds unfucked.'

He accepted my invitation to elaborate, and I laughed, I remember, at his elaborations. By the end of his aria, it was decided that I possessed a fucked voice, of the 'I'm such a happy fucker, I'll fuck anywhere and anyhow you care to fuck me' variety. And then Hadassah was ready to enjoy the golden sceptre.

We made love most of the night. Just before dawn, while I was summoning up the energy to get out of bed, Sammy spoke of my mother again. 'Why does she look at me as though I'm the first Jew she's ever clapped eyes on? She lives in St John's Wood, for God's sake, which isn't exactly uninhabited by the chosen race.'

'Oh, that's Mama,' I said. 'That's her way.'

'And that's a feeble reply. Is she really so cocooned from the world? And did she really believe, until I put her wise, that Esther's an English name?'

'Yes, she is, Sammy. And yes, she did, I'm afraid.'

'She's pitiful,' he said. 'The pity is I can't pity her.'

I washed and dressed hastily, and shoved some clothes and the books I needed into a bag, and kissed Sammy goodbye. I boarded the train with a minute to spare, and slumped into a seat, and slept for the entire journey.

'I'm sorry, Doctor Lady and Mr Gabriel.' Thus Stephen resumes, after a considerable silence:

But I shall have to speak some more of his stupid filth because that's how he is. Please remember that it's him, not me. I hope I've made that crystal clear. I don't want any confusion.

Well, the fact is, I ran away from my mum's husband's nice home a whole year before I ran away from it properly. I went across to Bradford. I stayed there a day and a night and then I got scared. I was tired as well through all the walking.

It was him who opened the front door. 'Your firstborn's come back with his tail between his legs,' he shouted out to my mum. 'You wicked boy,' she said, 'to cause us both such worry.'

The next time I was alone with him, he started in with, 'So you didn't care for Bradford, did you? Odd, that. I'd have thought Bradford was right up your coloured street. They say you're just a stone's throw from Calcutta, in Bradford.'

Was I deaf? he asked me. Or, rather, 'Are you fucking deaf, piccaninny?' I told him no, and he said I ought to have the good manners to fucking speak when I was being fucking spoken to. 'You can't even run away, can you? You don't even know how to run away properly.'

I'd know how one day, I said. I'd know how, and then I'd show him.

I won't dirty the air with the worst of it, but he swore at me after that the worst he'd ever sworn. I'll give you his drift. If I ran away again and came crawling back again, he'd knock me into fucking Kingdom Come, he promised me. 'And your mummy can bawl and cry as I'm walloping her black mistake –' I wasn't allowing that 'black', so I corrected him. He took no notice of me, which was typical. I was to remember that my mother had me when she was still wet behind the ears, and that my father was a fly-by-night who stuck his big black dick in every white hole that would open for him. My mother was on the look-out for novelty, and novelty's what she found, and I was the result. That was his drift, Doctor Lady and Mr Gabriel, minus you can well guess what.

I let him go on. And on, and on. When he drew breath, he asked me – Sambo, actually – if I was going to swear at him, like any other natural red-blooded boy would, and I told him no, of course not, I couldn't see the point in being so stupid.

That set his machine-gun off. He fuck-fuck-fucked at me, and I just listened – or rather, I tried not to. I've never seen such hate in anybody's face like the hate I saw in his that night, I swear to you.

When Sammy was in full flow – when I was the stuck-up, patronising Polish bitch who had never appreciated him; who had treated him as if he were nothing more subtle and sophisticated than a piece of East End rough – I could usually persuade myself that it was the gin, his alter ego, talking. Had I wanted to, I would have quoted his diatribe back at him, word for word, so familiar and monotonous had it become. I advised him, once, to make a record of it, to save himself the nightly trouble, and was rewarded with a snarl.

In vino veritas – the tag has to be amended to suit the intoxicated Sammy. *In vino malevolentia* better describes the drink-charged litany of accusations he regularly shouted at me. The most heinous of my sundry crimes, I heard, was that I practised under my Polish name, not my married one. I was ashamed to be called Elkin; I was ashamed to be thought Jewish – it was obvious.

'Potocki isn't my name, Sammy. It's my father's. Mine's Potocka. I'm Potocki at work because I'm grateful to Tata for his encouragement, and for no other sinister reason.' So I reminded him, when the litany was fresh on his lips, and on a couple of occasions later.

'What an arse-aching pedant you are. Potock*i*, not Potock*a*. *Vive la* sodding *différence*!'

I often silently cursed Maureen for dying with such awesome courage. She had set him too good an example. He could not scale her calm heights of humorous fortitude. Did he interpret that calmness – her hard-won acknowledgement that the fight was over, and lost – as a rejection of him? I think he did, eventually. He pitied his life without her.

'You *must* let me help you': how automatic, how ineffectual my response – heartfelt at first – came to sound.

'I will, Esther,' he surprised me by saying one evening. He was halfway through the litany. I had screamed my offer of help at him, and he had fallen suddenly silent. 'I will, Esther,'

130

he said at last. 'I will let you help me. What is it you propose to do?'

I told him my simple proposal. There was a clinic in Sussex about which various colleagues had spoken highly. I could arrange for him to be admitted to it if he were willing – and if he were willing to co-operate with the staff.

'Is it for rich soaks or poor ones?'

'I don't know,' I lied.

'Do they accept derelicts and down-and-outs?'

'Derelicts aren't willing to have treatment, Sammy. The place functions on a voluntary basis. The patients have to make the initial decision.'

He would make his decision, he said, but not just yet, not until the morning.

He was asleep when I left for the hospital the next day.

I was in the middle of a consultation when the receptionist interrupted me with the unlikely news that my husband was on the phone and insisted on speaking to me that very minute. He wouldn't leave a message. It was too urgent, too important for a message.

'I've made my decision, Esther.' The age of Hadassah was all but over by then.

'Have you?' I asked warily, bracing myself for an insult.

'I want you to go ahead.'

'You mean – ?'

'I mean that I am willing to be admitted. I'm eager. I'm keen.'

'Are you sure, Sammy?'

'Yes, yes, yes. I'm as sure as I'll ever be. Go ahead, Esther. Go ahead and have me put away.'

'It won't be for long.'

'It might be.'

He was wise to be realistic, I said.

He snorted. 'That's the Samuel in me coming out. There's only one snag, my big blonde beautiful wife. There's one obstacle blocking the road to my salvation.'

'Is there?'

'There is. It's called money. Who's footing the bill?'

'I am.' Anticipating his reaction, I continued: 'You can pay me back, Sammy.'

'You're an optimist.'

Things will be different tonight, I thought, after he rang off. This is his most elaborate practical joke so far. Or his most infantile.

Despite my misgivings, I contacted the director of the clinic that afternoon. I warned him that Sammy would probably revoke his decision nearer the time of admittance, and he observed that he was well accustomed to losing patients before the cure had even begun. 'I've known them arrive and depart in the same instant. It's in the nature of the disease.'

I drove Sammy to Sarton Hall, on the outskirts of Lewes. The fake-Jacobean manor house, built in 1910, stands at the end of a private road lined on both sides by aspens. There was no wind on that fine May morning, and as a consequence the aspens' leaves weren't brushing against each other, making the curious hissing noise which has earned the trees the nickname 'women's tongues'. We caught only the faintest rustle as we got out of the car and walked up the steps to the entrance.

'I don't want you to come in, Esther.'

I asked him why.

'No logical reason. I just don't want you with me. That's all. Pick me up again when I'm mended.'

I watched him stride into Sarton Hall. I waited a few minutes, in expectation of his reappearance, and then set off. I stopped at the gates, thinking he might be running after me down the alley of almost silent aspens, desperate to escape. But he wasn't, and I sighed with something quite like happiness at the realisation.

Sammy remained in the clinic for ten weeks. The longer he stayed at Sarton Hall, the more I grew convinced he was taking his treatment seriously. I did not need to guess what agonies of boredom he was enduring there, for Sammy was the most citified of people, the least likely ever to be seduced by the charms of country life. The prospect of green fields held no allure for him, while the creatures that occupied them – cows, particularly – rendered him senseless with terror.

'It's bulls you should be afraid of,' I'd said to him, on one of our rare excursions beyond London.

'*Should* be? Of course I'm scared of bulls. I'm bloody petrified of bulls. As far as I'm concerned, cows are bulls with tits.'

The director kept me informed of Sammy's steady progress. I learned that he had developed a friendship of sorts with an actor, with whom he occasionally went for a stroll in the grounds. I learned, too, that he was being competetive, playing what the director described as a 'murderous game of table tennis', and that he was beginning to smile in an open, as distinct from a sardonic, fashion.

It wasn't until the seventh week of his stay at Sarton Hall that I spoke to my newly smiling husband. I had left him, on his insistence, to his own devices: Esther the pesterer, as he'd recently referred to me, had done his bidding. Then, early one evening, he phoned me. My initial reaction, on registering his voice, was to wonder if he was drunk. Was I about to receive the litany at long distance?

'I'll be brief, Esther. The miracle seems to be happening.'

'That's wonderful, Sammy.'

'I thought you'd like to hear it from the sober horse's mouth.'

He added, in a rush, that he would pay me back the cost of his treatment. He had plans. Not of the pie-in-the-sky variety, but solid, sensible plans. He was looking to the future. He was going to bump-start his career.

He said goodbye to his Hadassah, for what was to be the very last time.

Three weeks later, the horse's mouth was no longer sober. It greeted me as I opened the door to our flat. I heard it say, from the darkness:

'I've returned. I'm home.'

I switched on the lights.

'I'm home, but I'm not dry, Esther. I'm pissed.'

I sat down beside him.

'Tell me, Sammy. Tell me.'

'What's to tell? I'm drinking again. Nothing unusual.'

The unusual thing, I noticed, was that he was drinking

again straight from the bottle. I got up and fetched him a glass.

'You prefer a little finesse, do you?'

'I suppose I do.'

'Is that your noble blood showing?'

'Probably.'

He filled the glass with gin and raised it to me. 'To the miracle that didn't happen. To yet another dismal failure.'

'No, Sammy.'

'Yes, Esther.'

I reminded him, calmly, of his solid, sensible plans.

'Oh, those, those. They're kaput. Completely and thoroughly and totally kaput.'

'Why's that?'

'Why? The television lounge at Sarton Hall is why. And the human detritus inside it. The dentist, the professor, the beautician, and the actor. Every single, shitty one of them. The actor's the shittiest, but only by a hair's breadth.'

The television lounge? The human detritus? What was he talking about?

What he was talking about, he answered, was the fact that his film (which was called *A Song, A Dance*, in case I'd forgotten) had been the Saturday Night Movie the night before last (a Saturday, appropriately) on the goggle-box.

'I watched it, Sammy. It's as beautiful as ever.'

'Ho hum. We watched it, too – the dentist, the professor, the beautician, the actor and me. It was the beautician, a vodka woman, who opened for the prosecution. "Why is the boy's mother always singing and dancing?" she wished to know. "Because singing and dancing's her job," mumbled the defence. "Point taken," the braying bitch conceded. "But if she can sing, it follows that she can speak as well. And she isn't speaking." Defence acknowledged the truth of her observation, and suggested politely that they could discuss the film once it was over. That was the normal procedure.'

'And did they?'

'They did. They tore into it. The prof, a whisky man, carried on where the bitch beautician left off. I had pushed dramatic

– or did he mean cinematic? – licence beyond its limits with my eschewal – my *eschewal*, yes – of dialogue. The dentist, also whisky, was forced to agree. Was I trying to be artistic? That was his question. "He was trying all right," the actor, a brandy and red wine man, chipped in. "And arty-farty's the result. God, that poor actress who played the plucky Jewish mother! The faces she had to pull because our friend here was too mean to provide her with words." And then the beautician bitch rejoined the fray, and then the four of them were at it, jumping in on each other with their honest opinions.'

What Sammy didn't say, what Sammy never revealed to me, was that he had gone berserk in the television lounge, and had needed to be restrained by a couple of male nurses, who pinned him to the floor, where he went on struggling for several minutes. He had foamed at the mouth. This information was passed on to me by the director of Sarton Hall when I contacted him on the day after Sammy's return.

'It was your brilliant idea to have me put in there.'

'Yes, Sammy, it was.'

'Well, don't have any more brilliant ideas. They only end in my humiliation.'

'That's absurd. That is really absurd.'

'Is it, Potocki? Is it?' He drained his glass and slammed it down on the table. 'Why don't you do something to make me stop hating you?'

'That's enough of Stanley's hatred,' Stephen remarks, after one of his shorter silences. 'For the nonce, anyhow. There's more to come, I warn you.' The next part of his tape is addressed to Gabriel. Stephen's tone is jauntily confiding:

Listen hard, Mr Gabriel. Last night I was – guess who I was, Mr Gabriel. I was Gabriel, actually. I met this man on the circuit and I knew from the moment I heard his voice that he'd appreciate a Gabriel. Which he did. It was my intuition made me choose, not brain. 'Hello, I'm Gabriel,' I told him, picking your funny name out of the air, and he came over all swoony. He asked me if I was an angel.

'I try to be,' I said. 'I do my best.'

You should have seen his house, Mr Gabriel. You should have seen his statues and his pictures. The luxury of it. The utter de luxe luxury.

'You aren't going to destroy anything, are you, Gabriel?' His voice, Mr Gabriel, was *whispery*. You could hear his breathing on every word. 'You aren't going to destroy anything, are you, Gabriel?'

'Me?' I said. 'Why should I do that?'

'Isn't there a demon inside you?'

'Me? Perhaps. Could be, Louis.' That's his name – Louis.

It clicked for me with 'demon'. I was on his wavelength straight away. Tonio, my teacher in this business, told me how to act with the talking punters. The secret with them is to let them spew – that was Tonio's, 'spew' – to let them spew it all out. The secret's for you to say as little as possible and to just stare at them. The less you say and the more you stare the better they like it, Tonio taught me.

I was on a winner with Louis, from the moment he mentioned demon. Who was to be me. This is going to be a pushover, I thought to myself.

'You have an angel's name,' said Louis. 'And the looks of one, with your lovely curly hair. But are you an angel underneath?'

I just stared at him. I just shrugged my shoulders.

'Don't answer me, Gabriel.'

Answer him? Why should I bother to answer him, when I'd only to stare? Which I did. Technique, Tonio called it. I was using Tonio's technique.

'You can be dangerous, can't you?'

'Suppose.' That's all I said.

'You suppose?' Then he was off again about the wicked gleam in my eyes, and what plan was I hatching, sitting there.

I began to undo the buttons on my sea-island cotton shirt. I kept my stare on him.

'What mischief are you up to? You won't say, will you? You'll surprise me, won't you?'

I slipped out of my one hundred per cent leather casuals and peeled off my silk socks.

'You're your own master, aren't you? You make the rules, don't you? It's you who has his finger on the trigger, isn't it?'

I got up, very slowly, with the good old stare still going strong. I kept it on him while I stripped.

'Me? Yeah.' That's all I had to say.

'Are you a cruel angel or a kind angel? Have you come down from heaven to be nasty to Louis?'

Spew on, Macduff, I thought.

Which he did, Mr Gabriel. Which he did for a half-hour. It was when he started on about my wings – my wings! – I knew it was time to put a stop to the spewing.

'Shut up, Louis,' I said. 'And lick my feet.'

That was exactly the right order for him. I lay back on his *di-van*, in the buff – as the Bish always called naked – and allowed rich little Louis to lick my feet. I could tell he was happy. I could tell by his noises.

I've you to thank, Mr Gabriel, actually, for last night. It was your name that achieved the object and accomplished the mission, as Tonio'd have said. If I'd told Louis I was a David or a Richard or even – *ho ho* – a Stephen, I never would have had such an easy ride. He wouldn't have come over all swoony if I'd been a Terence or a Martin or anybody ordinary. No, Mr Gabriel, me telling him I was a Gabriel was nothing short of inspired, though I say so myself. It was pure inspiration. It gave him the chance to spew his angel garbage – 'Where are your wings, Gabriel? Did you fall to earth without them?' – while yours truly treated him like he was my slave.

Thank you, Mr Gabriel, for lending me your Gabriel.

'Poor Louis,' said Gabriel. 'To be in need of a devilish angel.'

'You might as well say poor Gabriel, darling. After all,

you're in need of a dress, and a woman to get you out of it.'

'Not *any* woman, Esther. Only you.'

'And if you hadn't met me?'

'I would have gone on hoping. Against hope, probably. There must be another sympathetic woman somewhere in the big wide world.'

'I'm sure there is. She's multiplied by millions.'

Even so, as I remember that conversation, I pray that our child, should it be a boy, will not grow into a Louis or a Stephen. I offer up this prayer to whichever God is willing to hear it, among all those several gods we tend to implore – the faithful and the faithless alike.

This is the last of him, the finish, I promise you, Doctor Lady and Mr Gabriel. Stanley, I mean. My mum's husband.

I stayed in his nice home for more than a year after I ran away to Bradford and came back. There was one night he took my mum out on the town and I was left with the two twins and Donna. I had to put them to bed and see they behaved. Which they didn't. Jason and Kirk didn't is what I'm telling you, because Donna was still pretty babyish. They were only five, but they gave me *pan-de-mo-ni-um*. They gave me hell. They spilt the cocoa I cooked for them on my mum's new carpet, which I had to clean the best I could. Then they made a mess in the bathroom with their stripy toothpaste, and then they pinched me and kicked me when I tried to tuck them in. The worst came afterwards, when I thought they'd gone off to sleep. I was in my room, lying down in the dark with my eyes shut, when I heard my door being locked from the outside. I heard them laughing, Jason and Kirk, and calling me a stupid coon.

They were late getting home, my mum and him. The funny thing was I wasn't frightened, though I knew I was in for it, and in for it bad. 'What the fuck's going on?' he was shouting. 'Where the fuck are you?'

'I'm in here,' I said. 'Locked in.'

He opened my door and switched on the light.

'Who locked you in?'

'They did. The twins.'

'Why?'

I said he should ask Jason and Kirk.

'Why did you let them?'

I said I thought they were asleep.

'You're a useless fucking article, aren't you? I come home and find my kiddies staring at the fucking television at one in the fucking morning. They could've electrocuted themselves down there, left to themselves. It's a fucking miracle they weren't electrocuted, and no thanks to their half-brother.'

He lifted his hand up, and I waited. I never flinched, because I wasn't frightened.

'I ought to give you a thrashing.' He dropped his hand. 'And I will, soon enough. If it wasn't for your mother, I'd send you into Kingdom fucking Come this fucking minute.'

Well, he didn't send me there, Doctor Lady and Mr Gabriel, much as he wanted to. Which is why I'm here, in Jack's place, somewhere in London.

'Stephen,' my mum said to me one dinnertime (sorry — people like you call it lunch, and for the Bish it was *luncheon*), 'I think we should have a chat.' She was in her kitchen, on her own. Stanley was in the park with the three of them and a football.

'What about, Mum?'

About me and my stepfather, she said. She'd given up hoping that him and me would ever be close, but at least I could try and meet him halfway on a few things once in a blue moon, instead of ignoring him as I'd grown to do. 'I wish you'd stop pretending he isn't here. Because he is, and it's his money pays for our food and upkeep.'

'Yes, Mum.'

'You should be grateful, Stephen, and show your gratitude to him sometimes. He'd appreciate it if you did. Imagine what he must feel when he talks to you and you look right through him without saying a word. It isn't nice, love. It isn't kind.'

'No, Mum.'

'If you make an effort to be polite, I'm sure he will, too.'

Polite, I thought. Him, polite, with that fuck-fuck-fuck stuff, and Hottentot, and piccaninny, and Sambo, and coon – oh, yes, he's polite, I didn't say to her. I stayed – what's that word of yours, Doctor Lady? – *clandestine* on the subject.

And then she told me again, very quiet, what she hadn't told me for years and years – that love wasn't in it as regards her being married to him. Stanley was a good husband and a good father and a good provider, but love wasn't in it, not deep down. She couldn't ever love Stanley like she'd loved Hubert –

There it is, my dad's name. It's Hubert. I haven't been a Hubert on the circuit, and I don't intend to be, out of respect.

Anyway, although she couldn't love Stanley with a deep-down love, she was very content with the security he'd brought her. This nice home, for a start.

'If my dad turned up in Halifax, what would you do, Mum?' I asked her.

'Die of fright, I expect. Faint clean away from the shock.'

'Would you leave your nice home?'

'I'd have to do some serious thinking before I did that.'

'But would you?'

It was an impossible question, she said. Quite impossible.

And then there was him yelling, 'Yoo hoo!' and the twins and Donna running in and that was the end of our chat.

Dear Doctor Lady, I am now reaching my escape from his nice home, and that really will be the finish of him.

What I'm going to tell you, what I'm going to *divulge*, isn't *droll*, as the Bish used to say. Do you remember when you took me to meet your sweetheart, Mr Gabriel, and there was a funny bird, a black swan you said it was, on the River Thames – which is 'mightier by far than the humble Wandle' in the Bish's opinion. Anyhow, do you remember me seeing the swan and getting steamed up? Of course you do. Well, the reason I got steamed up was that he put me in mind of the blackbird who flew into Stanley's nice home and had trouble – terrible trouble – flying out.

Actually, in fact, he never got to fly out. He didn't have the luck.

It was a sunny day. I was sitting on the sofa in the lounge, reading the paper, when I happened to notice a blackbird was keeping me company. He was perched, bold as brass, on the arm of the sofa, peeping at me for a second and then not peeping at me in that funny quick-blinking way birds have got. I said hello to him. He made a tiny noise, and I thought for one daft minute he was saying hello back. Then he flew across to the television, and stood on the top.

I can't recall aright when his panic started, but it must have been soon afterwards. He flew from the television to the sideboard, from the sideboard to the lampshade, from the lampshade to the bookcase where Stanley keeps his *Cyclopaedia*, and he was chirp-chirping all the while. I went over and opened the window he'd come in at even wider so as to make it easier for him to fly out again, but would he take the hint? No, he wouldn't.

I opened the other window, too, but the blackbird flew nowhere near it. He was flying in a circle, and still chirping, but he didn't sound happy. Like a dopey idiot, I pointed to the open windows, thinking he would follow where my finger was showing him to go. But he didn't. Then I was panicking, too, because I couldn't make him understand the obvious.

I was shouting, 'Window, window! Window, window!' when he, Stanley, barged into the room.

'What's happening? Why all the fucking noise?'

'It's a bird,' I said.

'I can see for myself it's a fucking bird. What's it doing in the house?'

'He just flew in. He can't seem to get out.'

'I don't suppose it's occurred to you to grab hold of it. A normal lad would have caught it and thrown it into the garden, but not you.' Then he said to the blackbird, 'Come here, my beauty,' and the bird whizzed around for a bit and then stopped in the air and then landed on his — on Stanley's — shoulder.

'I've a knack,' he boasted, 'with our feathered friends. One of my mates on the site reckons I'm a proper Saint Francis of Assi with them.'

He had the bird on his hand, and the bird wasn't scared.

'My beauty,' he spoke to it. 'My beauty.'

'Thank God,' I said.

'What are you thanking Him for?'

'For saving the bird. For saving his life.'

'God had no part in it. It was me who saved the bird. *If* I saved it.'

What did he mean by 'if', I asked him.

'It's still in my hand. It's mine to do what I want with.' He smiled his smile at me. 'Entirely fucking mine.'

'You'll let him free,' I said. 'Won't you?'

He smiled his smile. 'No, I don't think I fucking will. Hottentot.'

He pressed his hand tight round the blackbird. Then he brought his other hand over, and with it he twisted the bird's neck.

'There's a present for you!'

He threw the bird at me. Which was dead, Doctor Lady and Mr Gabriel. The dead bird hit me full on the chest before he fell on the carpet.

'You can pick it up, as it's yours. I'll go to the bathroom and wash its shit off me.'

But not until he'd called me a cry-baby coon, a yellow-bellied nigger.

'It didn't deserve to live. It was stupid. It'd be alive if it'd had intelligence.'

When he'd finally gone, when I could hear the tap water running in the basin, I picked up the blackbird and put him out in the garden, under the bush of roses.

I dreamed about the blackbird that night. About his eyes, actually. His alive eyes first, and then his dead ones.

It was because of the dead ones, the ones which he, Stanley, had made dead, I decided to leave his nice home for good and all, yes, and for ever more.

And I did. And I have.

*   *   *

Stephen begins the second side of the first tape with a brief account of his schooldays. He might have been a prize pupil, he remarks, if things had turned out different – if his mother hadn't married and taken him to live in the nice home (that much-repeated phrase is always employed contemptuously); if his stepfather hadn't started to call him certain names; if his brain hadn't told him there was no point in book-learning and schoolwork so long as you were miserable.

He mentions only one of his teachers – a Mr Portman, whose lasting legacy to Stephen would appear to be the expression 'Listen hard and take heed'. Of his skills in the classroom, Stephen says nothing, beyond the fact of his insistence that the girls and boys listened hard to and took heed of whatever it was he was telling them. Mr Portman's speciality – his subject, or subjects – goes undisclosed.

It occurs to me, now, that I was not altogether happy at Dame Muriel's. I wish I could forget some of the teachers there as easily as Stephen seems to have forgotten those at his school in Halifax. How did Jane and Alice and I survive the censorious instruction of that ferociously devout trio of nuns – the Sisters Michaela, Imelda and Grania? For we have survived, and succeeded too, despite their efforts to persuade us of the vanity of earthly ambition.

'Tata, you are an atheist, aren't you?'

'You know I am, dearest. Why do you bother to ask?'

'I'm bothering to ask because I'm slightly confused. If you don't believe in God, why am I studying at a Catholic school?'

'Esther, you are my marvellous girl. That is the question I have been dying to hear on your lips since the day you donned the Muriel uniform. You may find my answer peculiar and my reasoning perverse, but no matter. It will be the truth.'

The truth he revealed to me when I was thirteen was that he had agreed initially to my enrolling at Dame Muriel's for no more subtle reason than his own cherished peace and quiet. 'It was what your mother wanted.' Having once acceded to Maria's demands, he then stopped to think about the consequences for his daughter, and eventually satisfied himself that they were not totally unfavourable. He had faith in her ability to resist indoctrination, on the evidence of the thousand and one questions she had put to him from infancy onwards. And now that faith had been justified, for she had asked the one truly significant question at last.

'You see, dearest, it's my conviction that the best learning is acquired by unlearning most of what you are taught in school. There are only so many irrefutable facts – all else is dogma, or mere supposition. You are making great progress as an unlearner, Esther. Do you understand me?'

'Yes, Tata.'

'Will you do me a favour, please?'

'Of course I will. What is it?'

'Try and limit the amount of shocks you afford your Mama. For my sake as much as hers. If you ration them to two per week, that leaves me with five whole days of tranquillity.'

His education disposed of in a few minutes of tape, Stephen goes on to assert that he sees the point of money. By the age of sixteen, he had saved enough to get him to London. He had delivered newspapers in the mornings, and washed cars at weekends, and hoarded a lot of the fivers his mother had given him. He was ready and prepared for escape:

I came down to London on the last train out of Halifax that evening. I bought myself a one-way ticket, because this time I was doing it properly. I had my promise to him to keep. My mum's firstborn wouldn't be crawling back with his tail between his legs. Definitely not.

On the train, though, I had to wonder what I was up to. I had nothing but the clothes I was wearing, and fifty-four pounds to see me through. I wasn't to know – how could I? – that Tonio would be waiting for me on the platform at King's Cross. Which he was, Doctor Lady, while the train moved closer and closer to the big city. He was waiting to introduce me, or someone else from Halifax –

because that Tuesday it was Halifax's turn – to the Bishop himself. But, as I say, I didn't know that Tonio would be there. I thought the police might be, after a frantic phone call from my mum. I had this idea she'd told them I was on the last train out of Halifax, running away from my nice home.

When that train stopped at King's Cross, I was too scared to get off. It was like I was froze to the seat. Like a block of ice, I was.

'Are you all right, son?' It was the ticket-collector asking me. 'This is King's Cross. This is the end of the line. Are you all right?'

'Me? Yes, thanks,' I said.

'You can't sleep on the train.'

I stood up, and said I wasn't planning to.

My feet touched the platform and, boy, was I scared now. I couldn't walk. I was froze to the ground like I'd just been froze to the seat.

'Hello,' said a voice. 'Need any help?'

'Me?'

'Yes, you. Where's your suitcase?'

'I don't have one.'

'That's odd. Somebody coming to meet you?'

'Me? Yes,' I lied. 'Any minute.'

'Mum, would it be? Dad? Aunt or uncle? Older brother or sister? Family friend?'

'Mind your own business.'

I looked into the voice's face, if you follow me, when I said that. He was young, and he was smiling. He had long, jet-black hair. He was very sure of himself, Doctor Lady. The cocky type.

'I make it my business when I see a person all alone and stranded. I'm sorry, but that's the kind of guy I am. I never walk past if I see a person in trouble. I always stop and offer help. I try to be a good Samaritan.'

He winked at me.

'I hope your somebody doesn't keep you waiting much longer,' he said, and walked away to where they take the

145

tickets. He stopped, and stood watching me. Five, ten minutes later, he was back.

'Do you think your somebody's forgotten you?'

'Me? Perhaps.'

'Who is this somebody?'

'Uncle,' I said, 'uncle' being the first word came into my head. 'My Uncle Joseph.'

'Where does he live?'

'Live?'

'Your Uncle Joseph. What's his address?'

'He never gave it to me.'

'That wasn't very considerate of your uncle, in my opinion. That wasn't very clever of him either.'

I don't know why I did, but I told him not to be rude about my Uncle Joseph. I mean, I didn't have any Uncle Joseph. I'd only just that moment made him up.

He said he'd intended no offence. What would I do, he asked, if my Uncle Joseph failed to arrive?

I was stuck – can you believe it, Doctor Lady? – for an answer. I hadn't a clue what to say. Another lie, I thought to myself, and I'll be in it deep. So I stayed dead dumb.

'Would you go to a hotel?'

'Me? Maybe.'

'The Ritz? The Savoy? The good old Dorchester?'

'Perhaps.'

You should have heard him laugh, Doctor Lady and Mr Gabriel. You should have seen him shake.

'The Ritz! The Savoy! The Dorchester! Him!' That's what he said while he was laughing and shaking. 'This one at the Ritz! I love it! I love it!'

'What are you loving?' I asked him. 'And why is it so funny?'

'Nothing, my friend.' He put out his hand to me, which had rings on it – three of them. 'My name's Anthony Innocent. What's yours?'

'Stephen,' I said. 'Stephen Eccles.' My mum was Eccles before she married you-know-who and became Mrs Patterson.

'Pleased to meet you, Steve.'

146

I wasn't Steve, I was Stephen, I corrected him. Stephen.

'My apologies, Stephen. My sincere apologies.' He looked at his watch. 'No sign of your uncle.'

'He's late.' That was the daft remark I made.

'He's *very* late, Stephen. It seems to me your Uncle Joseph has left his young nephew in the lurch.'

I had to agree with Anthony Innocent.

'I'm glad your Uncle Joseph isn't my Uncle Joseph. I don't approve of relatives who neglect their responsibilities.'

I had to agree with him again.

'Shall we give him another five minutes? And then, if he still hasn't turned up, shall we leave him to stew in his own juice?'

'Yes,' I said.

'And serve him right, too. Because it just so happens, Stephen, that I know a place where you can stay. It's where I stay. It's not the Savoy or the Ritz or the good old Dorchester, but it's clean and comfortable. I can arrange it so as you can hang out there as long as you want. I can pull strings, Stephen. I can make arrangements.'

'Can you?'

'You bet I can. That's my style. You can rely on your brand-new friend, Anthony Innocent. You're safe in my hands.' He winked at me. 'Shall we go?'

'OK,' I said.

'There's just one little snag, one little hurdle to leap over. My landlord has to approve of you first. He's on the station somewhere, on one of his rounds of mercy. He's a bishop, Stephen. A man of the cloth. I'll introduce you to him as soon as I can spot him.'

We were off of the platform by now, and in the station proper. There was a filthy old man sleeping full out on a bench, a tramp by the looks of him, and Anthony Innocent – he hadn't become Tonio yet – asked me if he, the tramp, was my Uncle Joseph.

'Him? Not likely.'

'I was pulling your leg, Stephen. He's the wrong colour, anyway.'

'My mum's white,' I said.

'Is she really, Stephen? You do surprise me. But not your father?'

'No, not my dad. Of course not.'

'You would be a miracle if he was white as well. You would be a kind of Jesus. You'd be the only black – '

'Brown,' I corrected him. 'I'm brown.'

'I beg your pardon, Stephen. You'd be the only brown boy ever to be born to white parents.'

'I'm no miracle. My dad's a Jamaican.'

'Pity about that. We might have made a fortune together – you as the miracle, and me as your manager. We'll strike it rich sometime.'

Are you listening, Doctor Lady and Mr Gabriel? I've been wasting my precious breath if you aren't. I hope you're still listening, because here he is: the Bishop of Wandle. I've got to him at last.

What follows is Stephen's account of his descent into hell.

If he were here beside me, he would snigger at my characteristically funny way of describing his time at the Bishop's palace. He'd say I wasn't allowed to talk like that. The clever Doctor Lady didn't understand. Hadn't she listened to the tapes?

(Yes, she has listened to the tapes, and read their contents, too, in Gabriel Harvey's careful transcriptions. She has studied them diligently. She has been moved and amused by them. And yet she wishes that they told a different story.)

If he were here beside me now, would I be able to convey to him the distress I feel at his becoming habituated to life in that bogus bishop's bogus palace? Probably not. Would he accept my circuitous – of necessity circuitous – offer to rescue him? It's doubtful.

Rescue him? How quaintly decent the notion sounds, how loftily philanthropic. But that's exactly what I want to do. Almost from the day he tried to befriend me, I detected in his sly, elusive nature a craving for enchantment. The delight he takes in unusual words and expressions – in the curious catch-phrases of Jack Saul; of his beloved Tonio – is evidence of this need. And with what relish, what misplaced relish, he speaks the Bishop's hothouse language. These are wasted talents.

If Stephen had been one of my hundreds of patients, I would not be thinking of him. Our relationship would have been brief and circumscribed. His life would have been his own affair, not mine. I would have remained Dr Potocki and not become his Doctor Lady, a recipient of his precious gift – the account, I persist in believing, of his descent into hell:

'That's him over there,' said Anthony Innocent. 'That's him, standing in front of the gentlemen's toilet, doing up his flies. Typical, I'm afraid. I spend my life reminding His Grace his zipper's undone. His thoughts, he says, are above, dwelling on higher matters.'

He laughed, but not as loudly as he'd laughed over the Ritz, Savoy and Dorchester stuff.

'Your Grace!' he called out. 'Your Grace!'

Anthony Innocent took me across to the Bishop, who was dressed religious in a purple shirt with a stiff white collar. He was wearing a gold cross.

'Ah, Anthony, you sound in cheerful spirits.' He had ever such a deep and booming voice. 'And who is this by your side?'

'Allow me to *effect an introduction*, Your Grace. This is Stephen, and he comes from Halifax. His Grace, meet Stephen; Stephen, meet His Grace, the Bishop of Wandle.'

'Good evening to you, Stephen. I say good evening, though I fear it is already good morrow.' He was speaking those funny words of his from the start. 'Are you alone in the great city?'

I said yes.

'He's missing his uncle, Your Grace. His Uncle Joseph was supposed to meet him off the train.'

'And have you been able to help poor Stephen, Anthony? Have you attempted to telephone his *errant* uncle?'

'Actually, Your Grace, I haven't. Seeing as how Stephen

doesn't know his uncle's address, I assumed he doesn't know his good old phone number either. Do you know his number, Stephen?'

I said I didn't.

'Dear, dear, dear,' went the Bishop. I'd never seen anyone with a face as red as his before, and nobody with such *watery* eyes. His eyes looked like they were swimming. 'What is to be done, Anthony?'

'May I venture a suggestion, Your Grace?'

'Please do, Anthony. Please do.'

'Well, Your Grace, and begging Your Grace's pardon, I took the liberty while I was chatting with Stephen here of suggesting that there might be a bed for him, and food and lodging, at Your Grace's palace.'

(Palace? Was I about to be taken to a Buckingham Palace kind of place? That's what went through my brain.)

'That *was* a liberty, Anthony. But tell me, dear boy, have you discovered whether or not poor Stephen is suitable?'

'I find him suitable, Your Grace.'

'And promising, Anthony?'

'Definitely promising, Your Grace.'

'Likely to be lucrative?'

I could have walked away while this was going on and neither one of them would have noticed. I'd no idea what *lucrative* meant then, but I stored the word in my brain – like I do, eh, Doctor Lady? – and I soon found out.

Anyway, 'Likely to be lucrative?' the Bishop asked him.

'Quite likely, Your Grace.'

'Only quite, Anthony?'

'Let's change *quite* to *very*, then. After a few private lessons from a certain teacher, he'll be *very*, Your Grace.'

'I trust your judgement, Anthony. At the moment he is a Heathcliff. A Heathcliff to the life.'

'I'm not on your wavelength, Your Grace. How can a boy look like a cliff on a heath?'

Then it was the Bishop's turn to laugh. You should have heard him. He shook, and his big fat tummy under his shirt was all floppy. He laughed till he choked, and Anthony

Innocent had to slap his back. Which he did, with another wink in my direction.

(Thanks to you, Doctor Lady, I now know who Heathcliff is. He isn't the dandy I am. I shouldn't think he's strong on ensembles.

Of course, we didn't have a clue why Tonio's remark set the Bishop off like that, and – of course – it's too late for me to tell Tonio the real reason now. That's life.)

The Bishop popped a *lozenge* into his mouth – 'I carry a tin everywhere, at all times, to ease the throat' – and offered me one as well. Which I accepted. It was a lemony cough sweet, and I allowed it to melt slowly instead of swallowing it down in one go, as I easily might have done, in the circumstances.

I mean, I was nervy, Doctor Lady and Mr Gabriel. I was nervy with this Bishop of Wandle, but I'd have been nervier with him alone by myself, without Anthony Innocent there. It was his winks steadied my nerves.

'Anthony, dear boy, I think we ought to *repair* to the palace. Poor Stephen must be tired and weary after his long journey from the industrial north.'

'I'm ready to repair when you are, Your Grace. How about you, Stephen?'

I'd guessed the Bishop's *repair* wasn't the kind my mum did with a needle and thread. His funny 'repair' meant 'go'. I said yes, I was ready.

'Do not mumble, Stephen. And I should be happier if you saw fit to address me as Your Grace.'

So I said my first 'Your Grace', and he patted me on the shoulder, the Bishop of Wandle.

'Reveal to me, Stephen, why your pockets are bulging. What have you stuffed inside them?'

'My socks, Your Grace, and my underpants.'

'How very mysterious. Do you always stuff your pockets with socks and underpants when you visit your Uncle Joseph?'

I had to say yes. It was feeble, I knew, but what else could I say?

'Each to his own, Your Grace,' said Anthony Innocent. 'We all have our good old foibles, don't we?'

'True, Anthony, true.'

We were walking out of the station, King's Cross, the three of us, when we came smack, face to face, bang up against a policeman. They've reported me missing, my mum and him, I thought, and he's come to get me, to send me back to Halifax.

But no, I was wrong, he hadn't come for me at all.

'Good evening, Reverend Father,' he said, with a friendly smile.

'Good evening to you, Officer.'

'Another runaway, I see.'

'Indeed, indeed. This young fellow's from Halifax. He appears to have a troublesome uncle. We shall endeavour, my devoted staff and I, to set him on the right path in life.'

'The more power to your elbow say I, Reverend Father.'

'Thank you, Officer.'

And out we went and straight into a taxi. Now this was odd, because the taxi-driver seemed to know the Bishop too, and was just as friendly to him. He spoke the same Reverend Father stuff, except that he called the Bishop a saint and said that if anyone deserved a place in heaven among the angels, it was him, the Bishop, and no mistake.

It was a rainy night, and dark, and the ride went on and on, and between them, the Bishop and the driver, they never drew breath. The Bishop mentioned my uncle again, who he said was a thoroughly bad character, and the driver said the likes of him, meaning my uncle, ought to be dropped on an island in the middle of the Atlantic Ocean and left there for nature to deal with. The Bishop clicked his teeth a bit, and spoke about showing pity and mercy even unto – that was his funny expression – even unto those who had done wrong. Then the taxi-driver called him a saint again, and the Bishop shook his head, and Anthony Innocent gave me one of his winks.

The taxi had to stop some time. Which it did, and after the Bishop had paid the driver there was more of the Reverend Father and saint carry-on before we got out.

We were stood in front of a huge building, which looked like a factory to me, not a palace. The entrance door was a small door inside a bigger one, if you follow me, and the Bishop opened it and let us in. That was just the beginning of it. Anthony Innocent turned on a light and the three of us went up a staircase. There was a locked door at the top. 'I have twice as many keys as Mrs Danvers,' said the Bishop in his funny voice, and laughed his laugh.

(Do you know who Mrs Danvers is, Doctor Lady? I don't, and Tonio didn't, and every time he asked the Bish who she is, the Bish only laughed his laugh and said, 'That would be telling, Anthony,' and never gave him a proper answer. I'm wondering now if she's another Heathcliff, Doctor Lady, in a book. I wouldn't put it past the Bish.)

I felt scared again, and nervy, because this palace I'd been promised wasn't like any palace I'd seen in films, and Buckingham in particular. I wouldn't be able to escape in the middle of the night, I realised, with so many doors to open. And, anyway, the Bishop had the keys. There were six of these doors to go through before we got to what Anthony Innocent called the living quarters. Talk about secret. Talk about *clandestine*.

Anyway, actually, the living quarters turned out to be quite de luxe. The first room I saw had carpets and chairs and a sofa and lamps. 'This is our reception area,' said the Bishop. 'This is where we chew the fat.'

'Eat?' I asked.

'No, no, no, dear boy, not *eat*. To "chew the fat" is to talk, to converse. We eat in the *refectory*.'

Then the Bishop showed me his office. There was a large shiny black table, and the gold chair which was behind it looked like a throne.

'His Grace does his *di-oce-san* business in here,' Anthony Innocent said. 'Don't you, Your Grace?'

'I most certainly do, Anthony. Oh, the problems that beset my flock!'

'You cope with them, Your Grace. You solve them.'

'I try to, Anthony.'

'Listen, Your Grace, shall I treat Stephen to his guided tour tomorrow? By the bright light of day?'

'An excellent suggestion, Anthony. The poor boy is tired and weary and in need of sleep.'

Which I was. I was yawning.

'Come with me, Stephen,' said Anthony Innocent.

'Good night, my child.' The Bishop stuck out his hand. 'Show Stephen how he must take leave of me, Anthony.'

I couldn't believe the next bit. Anthony Innocent bent over and kissed the Bishop's hand and then walked backwards out of the office. He said for me to do the same. Which I did, but only after Anthony Innocent told me it wouldn't poison me, the hand; it was only a good old human hand.

'He's learning, Your Grace.'

'He certainly is, Anthony. Good night to you, Stephen. Let us hope that your wicked uncle does not disturb your dreams.'

'Good night, Your Grace.'

Then I followed Anthony Innocent across the reception area and along a passage and up some stairs, and all the while he was saying to me, quiet and confidential, that he would personally see to it that I was A-OK; he would protect my welfare; he would make things easy for me.

'Here we are, Stephen. This is what the Bish – beg pardon, His Grace, the Bishop – calls the *dormitory*.'

It was a long and wide room with beds in it – five a side, ten altogether. Except for one, the beds were empty.

'That's Jack Saul snoring his head off. No one snores like Jack. Unless you do, Stephen.'

'Not to my knowledge.'

Anyway, there I was, just an hour and three-quarters since getting into King's Cross, standing in a dormitory instead of a bedroom, in a funny kind of palace in – I didn't know where.

'Where are we, Mr Innocent?'

'I'd say we are upstairs in the Bishop's palace, Stephen.'

'No. I mean, where in London?'

'We're in good old Wandsworth. On the south bank of the

154

mighty Thames. It's a poxy river as far as I'm concerned, but the Bish always says it's mighty.'

I was to have the bed next to his. 'Pride of place, Stephen.' There was a wardrobe with hangers in it, and a locker for my valuables. 'The Bish will discuss high finance with you in the morning, alias on the morrow. Have you got any money on you?'

I told him I had, and he wanted to know how much.

'Fifty-four pounds.'

'The Bish'll require fifty of those, for safe keeping. But I'll soon find work for you, if you're willing. I can teach you to be a regular earner.'

I was willing, and eager too, I said, but what was the work? Was it brain work, or was it manual?

'Your brain will come in handy,' he said, and winked.

But what kind of work was it?

'Don't yawn when you're speaking, or speak when you're yawning. I'll explain what the work is tomorrow.'

Which he didn't, really. It was days until he did.

'Get some shut-eye, Stephen. I have to prepare His Grace's nightcap and attend to his sausage requirements. You'll understand in due course.'

The toilet was at the other end of the dormitory. I tiptoed so as not to wake Jack Saul, and went in, and passed water, and then I brushed my teeth with my best toothbrush. I tiptoed back, and took off my clothes and jumped into bed, naked, and fell asleep with my money under the pillow.

You can imagine, can't you, Doctor Lady and Mr Gabriel, I didn't rest easy that night. Did I toss and did I turn. I kept coming awake and not recognising where I was, as I would have in Halifax. I kept coming awake and thinking: I'm in a palace, I'm in a funny palace, in London.

When I woke up properly in the morning, Anthony Innocent was talking about me to someone I guessed was Jack Saul. 'He's a half-and-half,' I heard him say. 'His dad supplied the coffee and his mum the cream.'

'Hello, Mr Innocent,' I said.

'You've had a lovely lie-in, Stephen. Just what the good

old doctor ordered. Allow me to effect an introduction to my friend and colleague, Jack Saul. Jack, this is Stephen; Stephen, this is Jack.'

'Hello, Mr Saul,' I said.

'*Mis-ter* Saul! Did you hear him, Ant? *Mis-ter* Saul!'

'I heard him, Jack. He's showing you respect. Aren't you, Stephen?'

Yes, I was.

'He's treating you like a gentleman. So enjoy the experience while you can.'

'Hello to you,' said Jack, with a grin all over his face.

'What's your morning *tipple*, Stephen?' This was Anthony Innocent. 'Tea, is it?'

Yes, it was, I answered him. Tea was my *tipple*. 'Tipple' was a new one for me. I'd not come across 'tipple' in Halifax.

'Fetch him a cup, will you, Jack? Sugar required, Stephen?'

The strange thing is, I don't care for sugar in my tea, nor in much else. I never have.

But I'm not allowed to tell you why it's a strange thing, Doctor Lady and Mr Gabriel. Not yet.

'No sugar, thanks,' I said, and Jack Saul went off out of the dormitory to fetch me a cup. While he was gone, Anthony Innocent said to me to stop saying Mr Innocent and Mr Saul. 'We're pals here, Stephen.' It was only the Bishop who expected to be *kow-towed* to, not us boys. 'You can call me Anthony, Stephen.'

'Anthony,' I said.

'No, on second thoughts, you can call me – ' He stopped to see if anybody was listening. 'You can actually call me Tonio. I'm giving you that privilege because I've taken a shine to you. I don't want you calling me Tony, or even Ant, which is what Jack does. Agreed and understood?'

'Tonio,' I said.

'That's me. I like the sound of it. I-talian. Listen, Stephen, it's our secret, eh? It's for when we're together, just us, not with them. And it's not to be spoken in front of the Bish – I beg his pardon, His Grace, the Bishop of Wandle. Are you with me? On my wavelength?'

'Yes, Tonio.'

'Have you got a name, Stephen – I mean, a name like mine, like Tonio?'

I said I had.

'Are you going to let me in on it?'

I had to think about it for a minute. I did have another name, I still do have, it was the one my mum gave me, but I wasn't sure I wanted to share it with him. Not yet. Not so soon.

But my brain told me to tell him. Which I did, and I could've bit my tongue off.

'That's unusual,' Tonio said.

Then Jack Saul came back with my cup – it was a mug, actually; with my mug of tea. There was breakfast to follow, but that would have to be taken downstairs in the dopey refectory.

'Eggs and bacon and some good old fried bread agreeable, Stephen?'

'Yes – ' I remembered not to call him Tonio. 'Yes, Anthony, thanks.'

'It's Anthony now, is it?' This was Jack Saul speaking. 'No more *Mis-ter* Innocent, Ant?'

'That's right, Jack. And no more Mr Saul for you neither. I think Stephen's going to be one of us.'

And the two of them left me to get washed and dressed, with Tonio saying he'd *rustle up* my eggs and bacon and fried bread and that I'd find the refectory at the bottom of the stairs, third door along.

It reminded me of school, the refectory did. The big table down the middle wasn't polished like the table in the Bishop's office. No, this table looked scrubbed. It was just plain wood. There wasn't a cloth on it, which my mum would have put on if it had been hers.

'Sit yourself down, Stephen, and tuck in.'

Weren't they eating, too? I asked.

'We rose with the lark,' said Jack. 'We've already had our fill.'

When Tonio offered me another cup of tea, I realised the

mug was up in the dormitory, by the bed I'd slept in. I said
I'd go and find it.

'Jack'll fetch it for you. That's no trouble, is it, Jack?'

'Course not.'

With Jack gone, Tonio called me by the name which you
two are not allowed to know. It was a beautiful day outside,
he told me: a perfect day for seeing the sights of good old
London town. After I'd had my tour of the palace, and my
session with His Grace, would I like him, Tonio, to show me
the landmarks of historical interest?

Yes, I said, I would.

'There's plenty of them.'

Jack brought me my mug, and I finished my breakfast, and
then Tonio took me to see the Bishop. He was sat on his gold
throne, with a big book for writing in open in front of him.
He had a pen in his hand.

'Good morning again, Your Grace, and beg pardon if we're
interrupting you.'

'Ah, Anthony, you catch me in the thick of the monthly
accounts. Figures, figures. And how is our new recruit?'

'He's had a lovely lie-in. Haven't you, Stephen?'

Yes, I answered, and remembered to say 'Your Grace'.

'Excellent. Anthony informs me that you have fifty pounds
on your person.'

I said that was correct, I had.

'May I suggest, dear boy, that you entrust them to me for
safe keeping?'

(That was always his expression – 'Entrust them to me for
safe keeping' – whenever we had some ten or twenty pound
notes to hand over. And when we did hand them over, you
should have seen the light come on in his watery eyes.)

Anyway, I gave him the fifty, which he said he'd put under
lock and key.

'Anthony will see to it that you are regularly supplied with
enough money for your daily needs.'

'I'll see to that with pleasure, Your Grace.'

'We share and share alike in the palace. That's our little
motto – isn't it, Anthony?'

'It is, Your Grace, definitely. With Your Grace's permission, I'd like to show Stephen Your Grace's chapel.'

'Go ahead.'

'And afterwards, Your Grace, I'd like to show him the sights of London.'

'An excellent idea, Anthony. But please, please ensure that Stephen does not get lost in the crowd.'

'Trust me, Your Grace.'

And then we had to take our leave again, just as we'd done before. We both of us kissed the Bishop's hand and walked backwards out of his office, with him smiling on us and nodding his head. I honestly couldn't believe I was doing it.

We went through the reception area and along a passage and past the refectory and Tonio stopped outside two doors – double doors – and said, 'Wait till you see this, Stephen.'

(I'm saying 'Stephen', but it was my mum's name for me he really used.)

He opened the doors, and there it was, the Bishop's chapel. It was like a church, but smaller; smaller than the Methodist one my mum and me went to at Christmas, before *he* arrived. And it was *much* smaller than the Church of England church where my mum and him were married, with my mum all in white, and certain of the people – the *congregation*, I mean – laughing. It didn't have the big columns, nor the organ.

There was an altar, though, and there was a *pulpit*, and there were four rows of benches, and a dark sort of wooden box, which I had to ask Tonio to tell me what it was. 'That's a confessional,' he told me. 'That's a *bona fide* confessional, alias the real thing. The Bishop squeezes himself inside – it's a tight fit for His Grace with that great gut of his – and we sit on the outside, one at a time, and talk to him through the grille.'

What, I wanted to know, did they talk to him about?

'We confess,' Tonio said. 'Our sins. If we have any.'

'What kind of sins?'

'All kinds, Stephen. You'll understand in due course.'

Which I would, Doctor Lady and Mr Gabriel. Which I did.

You should have heard him 'Ooh'-ing and 'Aah'-ing when one of us was confessing what we'd been up to. You should have heard his funny noises.

But that's jumping the gun, which I mustn't.

'Ready for London, then?' This was Tonio. 'Ready for the sights?'

Yes, I said, I was.

I have to tell you the palace looked even more funny by day than it did by night. You don't picture a palace being up above a sort of garage, but this one was. After Tonio'd opened all the doors, and we'd gone down all the stairs, we were in this huge space, which only had an old car in it. 'Property of the Bishop,' Tonio said. There was room to spare for another fifteen of them, I remember I thought.

When we were out in the sunshine, I could see that the palace – the building the palace was in – took up most of the street. There were no houses. Where we were, Tonio said, was a wharf. I had to ask him what a wharf is, not ever having been in one in Halifax. 'A wharf's like a dock,' he told me. 'But a dock's near water,' I said. 'So are we, Stephen. The mighty Thames is just around the corner.'

Which it was. We walked across Wandsworth Bridge and then we got on a bus going into what Tonio called 'the good old West End'. We sat on the top – no, of course we didn't; I mean, we sat upstairs – and Tonio lit a cigarette and offered me one but I told him no thanks, I never smoke. He paid our fares and said I wasn't to worry about the money I'd given to the Bishop. I'd have a roof over my head and food to eat and there was no problem with work. 'It's easy as falling off a log, Stephen. Easier. You'll soon find out how easy it is.'

The bus went through Fulham, which had no sights to speak of, and Chelsea next, along King's Road, and then to Hyde Park and on to Piccadilly, where we got off. Tonio pointed out Eros with his wings, who – according to the Bish, Tonio told me – is not the God of Love, like most people think, but the angel of Christian Charity.

(Do I know something you don't, Doctor Lady and Mr Gabriel? That would be a surprise, wouldn't it?)

'He's nothing much, is he?' This was Tonio, pointing at Eros, and I had to agree with him. 'Let's go to the good old Tower of London and look at something really historical.' He stopped a taxi, and he pushed me in, saying we might as well travel in style as he was feeling flush. And then he told me again that he'd see to it that I was A-OK; he was my friend Tonio and I was his friend . . . well, Stephen to you two, for the nonce.

We had an ice-cream each before we went into the Tower. We had to join a queue of foreigners, from all over abroad – Chinese or Japanese; and Germans, Tonio said, and Americans. Tonio paid for our tickets and we followed the foreigners inside. We saw the dungeons, and one of them had a funny name because the prisoner who was locked up in it wasn't able to stand nor lie down either. He had to crouch. In history. We saw chapels, too, that were different from the Bish's, and the Crown Jewels themselves – diamonds and pearls and rubies, and the Great Sword of State. 'The Bish would love to get his hands on these,' said Tonio. 'Specially the crowns.'

In St Paul's Cathedral, which we visited after, Tonio paid for us to go up to the Whispering Gallery, where he stood on one side of it and I stood way across on the other and he whispered into his wall and I heard every word, and then I whispered into my wall and he caught what I said. 'That's what's known as a phenomenon, Stephen, on account of its being phenomenal.'

We were both hungry by now, and Tonio's tummy was rumbling, so we *repaired* to a place in the Strand which Tonio said was cheap and cheerful, and he bought us both a hamburger and himself a Coke and me a grapefruit juice. Quite *frugal* it was, our meal, Doctor Lady, though not as frugal as tomatoes, and the place wasn't a *bistro*. It stank – or is it stunk? – actually. It stank or stunk of meat and onions, but onions most. You and your darling, your sweetheart, Mr Gabriel, would never have *repaired* to it. No, not you.

'Do you really have an Uncle Joseph?' Tonio asked me, I

161

remember, while the man in the funny chef's hat was *fixing* our hamburgers.

I said yes, I had.

'You were kidding me, Stephen. Admit it. You were pulling my leg.'

Yes, well, I did admit it. I'd made Uncle Joseph up on the spur of the moment. Out of panic.

'I won't tell His Grace, the Bishop of Wandle,' Tonio promised. 'I won't let on that you don't have an uncle. Your secret's safe with me.'

He wanted to hear why I'd run away from Halifax. Was it because of my mum and dad?

No, it wasn't; it wasn't because of them. It was *him*, I told Tonio; the man my mum hadn't the courage to say no to; the one man in the world she should have given the brush-off, but didn't. I told Tonio about the Hottentot and piccaninny and coon stuff, and about the twins and Donna – but not about the bird. Which I couldn't allow myself to tell that first day with Tonio. I was too close to it.

'You did right, Stephen. I don't like the sound of him. I don't like the sound of him at all.'

I'd had enough of talking about *him*, so I asked Tonio if he had run away from his home like I had.

Yes, he had, three years previous. It was his own father, his own flesh and blood he'd got shot of, he said. He was a bloody tyrant, his father, a bloody pig-headed bully.

(You should have seen him at Tonio's funeral, Doctor Lady. You should have seen him crying. You should have seen his tears, Tonio's dad's, and how they wouldn't stop falling. And you should have heard what his daughter, Tonio's sister, said to him.)

But I mustn't jump the gun. We finished our quite frugal meal and then we walked to Trafalgar Square, where Tonio showed me Nelson's Column. It's Jack's opinion that Nelson's Column is the most dopey statue in London: 'You'd have to be a giant – and who's a giant? – to get a look at his face, he's up in the air so high,' Jack says. 'The bloke who built him must have been totally dopey.'

Tonio said we ought to be making tracks back to the palace and catching the bus before the rush hour started. Piccadilly's only minutes from Trafalgar Square, and when we reached it Tonio said his bladder was bursting, and I said so was mine. We went down to the gentlemen's toilet in the underground station and once we were inside I couldn't help noticing that a couple of men nodded at Tonio, and another smiled, and that Tonio nodded and smiled too. 'Business acquaintances,' said Tonio, while we passed water. 'Useful contacts. Not big spenders, but reliable.'

It wasn't dark yet when we turned into the wharf, and I saw there were words on the outside of the building the palace was in. 'J.T. Montagu,' I read. 'Furniture Removals and Depository. Established 1839.'

'What's a depository, Tonio?'

'A depository, my friend, is a place where things are *deposited*, alias stored. That's what a depository is. Understood?'

Yes, I understood, but what I didn't understand was why the Bishop of Wandle had his palace inside it.

'Needs must, Stephen, if you catch my drift. This here depository was empty for ages, and when it came up for grabs on the market, His Grace made an offer. He bought it at an auction, wearing his plain clothes. Family money, he said. They weren't to know what he was going to use it for – '

Tonio stopped speaking, and smiled, and I had to remind him to tell me what they weren't to know he was going to use it for.

'Why, religious purposes, of course.' Tonio let out his laugh, like he had with the Ritz, Savoy and Dorchester. 'For religious purposes, my dear Stephen. What else?'

He laughed some more, and then he rang the bell – the bell to the palace, I mean – three times. Then he rang it two times – alias twice, as Tonio used to say.

'This is the only way you can get in, Stephen, short of having a set of keys. It's simple. You ring three times, wait a second, and then you ring two times, alias twice. Then you have to wait again, before one of the lads comes down and opens up.'

The door was opened that first day by a boy I hadn't met.

'Allow me to effect an introduction,' said Tonio. 'Brendan, this is Stephen; Stephen, this is Brendan.'

'Hi there,' said Brendan, who – as you'll probably guess, Doctor Lady and Mr Gabriel – was Irish. *Is* Irish, I should say, because Brendan is still in the land of the living as far as I know, even though he's left the circuit. There's a rumour that he's married now with a kiddy and has put his wicked past – *ho ho* – behind him. Anyhow, Brendan had dark-red hair in thick curls and those spots on his face that aren't spots, but freckles. Brendan was freckled.

'The Bishop's just heard my confession, Tony,' said Brendan. 'I didn't have much to confess, so I spun it out a little. I made the punter sound far worse than he was. Told the Bishop I had to beat him up, which wasn't true at all.'

'I bet His Grace loved that, eh, Brendan?'

'Seventh heaven, Tony. He was in seventh heaven. Is the new boy *aware*?'

'Not quite. He will be.'

'Breaking him in slowly, are you?'

'That's my method, Brendan.'

We went in, and up the stairs, and through the six doors and into the reception area, where the Bishop was standing in his *regalia*. He was wearing his *alb*, Doctor Lady, and his girdle, and his stole, and his cope, and his *skullcap*, too, but without the mitre. Impressed? I learned those words in the palace, Doctor Lady. I can't imagine I'd ever have learned them if I hadn't lived in the palace.

'Good evening, Your Grace. I wasn't expecting to see you in your finery.'

'My whim, Anthony, my whim. I felt the urge to put everything on. Brendan assisted me after I heard his *riveting* confession.'

Tonio nudged me with his elbow, and I took the hint. 'Good evening, Your Grace,' I said.

'And good evening to you, Stephen. Have you had a pleasant day seeing the sights?'

I said I had, yes thank you, Your Grace.

'Begging Your Grace's pardon' – this was Tonio – 'but has Your Grace forgotten your mitre?'

'You are always so observant, Anthony. No, I haven't forgotten my mitre. I have a slight headache, and decided not to don it. Tell me, Stephen, what do you think of my *ensemble*?'

I had no idea what to answer him. I stared at the Bishop, and Tonio and Brendan sort of giggled.

'He doesn't know what an ensemble is, Your Grace,' said Brendan. 'And neither did I till I came here.'

'I shall enlighten him, then. An *ensemble* is a person's complete outfit of clothes. This is my bishop's ensemble, Stephen.'

'Minus your mitre, Your Grace.'

'Exactly, Anthony.'

It was Tonio's turn to do the cooking that night, and he went off to the kitchen behind the refectory. The Bish asked me if I was a cook, and I said no, and he said I must learn to become a cook because everybody in the palace had to pull his weight. 'Team spirit, Stephen.' He was sitting down by now, with his 'skirts up', as he said, and having a 'well-earned rest'.

'Be a dear boy, Brendan, and fill my goblet to the brim with the clear liquid.'

(The Bish always called vodka, to which he was very partial, the 'clear liquid'. I never found out why.)

'At the double,' said Brendan.

The Bish could easily have poured the drink for himself because the bottle and the glass were both on the table in front of him, but he enjoyed being waited on hand and foot. It was what he deserved, as the shepherd of the flock – that was his belief.

'Stephen, you are curious, perhaps, to *ascertain* why I am Bishop of Wandle?'

Ascertain had me stumped. I looked into his watery eyes and just said, 'Yes, Your Grace.'

'The Wandle is a London river. A humble river – humbler by far than the mighty Thames.'

'I've seen the Thames.' This was me. 'Today, Your Grace.'

'Excellent. Now, if you wish to see the Wandle, you will need to be something of a detective. It trickles through Surrey and south London, and does most of its trickling under the ground. It was not ever thus.'

Then he said that six hundred years ago there was a famous *argy-bargy* between the bleachers of cloth and the hat-makers of Wandsworth as to which had the rights to the waters of Wandle. The bleachers won the battle, and the hat-makers disappeared, and did not come back until four hundred years later.

'Not the *same* hat-makers, Stephen, of course. Their great-great-great-great-great-great-grandchildren. They supplied the hats for the cardinals in Rome.'

I bet I know as much about the humble Wandle as you two clever people do, the times I had to hear the Bish spew on about it. It was only Tonio could ever shut him up. 'Beg pardon, Your Grace, but Your Grace's needle is stuck. The good old Wandle is getting on your acolyte's nerves, alias his wick.'

And then the Bish would say he was sorry in his quiet voice, for he loved Tonio if he loved anybody, and Tonio had this power over him which no one else was allowed to have. The horrible Nick had power over him, but his was different – his was horrible, in a word.

Anyway, there was more River Wandle stuff from the Bish before Tonio came back and said, 'Dinner is served, Your Grace,' and we followed him, the Bish, into the refectory. There was only the three of us – Tonio, Brendan, and me – besides the Bish, and it was Tonio who told me I couldn't sit down at table until His Grace'd said grace and sat down himself.

'*Divest* me, Brendan dear boy, of my outer robe,' said the Bish. Which Brendan did divest him of straight away, and put it on an empty chair. 'That's comfier.'

The Bish was at the top, of course, him being who he was.

'For what we are about to receive may the Lord make us

truly thankful,' we had to say, and then, 'Amen,' and then the Bish told us to be seated.

'What have you prepared for us, Anthony?'

'Steaks, Your Grace. And chips. And fresh garden peas. And one of your favourite desserts – rice pudding with a dollop of strawberry jam. And there's a nice chunk of Canadian farmhouse Cheddar cheese, with assorted biscuits.'

'Yum yum, Anthony. My taste buds inform me that a glass or two of our red communion wine would accompany such delicious fare most agreeably.'

'Begging Your Grace's pardon, but I've already taken the liberty of opening a bottle of same. Your Grace does like your red to breathe.'

'Excellent fellow.'

(Have I made it clear to you, Doctor Lady and Mr Gabriel, that it was Tonio who called the Bishop the Bish? Not to his face, mind. Never to his face.)

Anyway, the Bish asked me if I would care to *imbibe* a *modicum* of his wine, but I said no thanks, I'd stick to water. Tonio *imbibed* some, though, and Brendan drank a lager. Or ought I to say he imbibed it as well? Can you *imbibe* lager? You're the experts.

Brendan and me had to do the dishes afterwards. He washed and I dried, with a tea towel showing Westminster Abbey on it. 'It's just my luck to be on sausage duty,' he said, 'when His blinking Holiness is drunk as a skunk. He'll be taking for ever, he will, and my hand'll be aching, it will, from the effort. Just my lousy luck, when I'm dying for a kip.'

What, I wanted to know, was sausage duty?

'Are you telling me that Tony hasn't told you?'

Yes, I was.

'In that case, Stephen, I'd rather not answer. I'd rather leave it to Tony to explain. He has the gift.'

It sounded funny, whatever it was, I said.

'Funny, Stephen? It's funny all right. It's funny ha ha and it's funny peculiar.'

I could see that the Bish had lost his brain when I went to his office, as Tonio told me I should, to wish him good night.

He was giggling to himself and when he lifted his glass – his *goblet*, he always said – to have a drink, the clear liquid, alias vodka, missed his mouth and spilt down his shirt. 'Oh heck!' he said. 'Oh botheration!'

'Beg pardon, Your Grace. The new boy, Stephen, has come to take his leave.'

'Ah, yes. The tinted fellow. Sweet dreams, Stephen.'

'Good night, Your Grace.'

Then I kissed his hand, and walked out backwards.

The short silence that ensues is the only one Stephen allows himself on this side of the tape. After reminding Doctor Lady and Mr Gabriel that he never could have said what he's saying to their faces, he continues:

I'd gone to bed and I'd gone to sleep, and when I woke up it was in the dark, and I was in the dormitory, of course, where else, and next thing I was crying. My brain was ordering me not to, but I couldn't stop myself. My mum says it's wrong for a boy or a man to cry – that's a woman's privilege – and here I was doing wrong. What was funny was that I didn't know why I was crying like I was – it just seemed to be happening of its own accord. Yes, that's how it was – of its own accord.

'What's up, Stephen? What's the trouble?' This was Tonio. 'Are you homesick?'

No, I said, I wasn't.

'Move over.' He got into my bed and put his arm round me. 'There, there,' he said. He whispered, actually. 'Relax, relax. I'll see you're safe. You'll be A-OK. You'll survive.'

I stopped – it stopped, rather – after a while, and not before time. I was ashamed of myself, I honestly was. I was too ashamed to speak.

'I'll stay with you, Stephen.'

(Except it wasn't 'Stephen' he called me.)

Tonio stayed with me for hours, until it was almost

daylight. Which was when he did with his hand for me what I'd only ever done with my own hand for myself, if you get the picture. Of course you do.

That second morning of mine in the palace, the Bish was in a very bad state. You should have heard him groaning. You'd have thought he was at death's door itself. Tonio had to fetch a bowl from the kitchen into the bedroom for the Bish to throw up in. 'Two fingers down Your Grace's throat will do the trick, Your Grace,' Tonio said to him, and winking at Brendan and me while we watched.

'Oh, Anthony, must I?'

'I'd must if I was you, Your Grace. What's inside Your Grace's guts – beg pardon the vulgarity – would be better off in the basin, in my opinion.'

'Here goes, then,' said the Bish, and put two of his fat fingers in his mouth. He soon brought them out again. 'It's agony, Anthony.'

'I never would have thought, Your Grace, that you're a coward. Not you, of all people.'

This gave the Bish the hump, as Tonio guessed it would, so he shoved his fingers in and then, whoosh, up came his sick, bright-yellow.

'There's a brave Your Grace. Shall we try once more?'

Which the Bish did, but there wasn't so much of the yellow muck now.

Sick or no sick, the Bish never really learned his lesson, and lost his brain night after night, and usually suffered the consequences. It wasn't as if Tonio didn't warn him. 'Beg pardon, Your Grace,' he'd go, 'but hasn't Your Grace had a skinful already?' And the Bish would laugh his funny laugh, or shake his head, depending on his mood.

Anyway, Tonio left the Bish to sleep it off and we had some breakfast and then Brendan and me spent the morning doing women's work: sweeping the floors and dusting and polishing the furniture. I was given the Bish's office table to polish, which I did and made it shine. Tonio collected all the rubbish – 'the Bish's dead soldiers, alias his empties' – and stuffed it into black plastic bags, and the two of us – Tonio and me – lugged them down the stairs and round the corner and deposited them – 'Let's *deposit* them here' – on the steps of another huge building which Tonio said was due to be knocked down, alias demolished.

I went shopping with Tonio afterwards, in the market in Battersea, which isn't far from Wandsworth, as the good old crow flies. That's Tonio's – 'as the good old crow flies'. Since it was a Friday, the Bish had to have fish for his dinner, so we stopped at this stall where the woman with a moustache who owned it asked Tonio if the Right Reverend was prospering. 'He's prospering, thank you, Mrs Hopkinson, he's blooming.' Mrs Hopkinson said she was happy to hear it. And how was the Right Reverend's beautiful, *particular* cat? Fluff, Tonio told her, was blooming, too. 'I'm not surprised, with his fancy appetite. He must be packed with vitamins.' Then Tonio said it was because of her that Fluff was so healthy, and she laughed and slapped him on the chest, and wondered how she could oblige the Right Reverend gentleman today. With cod or haddock, Tonio answered her. Either would do nicely. Mrs Hopkinson sliced off a big bit of cod and a big bit of haddock, and then she threw in a few scraps of smoked salmon, free of charge, for His Highness, Fluff, the spoilt Siamese.

'Has the Right Reverend taken you in under his cloak, youngster?' This was Mrs Hopkinson talking to me while she wrapped the fish.

'Yes, he has, Mrs H,' said Tonio. 'This very week, Stephen's from a broken home in Halifax.'

'The poor mite,' said Mrs Hopkinson. 'Still, with the Right Reverend to look after him, he's bound to end up a credit to the community. Like you are, Tony.'

'Virtue's its own reward, Mrs H. We'll make sure that Stephen does well for himself.'

Tonio paid her, and she gave him his change. 'Don't forget to pass on my respects to the Right Reverend, and to stroke the pussy cat for me,' she said, and shook Tonio's hand. 'See you next week, love.'

Once we were out of the market, Tonio sniffed the hand

Mrs Hopkinson had shook. 'It stinks now, Stephen.' Then he answered the question I was going to ask him even before I asked it. 'The Bish's pussy cat's about as real as your Uncle Joseph is. The crafty old sod invented Fluff and told Mrs Hopkinson he was very *particular* in his tastes. "Would you believe, dear lady, that Fluff has a *veritable* passion for smoked salmon?" The result is, the Bish gets to eat his favourite grub every Friday, thanks to Fluff, the cat that never was.'

It was while we were on our way back to the palace that Tonio started to explain about the sausage. I mean, the 'sausage requirements'; the 'sausage duty'. The Bish, he said, seldom called a good old spade a spade, and it was the same with his cock. Other people – well, men, actually – had cocks, but not the Bish. 'The Bish's is a sausage, Stephen. He calls his cock a sausage.'

'Why's that?'

'Search me. It's his *whim*, you might say. He has plenty of those – whims. He wouldn't be the Bish if he hadn't.'

'So what's sausage duty, then?'

'You're the one should be named Innocent, not me. Listen. It's like what I did for you this morning, Stephen, only it's for the Bish instead. Are you on my wavelength? It's the price we have to pay for staying in the palace – *obliging* His Grace before bedtime. I can do it with my eyes shut now. Second nature. That's sausage duty, in a nutshell.'

'Will I have to do it?'

'Definitely. But only twice a week, at the most. It depends how many of us are in residence. Myself, I prefer to get my work done during the day, and sleep in my own bed at the palace, but some of the other lads are different. They're night owls. *Ergo*, as the Bish says, Anthony the acolyte is usually lumbered with the sausage.'

(An acolyte, for your information, just in case you don't know, is an attendant. He's a faithful follower. And that's what the Bish thought Tonio was – faithful. As much as he thought anybody was faithful.)

Anyway, that Friday evening, after we'd had our steamed

171

fish, the four of us – Tonio, Brendan, Jack and me – and after His Grace'd had his steamed fish *and* his smoked salmon ('Thanks be to Fluff,' he wobbled in his funny sing-song voice), and he'd changed from the white communion wine back to the clear liquid, we all of us went to the reception area – if you're still with me – and flopped around and played the Bish's favourite game, Naked Knowledge.

It was the Bish's favourite game because it was him who asked the questions and us who couldn't find the answers.

The Bish said, 'I'll begin with you, Anthony.' Which he did with, 'What is the capital of France, dear boy?'

'That's an easy one, Your Grace. Why, the capital of France is good old gay Paree.'

'Excellent. Now, Brendan, here's one for you. Which king of England, reckless fellow, burnt the cakes?'

'Alfred, Your Grace. That would be Alfred.'

'It would, indeed. And now, Jack, it's your turn. Tell me, if you can, the name of the popular singer who achieved success with "Blue Suede Shoes".'

'Elvis Presley, Your Grace. Elvis the pelvis himself.'

'Exactly so. Finally, Stephen, do you know who tried to blow up the Houses of Parliament with gunpowder?'

Which I did know, and I said it was Guy Fawkes, and the Bish was pleased with me.

'The second round will be a trifle more difficult. Anthony, dear boy, who painted the Mona Lisa?'

'The girl with the mystic smile? It was Leonardo, Your Grace, if my memory serves me aright.'

'It does, Anthony. It most certainly does.'

It was with the next question, which Brendan couldn't answer, that I twigged what the game was about and why it was *naked*.

'Remove your shoes, Brendan. That is the penalty.'

'Sure thing, Your Grace.' And Brendan took off his shoes.

'Let's see if Jack fares better,' said the Bish. 'Think carefully, dear boy. What is the Diet of Worms?'

Jack did think carefully. If what he looked like was anything to go by, he was really racking his brain. 'The

Diet of Worms, Your Grace, is what a fish has to eat when he's caught.'

Well, you should have heard him laugh, the Bish, when Jack said that. He laughed till he choked, and Tonio had to slap his back and say, 'Steady on, Your Grace, or you'll be having a seizure.'

'I'm afraid you are wrong, Jack.' This was the Bish as soon as he'd stopped laughing. 'You are *gloriously* wrong, and you must pay the penalty with your shirt.'

Which Jack had to do, it being the rule in Naked Knowledge that if you don't give the correct answer you have to undress.

Then it was me again. 'Stephen, dear boy, how did Joan of Arc die?'

'Joan of Arc?'

'Yes, Stephen.'

'How did she die?'

'Precisely.'

'Well, Your Grace, I suppose she died through want of breath.'

That didn't satisfy the Bish, although she must have died through want of breath, because everybody does. No, he'd wanted me to say she'd been burnt as a *heretic*. Which he said she wasn't, actually.

'Let's start with your shoes, Stephen.'

From then on, none of us, not even Tonio, answered the Bish correctly. He was in his element, drinking the clear liquid and throwing us lots of questions about people with funny foreign names – *Neb-u-chad-nezz-ar*, I mean, and *Tu-tan-kha-mun*, and similar. And we were each of us struck dumb.

Tonio, Brendan, Jack and me soon had nothing on.

'You're in the buff,' said the Bish. 'In the lovely, lovely buff. And all because you didn't concentrate at school. What lazy fellows you were.'

'You're our teacher now, Your Grace. I had no idea it was good old *Neb-u-chad-nezz-ar* who conquered and destroyed Jerusalem and shoved the Jews off to Babylon until you told us this evening, but I'm glad you did. I feel that bit more clever as a result.'

'Excellently said, Anthony.'

'Beg pardon, Your Grace, may I ask Your Grace if he likes the look of Stephen in the buff?'

'You may ask, Anthony, and I shall reply. His skin is very silky and a delight to gaze upon. I am *tickled*, I have to say, by the ring of white on his chest. Nature's afterthought, is it? Or her forethought, perhaps – and then she changes her mind. Yes, it tickles me, Anthony.'

'And his sausage, Your Grace?'

'His sausage appears to be household average. It wouldn't dishonour the regiment, but it is not in the same league as Jack's.'

'Nobody's is,' said Tonio.

'True, Anthony, true.'

(Listen hard and take heed, Doctor Lady and Mr Gabriel. Jack's sausage, alias his cock, or whatever, is enormous, and I do mean it's enormous. It's longer and thicker than a toddler's arm – that was Tonio's opinion. The Bish used to call it the Eighth Wonder of the World, but Jack himself thinks it's dopey. 'It's dopey having a cock this big,' Jack's always saying.)

'And what about Stephen's peach, Your Grace?'

'Ah yes, his peach. I am going to surprise you, Anthony. Stephen's peach is silkier and shinier than the other peaches present, and so I shall refer to it as Stephen's nectarine. The nectarine is a kind of peach, but with a smoother skin than its more familiar relation.'

(My nectarine, if you haven't guessed, is my bottom. My behind. I ate a nectarine on the day of the frugal tomatoes and nearly had hysterics. Do you remember, Doctor Lady?)

Tonio gave me my first lesson that Friday evening. The Bish had lost his brain and was flat out in his four-poster, but he still wanted his sausage stroked. And Tonio showed me the best way to stroke it, while the Bish made his funny noises. You should have heard him moaning and groaning. 'Oh, Anthony, Anthony,' he said.

174

'That's me, Your Grace. I'm Anthony, your acolyte.'

'You're a wonderful fellow.'

'I only try to do what's best for everybody, Your Grace. And virtue, as they say, is its own reward.'

And Tonio winked at me, and I winked back.

Anyway, anyhow, I'm tired of talking and I'm hungry and thirsty and so that's it for the nonce, Doctor Lady and Mr Gabriel. For the good old nonce.

You two could never play Naked Knowledge, could you? You have the answers to everything. You wouldn't be struck dumb over *Neb-u-chad-nezz-ar*.

You'd be in your clothes for hours and hours.

The first side of the second tape opens with Stephen informing us that he is wearing a fresh ensemble. 'Quite a sober one, actually, though I have allowed myself a splash of colour. There's a red silk handkerchief peeping out of the breast pocket of my blazer.' He wouldn't look seriously wrong, he adds, in a room with a chandelier.

'Where did I love you and leave you yesterday?' he asks. Then, after a rather stagey pause, he provides the answer:

On the Bish's four-poster it was, wasn't it, with the Bish going swoony while Tonio attended to his sausage requirements. Are you thinking, you two, what I think you're thinking? That I must have been – *ought* to have been – shocked, disgusted?

Well, I was disgusted, but the funny thing is I wasn't disgusted for very long. It wasn't a pretty sight, the Bish spread out, with his great big gut sticking up in the air. You definitely would have had to have lost your brain to ever think it was – a pretty sight, I mean. No, it was disgusting to start with, and then it was pathetic, really, to see this fat old man in such a state. And when Tonio winked at me I knew how stupid and pathetic the Bish was, actually, and would go on being, and that I could get by in his palace just so long as I took Tonio's advice. I hadn't much to fear with Tonio around, I told myself. That I already knew for certain.

'You'll be my star pupil, Stephen,' said Tonio. Which I probably was, because I listened to him like I'd listened to Mr Portman in the school in Halifax. 'I'll teach you what I've learnt,' he promised. 'The Anthony Innocent technique.'

Tonio said that there were men out there, meaning the rest of London beyond the palace, who needed what the Bish needed every night, only with differences. They needed it so bad, they were prepared to pay for it. The trick was to take as much money from them while giving as little as possible, and this trick was one that he, the Bish's acolyte, had got off to perfection. 'My trick with the tricks, I call it. Judgement, Stephen. That's what you have to acquire. Judgement.'

'He's *surly*, Anthony.' This was the Bish, referring to me. 'There's still a bit of the Heathcliff in him.'

'Surly I can follow, Your Grace, but as to the heath cliff, I'm not on Your Grace's wavelength.'

The Bish laughed his funny laugh, and then he said that I, Stephen, could do with a little fine tuning.

'Don't expect to be a *Strad-i-var-i-us* like Anthony, but with a little fine tuning you'll pass master. Anthony will raise you to concert pitch – won't you, Anthony?'

'Have I ever failed Your Grace? I'll tune him up for you. I'll make him playable.'

The Bish laughed his funny laugh again, and took a swig from his goblet.

Believe it or not, Doctor Lady and Mr Gabriel, but the Bish had decided that I'd got a touch of class. He thought I might appeal to a more artistic type of punter because of my *soulful* eyes. Jack and Brendan were best left untuned, he said, along with Ray and Wally and the other, rougher boys who sometimes stayed at the palace.

I'd been there a whole week by now when one day Tonio said, 'You're coming with me, Stephen. Let's find out what the big city has to offer.'

I still only had the clothes I'd come down from Halifax in.

This was before I developed my taste – my *penchant* – for ensembles.

We rode on the bus to Piccadilly, and Tonio kept telling me not to worry and that I'd be A-OK. He would show me the good old ropes and teach me a lesson or two in technique.

It was three in the afternoon by the time we reached the West End. 'If I mention Jennifer or Lily, Stephen, it means we're not stopping here. We're moving on. Understood?'

Yes, I said, I supposed I understood, but who were Jennifer and Lily?

'I'll explain later.'

We went to the gentlemen's toilet in the underground and stood next to each other, and Tonio looked this way and that, and whistled a tune, and then he said, very quiet, 'Jennifer's about. We're off. Pronto.'

We were to leave together casually. Which we did, and went up the stairs and into Piccadilly and from there we walked into Soho, and Tonio bought us an apple each in the market and while we were eating them he explained that Jennifer is short for Jennifer Justice and Lily is short for Lily Law and that Justice and Law are the boys in blue, alias the police.

'So if I say to you, "That bloke looks like Jennifer's brother," or, "He could be Lily's twin," you ought to be on my wavelength straight away – *tout de suite*, or even *suiter*.'

That was one of Tonio's – *tout de suite*, or even *suiter*.

'The blond guy in the bogs, smiling at everyone – he had Jennifer written all over him. In letters of flame.'

'How could you tell, Tonio?'

'Instinct, Stephen. He was overdoing the friendliness. He had the confidence of somebody who knows he isn't going to be arrested. Besides, he's got a Jennifer face.'

'What's a Jennifer face?'

'It comes in all shapes and sizes, Stephen, fat and thin, but it always has the same snotty expression. I understand what I'm talking about, though thousands wouldn't.'

Wherever we went that afternoon, Tonio spotted a Jennifer

or a Lily, and it wasn't until the pubs opened at five-thirty that Tonio said he felt free to do a bit of work. 'This one's on the circuit,' he said as he led me into a pub which was very dark inside with pictures of boxers from long ago on the walls.

'Is your chum eighteen?' the barman asked Tonio.

'Eighteen years, seven months, four days, nine hours and six minutes,' Tonio answered him. 'At the last count and to be precise.'

The barman smiled at this, and Tonio bought a pint of beer for himself and an orange juice for me, and we went and parked ourselves in a corner, opposite the entrance.

'Are you scared, Stephen?'

I said no. Which was a lie.

'Yes, you are. I was scared the first few times. Until I became used to it.'

'All right, then. Yes, I'm scared.'

'No need to be. You're in the company of an expert.'

We stayed there for a while and nothing seemed to be happening, apart from this one man who kept gaping at us. 'Ignore him,' Tonio said.

'He's not a Jennifer, is he?'

'No, nothing like. He's just a bit too full of himself. He's wondering why I haven't responded, and the reason's money. Ergo, as the Bish says, he doesn't want to pay for my lovely services. Or yours, Stephen. He thinks he's God's gift; the bee's good old knees. Not for Anthony Innocent, he isn't.'

God's gift saw he was getting nowhere fast with us, and stopped his gaping, and then the door was opened by a tall man in a smart suit who popped his head into the pub, saw Tonio, nodded to him, very quick, and took his head away, and closed the door without coming in.

'Business beckons,' said Tonio. 'We're on the move.'

Up we got and as we were leaving Tonio gave God's gift a cheeky little goodbye wave, and out we went into the street where the tall man was waiting for us. He was pretending to be interested in something in a shop window, actually. 'Stay here for a minute, Stephen. I have to discuss arrangements with him.' Which he did. What we had to do was to walk behind the man, not alongside him. Tonio had catered for him before and he was safe, and I should consider myself the luckiest young man in London to be starting my career so easily.

Anyway, this man lived in a block of flats off Charing Cross Road. His flat was at the very top, and I said I'd prefer to use the stairs up rather than the lift because lifts give me claustrophobia. He had a view over the city, which we had a glimpse of until he pulled the curtains. It was very neat and tidy, with no mess. The books on his bookshelves were to do with famous trials – murders, mostly – and they were all the same colour, red. And there were photographs on his desk – of him on his wedding day with his wife in white, like my Mum had been; and of her with him again, dressed normal, with two kiddies, a boy and a girl.

He said nothing, the man – not a word. 'The usual?' Tonio asked him, and he nodded. 'The soap's in the bathroom?' The man nodded. Tonio signalled to me to go with him, so I did.

'He likes the taste of goat's milk soap, does our talkative friend,' Tonio said, taking out his cock in the bathroom and washing it at the basin. He worked the goat's milk soap into what he called a 'lovely lather' and told me to wash mine in it, too. Which I did, and then Tonio said he'd quickly put me in the picture. I was to watch what he did, carefully, because I'd have to do exactly the same when it was my turn. I was to make no sound whatsoever while the man was eating his dinner. 'That's us, Stephen. We're his dinner.'

The man handed Tonio a newspaper as soon as we were back in the room with the murder books. Tonio sat down in a leather armchair and started to read the paper. I watched him carefully, like he'd told me to. The next thing was, the man was on his knees on the floor and undoing the zip on Tonio's trousers. Then he pulled out Tonio's cock and began to lick it. Tonio went on reading the paper just as though the man wasn't there. He turned the pages slowly, one by one. I couldn't see Tonio's cock any more because the man had the whole of it in his mouth.

Well, Doctor Lady and Mr Gabriel, the man finished munching – that was Tonio's word, 'munching' – and lay down on the carpet with his eyes shut as if he was about to go off to sleep. Tonio stood up and pointed to the armchair, which I went and sat in. He passed me the newspaper. It was the *Daily Telegraph*, in case you're interested.

This is funny, but I can still remember what I was reading while the man was munching me. It was inside the paper, not on the front page, and it was the story of a woman who fell in love with a plumber who came to unblock her drains. She persuaded the plumber to kill her husband, who was a millionaire. The plumber pretended to be a burglar, and broke into the house and shot the millionaire, but the bullet missed killing him. He survived.

'Good work,' said Tonio, once the man was in his bathroom, gargling. 'That was painless, wasn't it?'

Which I had to agree it really was.

The man still said nothing when he paid Tonio for us catering to him. 'See you around,' said Tonio. The man nodded. We left.

'Has Stephen been *initiated*?' This was the Bish, the moment we were back in the palace.

'Yea, verily, he has, Your Grace.' Although the Bish tut-tutted, and said, 'Naughty Anthony,' he always loved Tonio's 'Yea, verily' stuff. 'The West End was riddled with Jennifers this afternoon, and I was in two minds whether to carry on or shut up shop when who should put his head in at the door of the Needle and Compass but the Muncher from the Mansions. He had a catering job to offer us, and we accepted.'

'Excellent, Anthony. Excellent, Stephen. And the payment?'

'Three tenners, Your Grace, alias thirty pounds.'

'He had a bargain.'

'True, Your Grace. A double helping, you might say. Still, it does no harm in the long run to keep certain customers happy.'

'Such wisdom on such young shoulders.' Then the Bish turned to me. 'You must be ready to confess your sins.'

180

I said I was. Tonio had warned me on the bus that the Bish would want to hear me in his box. It would tickle him, listening to a brand-new sinner. 'It'll be a good old novelty for him.'

'Oh my, it's becoming a tighter fit with every passing day. I fear I shall have to fast.' This was the Bish, trying to squeeze into his confessional. 'Roll on, Lent, and semi-starvation.'

I was tongue-tied at the start, I honestly was.

'What do you wish to confess, my son?'

I answered him that I wasn't sure.

'Have you done something rude?'

Strictly speaking, I hadn't – done something rude. It was the man who nodded. He was the one.

'Did you permit him to be rude?'

Yes, I did permit him, I said, after watching Anthony.

'Was Anthony setting a naughty example?'

I answered him yes, which I could tell was what he wanted.

'This man who nods. Describe him.'

'He's tall and thin, Your Grace.'

'Enviable fellow. And?'

'He has hairs coming out of his nose.'

'Dear, dear. You saw nothing more of him?'

Not really, I said. Not his body. He didn't take his clothes off.

'Why?'

'He didn't have to, Your Grace. He was happy using his mouth.'

'How did this wicked, nodding man use his mouth?'

The Bish was gasping by now. You could hear his breath when he wasn't speaking.

'On our cocks, Your Grace.'

'On your sausages, please, dear boy.'

'On our sausages, then, Your Grace.'

'And you enjoyed it? What he did to you with his mouth?'

'It was all right.'

'Only all right?'

'Well, it was quite nice. I mean, I didn't have to look at him. I was reading the paper.'

181

So I had to explain about the newspaper, and me not making any sound whatsoever, and the washing in the goat's milk soap – which the Bish said was most hygienic.

He asked me over and over if I'd enjoyed what the wicked, nodding man had done to me with his mouth, and in the end I said yes, I had, very much, just to stop him from asking me yet again.

'Say after me, "I am a terribly sinful boy and I must repent."'

Which I did say, and he said I could go, and he hoped in his heart of hearts that I would have no reason to confess to him in the future.

'Is that it, then, Your Grace?'

'It is, dear boy, for the nonce. Send Anthony to me, if you would be so kind.'

(Anyway, that's how my terribly sinful life – *ho ho* – got started. That's how, with me reading the paper in a leather armchair, while . . . But I've told you what happened while.)

When I think about it, there wasn't much to the 'fine tuning'. Tonio said I should only look my usual surly self if the punters required it. I'd learn how to tell which ones did: 'Some of them fancy being glared at.' Otherwise, I should try to smile, be easy-going, devil-may-care. I have to say I didn't find it easy being easy-going, specially those first few times without Tonio, on my own, though I did do my best not to seem as scared as I was feeling.

And my clothes, I had to do something about my clothes, if I really wanted to appeal to the artistic types. The Bish was very concerned that I was still wearing what I'd been wearing when I came to London to meet my Uncle Joseph.

'I have given Anthony an allowance with which to *purchase* a new outfit for you. You will spend wisely, Anthony, won't you? And prudently?'

'Trust me, Your Grace. If anyone has an eye for a bargain it's your acolyte.'

'Indeed, indeed, Anthony.'

The two of us kissed the Bish's hand, and walked out of his office backwards, according to the custom.

We made straight for Chelsea, where Tonio said we might find something snazzy. Not *too* snazzy, or the Bish'd be upset. 'He doesn't approve of us making a spectacle of ourselves. He's a fine one to talk, with his alb and his cope and his mitre. With his good old regalia. With his ensemble.'

'Is the Bish a real bishop, Tonio?'

'Who's to know? He showed me a certificate once, in blue and gold, which had written on it that he'd been *ordained*. But it could be a fake. I wouldn't put it past him.'

I wondered why it was that, although the Bish had a chapel, he didn't hold any services in it. Not even on a Sunday.

'Don't worry, Stephen. The Bish'll be holding a service again when he's in the mood, complete with a sermon from the pulpit. It all depends on his whim and how much of the clear liquid he's poured down his throat.'

We went from shop to shop, the entire length of the King's Road, both ways, that Tuesday. I'd never seen so many different kinds of clothes before, not in so many colours. 'Too expensive,' Tonio kept saying when I said I liked this or that shirt, or a pair of corduroys, or a jacket or a coat.

'You'll empty the kitty in one fell swoop, Stephen. Let's take our time and pick and choose.'

Which we did, and thanks to Tonio we bought enough for two separate ensembles. I say 'we' even though he paid, but I reckoned that some of the money must have been mine, from the fifty pounds I'd handed over to the Bish and from what I'd earned by reading the newspaper for the man who munched me. I mean, I wasn't accepting charity.

Anyway, anyhow, that's when the rot set in, to borrow Tonio's expression. I'm referring to my taste, my *penchant*, for beautiful clothes. It was just as if I was a new person, a whole new Stephen, the moment I put on that very first London ensemble. I couldn't bear those Halifax clothes any more, specially the boring shoes and socks. I wanted rid of them.

I was for throwing them out, but the Bish wouldn't

let me. 'There are plenty of other deserving lads in this wretched world, Stephen. "Thrift, thrift, Horatio,"' he said, and laughed.

'Beg pardon, Your Grace, but why did you call Stephen here Horatio?'

'Oh, Anthony, that would be telling.'

'Is he like your friend Mrs Danvers, then, Your Grace?'

'Horatio? Yes, I suppose he is. Horatio's a *chatelaine*, I suppose, in his way. He's very like Mrs Danvers, now that I think about it.' And then the Bish had a laughing fit, and Tonio stuck a finger to the side of his head to show me he thought the Bish had a screw loose.

(I meant to ask you what a 'chatelaine' is, Doctor Lady, but I forgot to. I can't find it in my pocket dictionary.)

I wore some of my Chelsea togs the next time I travelled up West with Tonio. He was in two minds, he said, on the bus, puffing on his cigarette, whether or not to throw me in at the deep end – in other words, allow me to go it alone. He'd see how the lie of the land was before he came to a decision. I would be A-OK, whatever happened.

It was an afternoon again, Tonio being mostly a day worker. Manoeuvres – that was Tonio's, 'manoeuvres' – began in the gentlemen's toilet at Piccadilly. 'No sign or sniff of Jennifers today, Stephen. They must be looking out for real criminals, for a change. Wonder of good old wonders!'

There were no Jennifers, but there weren't any clients either, it was Tonio's opinion. The sound of money wasn't in the air. The cash registers were always silent when the something-for-nothing brigade was on patrol. Manoeuvres would have to be shifted to another place on the circuit.

As it turned out, we didn't have to shift very far. It was in Piccadilly itself, outside the large chemist's, that this man who knew Tonio stopped him for a chat. When I say he knew him, I mean he knew him in a business sense. He called Tonio Derek.

'May I effect an introduction?' This was Tonio, of course. 'Mr White, meet Michael; Michael, meet Mr White.'

(Yes, I was Michael, just as Tonio was Derek. 'Take my

advice, Stephen, and always give the punters a false name, alias an alias. It's a kind of protection, as well as a kind of camouflage.' What was *camouflage*? 'Camouflage, my young friend, is like a disguise. You've heard of animals staying stock still and merging with their surroundings? That's camouflage. Being human, we can't manage that. We cover our tracks differently. We say we're someone we're not.' Well, Doctor Lady and Mr Gabriel, I've taken Tonio's advice. I've protected myself with camouflage. That's how I've covered my tracks.)

'Hello, Michael.' This was Mr White.

'Hello,' I said.

'Is Michael fresh on the scene, Derek?'

'As a daisy, Mr White.'

'Is he available?'

'Depends, doesn't it? On the price, and what you want for it.'

'I want to rim him, Derek.'

'So far so good – or should I say peculiar? How much?'

'Twenty.'

'He's yours.'

'There's one condition, Derek. Do you know if he's been rimmed already?'

'I can safely tell you hasn't. He's only just down from Halifax. I can't imagine he'd have been rimmed up there.'

'Check, would you.'

Tonio turned to me and asked, very quiet, if anyone had ever eaten my nectarine. It took me a minute to click what he meant.

'No,' I said, or shouted, rather. 'No, nobody has. Why would they? What are you talking about?'

'He's shocked, isn't he?' Mr White said to Tonio. 'He's disgusted. That's wonderful.'

Tonio told me to go with Mr White, who would treat me A-OK. I said it was disgusting, what he wanted to do, and Tonio said, 'Let him. It's not going to hurt you, Michael. There's a first time, as they say, for everything. I'll be waiting for you in the Needle and Compass.'

I went off with Mr White, to a small hotel where the woman behind the desk seemed to know him and gave him the key without him having to ask for it. He wasn't as old as the man who nodded, and he actually spoke to me. He'd never set foot in Halifax, he said. Was it worth a visit? And so on, and so forth. Polite conversation.

The room was on the second floor, at the end of the passage. It was really gloomy and dingy inside, because the only thing you could see from the window was a black brick wall. That was the view.

'Shall we get started, Mike?'

'Michael,' I corrected him. 'My name's Michael.'

Then we got started. He did, I mean. 'May I undress you, Michael?' And before I could answer him yes or no, he reminded me, Michael, that he was paying, and him undressing me was part of the deal. So I stood there while he stripped the clothes from off me, one after another.

'Don't be frightened, Michael.'

I'll spare you all the details, Doctor Lady and Mr Gabriel, because strictly speaking they're my affair, not yours, and anyway you don't want to have to listen to me telling you how he licked my bottom for over an hour. Which he did do – to his heart's content, he told me after. Anyway, while I was on the bed in the hotel, I thought of my mum and what she'd be thinking if she knew where I was and what was happening to me, and I wondered if she'd tear Mr White limb from limb, like she'd once promised to if any stranger dared lay a finger on her son.

'I haven't finished yet.' This was Mr White. 'I'm just coming up for air. Taking a breather.'

He came up for air and took a breather three times before he'd decided he'd done it to his heart's content. He was so content, actually, that he gave me an extra ten pounds. And I said to him, which was a surprise to my brain, that if he wanted to do it some other time he could, for the same price, with or without the extra.

'Thanks, but no thanks, Michael. It's only fresh, unrimmed

186

bums that appeal to me. As yours was, at four o'clock this afternoon. You've lost your freshness for me now.'

And that was that. Tonio was in the Needle and Compass, as arranged, and I had an orange juice to celebrate what Tonio said was a successful mission accomplished. 'You'll soon be quite the expert, Stephen. Specially where catering jobs are concerned.'

The Bish, while I was confessing that evening, couldn't get enough of Mr White. I wasn't allowed to spare him a single detail. I had to tell him everything I remembered about the *brazen* fellow, and then he asked me to repeat it word for word. It was the freshness stuff that tickled him most. 'How *droll*,' he said. 'How very, very *droll*.'

As for the ten pound note, I kept it, since it was Mr White's present to me. I opened my ensemble kitty with it. Tonio said the punter who paid you over and above the agreed charge was one in a thousand – therefore, alias *ergo*, I should take advantage 'while the good old going is good, Stephen'.

(Except that it wasn't 'Stephen' he called me.)

That same evening of the Mr White confession, we were eating our supper in the refectory when the Bish began to chuckle to himself. We all thought this was funny peculiar because nobody was speaking.

'Beg pardon, Your Grace, but would Your Grace consider sharing the joke with us?'

'I'm not sure that I can, Anthony. The secrets of the confessional must ever remain secret. That is *episcopal* law.'

'Was it something I confessed, Your Grace? Something Your Grace found amusing?'

'No, Anthony. You are not the cause of my mirth. Not you, dear boy.'

'Then who is it, Your Grace? Stephen? Brendan? Jack? Don't be a spoilsport, Your Grace.'

'Tempt me no further, Anthony. My lips are sealed.'

My theory is that what he was chuckling at was Mr White's freshness remark, but I wouldn't pledge my life on it. That's my theory, anyway, if you want it, which you most likely don't.

You'll have gathered by now, you two, that I was settling in at the palace. I'd become one of the Bish's sheep, one of his little flock. With Tonio's help I'd even begun to do a spot of cooking. Not up to your standards, Mr Gabriel. I mean, the world would end before I baked a lemon tart like yours, or anything similar. That's a compliment. You ought to be the chef in a big restaurant with chandeliers, in my opinion.

Anyway, the Bish ate the food I cooked for us, and always said it was worth saying grace over. 'Delicious *provender*, Stephen.' Him and his 'provender'! He also said that, Anthony apart, I was the tidiest boy who'd ever lodged at the Palace of Wandle. So you see, funny as it was, and it *was* funny – having to do sausage duty was funny – the palace was a kind of home for me, already.

A person can get used to almost anything if he has to. I speak from experience. And, anyway, it's not as though I had to shake the Bish's sausage every night of the week. Sometimes, Ray and Wally – 'my rough diamonds', the Bish called them – came to stay when they were on parole from the place in the country for young offenders they'd been shoved in, and they were happy to oblige the Bish. Wally and Ray never answered a single, solitary question right, not even the dead easy questions, when we played Naked Knowledge, so they were always the first to be in the buff, 'in the lovely, lovely buff'.

There was only one of us, except that he wasn't really one of us, who ever complained about sausage duty, and that was the Honourable Grenville. He never was or would be a Honourable, but that's what Tonio decided he was. 'I bet he was born with a silver spoon in his mouth. You can't have a name like Grenville without a good old Honourable stuck in front of it.'

Tonio said he'd had his doubts about Grenville the very night he and the Bish had picked him up at Euston Station. 'My instinct kept telling me he wouldn't belong – not with that cut-glass voice and that snotty look on his pasty face. When I warned the Bish I sensed Grenville spelt trouble, the

Bish ticked me off for being uncharitable. He's changed his tune now.'

The Bish changed his tune the evening the Honourable Grenville refused point blank to satisfy his sausage requirements. 'Shake the revolting pink thing yourself, or order one of your common bloody *minions* to do it.'

'Grenville, dear boy, what are you saying?'

'Your Grace isn't deaf.'

The Bish had seemed all set to lose his brain until the Honourable Grenville spoke, but not any more. The clear liquid might have been water.

'No, I am certainly not deaf, Grenville. I very much wish I had not heard the vile words you addressed to me a moment ago. An apology, if you please.'

'Your Grace can whistle for an apology. I've no intention of apologising.'

'Think, Grenville. Think carefully before you speak again.'

The Honourable Grenville shrugged his skinny shoulders and turned his back on the Bish.

'If you choose not to obey the rules, Grenville, you will have to leave the palace, I am serious.'

'Come on, Gren.' This was Jack. 'Play fair with His Grace. He's been pretty kind to you.'

Well, the Honourable Grenville went crazy when Jack said that. He went completely bananas. He flipped his lid. He screamed at us that the Bishop of Wandle wasn't kind. The Bishop of Wandle was a great fat ugly dirty slug with a revolting pink thing. The kindness of the Bishop of Wandle was a sham, a fraud, a fake, and so was the Bishop of Wandle.

You'd have expected the Bish to go crazy back at him, but no, oh, no, he was as frosty as ice, as cool – Tonio said later – 'as a good old cucumber'. He waited for the Honourable Grenville to burn himself out. 'May I remind you of the pitiful state you were in when Anthony and I first met you? You were shaking then, but not from anger. You hadn't eaten for days. On your own admission, you had tried to sell your puny body to a man who hit you and hit you and left you almost for dead. And here you are, insulting me in front of my faithful and grateful flock. Think, Grenville. Think of the benefits you have received during your stay here.'

Then the Bish offered him, the Honourable Grenville, a second and final chance to apologise to everyone present.

'No.' That was the Honourable Grenville, and that was all he said. Just the one 'No'.

'Get rid of him, Anthony. Escort him off the premises. Give him his return fare to *purgatory*.'

And that was the last we saw, but not heard, of him.

I've really and truly jumped the gun with the Honourable Grenville, haven't I, Doctor Lady and Mr Gabriel. There's method in my madness, though. Be patient with me, and you'll soon learn why.

The Honourable Grenville stayed at the palace for two weeks. He didn't fit in with the rest of us from the start, and he didn't make much effort to either.

Anyway, there he was in the dormitory, fast asleep one morning when I woke up. 'Have you seen the streak of English piss?' Tonio asked me in the kitchen a few minutes afterwards. 'The Bish and myself brought him back from Euston last night, and I don't think we should have bothered. He speaks la-di-da.'

'Where's he from?'

'Not Halifax, that's for sure. Surrey, actually, if he's to be believed. His father, he says, owns a mansion, not a house, with a tennis court and a swimming pool.'

'What's he doing here, then?'

'That's what I'm wondering too. His parents threw him out, he says.'

'Why, Tonio?'

'For failing his exams, he says. For taking drugs at school. You'll never guess his name, Stephen.'

He was right, of course, Grenville's name being Grenville. I mean, how many Grenvilles do you have as friends, Doctor Lady? Gabriel's funny enough – as a name, that is – but *Grenville*. I mean!

That's when Tonio said he bet Grenville was called the

Honourable and that he was born with a silver spoon in his mouth. It was only the two of us ever used the Honourable. It was our secret, our joke.

Anyway, Grenville made it plain from the moment I met him in the refectory that I was beneath him. He made it plain he thought I was his inferior, just by the way he looked at me. Or didn't look at me, I should say. When he did bother to glance in my direction, it was as if I wasn't there.

'We must fatten Grenville up,' said the Bish. 'We must help him regain his strength.'

'No problem in that department, Your Grace. He scoffed his breakfast as quick as a dog scoffs, and then he had the good old gall to ask for more.'

'The poor boy needs to rest, to relax. He has suffered, Anthony. He will be an asset to us once he is restored to health.'

'I sincerely hope so, Your Grace.'

'Oh, Anthony, what a doubting Thomas you are.'

'Who's Thomas, Your Grace?' This was me. I thought he'd do his 'that would be telling' stuff like he'd done, and always did do, with Heathcliff, Mrs Danvers and Horatio, but he actually gave me an answer instead.

Which I won't bother you two with, but if you were to ask me who Thomas was, I could tell you straight off. Real name Didymus. Right? His story's in St John's Gospel. Right? Chapter 20. Verses 24 to 31. Am I right or am I right? Of course I am. Because, after that day, whenever I was alone in the palace with just the Bish, he'd say, 'Tell me, dear boy, who is doubting Thomas?' and I'd tell him straight off exactly what he'd told me in the first place.

Well, anyway, Grenville filled his face with the food the rest of us cooked, and drank the Bish's communion wine, red and white, and had his bed made for him by yours truly, and only helped with washing and drying the one single solitary time in the whole two weeks he was at the palace. You'd have thought we were his servants, and him our boss.

He was polite as he could be, which wasn't much, with the Bish himself. He wiped his sneer off a bit when the real boss was talking to him. The funny thing was that he never corrected Jack, who called him 'Gren' from the word go. I'd have thought if you had a name as posh as Grenville you wouldn't want it turned into something common like Gren. I mean, Jack knew better than to call me Steve. He still does, know better.

On the first Friday evening the Honourable G was with us, the Bish was in a jolly mood because Mrs Hopkinson had been particularly generous to his particular cat, Fluff: *ergo*, the Bish had eaten *lashings* – that was what he said, *lashings* – of smoked salmon. 'Thanks be to Fluff,' he'd wobbled.

'I am going to put you to the test, Grenville,' said the Bish. 'It being Friday, we shall be playing Naked Knowledge, a delightful game I myself invented in an idle moment. We play it on Fridays because we eat fish then, and fish is the food that does our brain cells most good. Since you have had the benefit, dear boy, of an expensive education, it *behoves* me to ask you more difficult questions.'

Well, the Bish started off with his Diet of Worms one, and it flummoxed the Honourable G just as it had flummoxed Jack. 'Shame on you, Grenville,' said the Bish with a laugh. 'You must pay the penalty for your ignorance.'

The Honourable Grenville wasn't happy with the rules of Naked Knowledge, and told the Bish he had no intention of removing his clothes. Which was a bit rich when you think about it, because all the clothes he had on were cast-offs kept by the Bish for the likes of him, including the shirt I was wearing when I came down to London from Halifax. The Bish said nothing of this, but it's what we were thinking.

'It's only a dopey game, Gren,' said Jack.

The Bish clapped his fat hands. 'I have the perfect solution. Jack and Brendan, strong lads both, will perform for Grenville the little task he is reluctant to perform for himself. *Ergo*, they will undress him.'

Which they did, with Jack saying, 'Come on, Bren,' each time they took something of Grenville's off.

(You'll have gathered that Brendan didn't mind Jack calling him Bren. I would have minded, but that's me. I'm choosy.)

Grenville kicked up a fight to begin with, but Jack and Brendan were far too strong for him, and soon he was in the buff alongside the rest of us. The Bish spewed his 'lovely, lovely buff' stuff, but honestly and truth to tell, Grenville was a total weed. He looked shocking with nothing on. There were nasty bumps and streaks of blue on his skinny legs, and pimples on his chest and back and down his arms.

'He's like a skelington,' said Jack.

'Skeleton, dear boy, *skel-e-ton*. How very rude of you. Please repeat the correct word and apologise to Grenville.'

'Skeleton, Your Grace. And I'm sorry, Gren.'

(He's a skeleton now, all right, is Grenville. He's bones under the ground in a grave someplace. But I don't have to tell you, Mr Gabriel. You must have read about him in the papers.)

Tonio showed the Honourable Grenville the best way to shake the Bish's sausage once Brendan and Jack and me were up in the dormitory. 'He held it like it was a turd,' Tonio told me. 'I had to put my hand over his, to get a grip on it.' There were plenty of nights when none of us really wanted to go on sausage duty, and we used to have a moan about it among ourselves, but we always went ahead and did it, because our motto was share and share alike – or 'shake and shake alike' which was Tonio's joke – and because we in the flock knew which side our bread was buttered.

It was on the next Friday that the Honourable Grenville refused point blank to touch the 'revolting pink thing' and was given his 'return fare to purgatory'.

He definitely wore smarter clothes going from the palace than he'd worn coming to it, for all they were cast-offs.

'Good riddance to the streak of English piss, if you'll pardon the vulgarity Your Grace,' said Tonio when he came back to the reception area after seeing the Honourable Grenville off the premises. 'Good bloody good old riddance.'

'You are pardoned, dear Anthony. Fill my goblet to the brim, Brendan. I have a sorrow to drown.'

'At the double, Your Grace.'

The Bish drowned more than one sorrow by my reckoning,

by all our reckonings. 'A thousand, minimum,' said Tonio. 'Enough for the Atlantic.'

Shut-eye wasn't on the cards for us until the Bish was done with his drowning. And he wasn't done with it for ages. He even ordered Brendan to fetch another bottle.

'Beg pardon, Your Grace, but hasn't Your Grace passed his limit?' This was Tonio, of course. 'Haven't you had your skinful?'

'No, Anthony, I haven't. Would that I had had!'

'I'm worried about Your Grace's good old beauty sleep, and about the state of his head in the morning. Alias on the morrow.'

'You are an excellent fellow, Anthony – sweet and kind and thoughtful. Do not worry on my behalf. There is no need for worry. Rest assured.'

(Do you remember, Doctor Lady, the meal – the lunch – we had together, when I was frugal with the tomatoes? I remember it, and I remember how you told me your husband drank himself to death, and I asked you had he let himself lose his brain, and you said that was one *diagnosis*. I learned *diagnosis* from you. Well, then, all I can say to you, Doctor Lady, having watched the Bish with his brain lost more times than I could count, is that your husband, Samuel, must have drank gallons and gallons and gallons to make himself die. And I do mean gallons, having watched the Bish.)

Anyway, even Tonio was amazed by what happened next. The Bish stood up and ordered Brendan and Jack to bring him his bishop's robes. 'At once, at once.'

'Your Grace, it's past midnight.'

'Time, time,' said the Bish. 'Who cares for time? Bring me my robes.'

So Jack and Brendan went to his office and brought him his complete bishop's ensemble to the reception area, where they both helped him into it. He was swaying, but he wasn't falling over.

'To the chapel.'

'Beg pardon, Your Grace, but isn't it a bit late for the chapel?'

'Late, Anthony? Late? I have a sermon to deliver from my pulpit, at this precise moment. Now.'

The Bish held out his goblet for Brendan to fill up, which he did, 'at the double', and then he, the Bish, swigged the clear liquid down without stopping for breath, and then, 'I am prepared,' he said, and off we went behind him.

You should have seen him prancing into his chapel. You should have heard him wobbling his funny stuff, and you should have watched him, like we had to, while he tried to get up the steps to his pulpit, which took him an *eternity*, what with all the drink inside him and the bottom of his cope catching on a big splinter. It really was hard for us not to laugh. Honestly.

'This is dopey,' said Jack.

Anyway, the Bish started on with his 'dearly beloved brethren' stuff, and then he said we should thank our lucky stars the ungrateful Grenville had been sent packing from our palace with a flea in his ear by our acolyte Anthony. Then he said it all over again. Then he said he was our shepherd and we should not want and Grenville was a black sheep and a disgrace to the flock, who had been sent packing from our palace of Wandle, by the mighty Thames, and we should thank our lucky stars that Anthony had seen him off the premises with his return fare to purgatory as well as a flea in his ear, which no one deserved more than Grenville, who was a black sheep and a disgrace to the flock, and we should all, each and every one of us, thank our lucky stars that he had been sent packing from our palace of Wandle with a flea in his ear by our acolyte Anthony because he was ungrateful, which is why he'd been sent packing from our palace of Wandle –

'By the mighty Thames, Your Grace,' Tonio chipped in.

'Exactly,' said the Bish, and then he said, 'Yes, indeed,' three or four times, and, 'Yea, verily,' and then he stared down at us, with his mouth wide open.

'Beg pardon, Your Grace, but may I humbly suggest Your Grace puts a good old sock in it?'

The Bish stared down a bit longer with his mouth still

195

wide open. 'Oh, Anthony,' he said, and burst out laughing. He actually had hysterics, right there in his pulpit.

'Come along, Your Grace,' said Tonio, when the Bish's fit was finished. 'That was a lovely sermon, that was, and we all enjoyed it. Didn't we, flock?'

'Yes,' we answered – Jack and Brendan and myself.

'Another satisfied congregation, Your Grace,' said Tonio, with a wink at me. The four of us undressed the Bish and put him to bed.

'I failed with Grenville, Anthony.'

'Never mind, Your Grace. There'll be others for sure and better-looking, too.'

'I feel pooped, Anthony. I feel thoroughly shagged,' said the Bish, and went straight off to sleep. Which meant that none of us had to do sausage duty, which was a real relief.

'It would have been murder doing it tonight, with him in that condition,' said Brendan. 'It would have been diabolical murder.'

It's at this point that Stephen allows himself another of his disgressions.

There must have been hundreds, he tells us – 'hundreds and hundreds'. And the funny thing is, he goes on to say, is that Tonio had warned him at the start of it, when he was teaching him the ropes, that after a time the hundreds would all *merge* into one. 'They'll become like the same person, Stephen. I often think to myself that there's just one single solitary punter in the world who's been multiplied and multiplied.'

Then Stephen remembers an 'exception to the good old rule': a man he went with in the days when his ensembles weren't the ensembles they are now. He remembers the man because nothing happened between them in the way of business – it was the man's attitude; it was what the man said.

The man – an American who was staying in a de luxe hotel with gold taps in the bathrooms – had the nerve to call Stephen, who had introduced himself as Robert, 'Bob'. Stephen had corrected him, in his customary manner, insisting that his name

196

was Robert. The American asked if he was kidding, and Stephen replied that he, Robert, wasn't.

Stephen remembers the American glaring at him: 'You're Bob for me. I'm paying for Bob, not Robert.' To which Stephen answered that he, Robert, was Robert or he was nothing. 'You're Bob,' it seems the American persisted. 'I'm buying what you're selling, and I'm buying Bob. It's me has the dough, smart ass.'

Stephen remembers that he stood his ground, and that when the American ordered Bob to undress, Stephen told him there wasn't a Bob to undress, only Robert.

Stephen remembers the American turning nasty and calling him a whore, and reminding him, the Bob he wasn't, that whores did what they were paid to do, and he was paying him, Bob, and he was telling him, Bob, to undress this instant, and –

'Ask Robert and he might,' Stephen remembers saying.

But the man could not and would not ask Robert, and so Stephen left him, without the promised twenty pounds in his pocket.

'I reckon it was money well lost. In the circumstances.'

The digression over, Stephen returns to the palace of Wandle and its presiding Bishop. He begins with a caution:

I must warn you now, Doctor Lady and Mr Gabriel, that you are about to receive an earful. You have been warned. The reason why is that I intend to tell you all you will ever wish to know about Nick, the horrible Nick, who I only met the once, but once was enough to last me my entire lifetime.

'There's bound to be trouble in the good old corral tonight, Stephen. The Bish has sent for Nick.'

Who was Nick? I wondered.

'Nick, my dear young friend, is a bruiser, a basher. He's ugly as sin, though I'd say myself he's uglier. Handsome he is not. He's got one slimy squiggle stuck on his head pretending to be his hair, and his teeth come in shades of brown. His teeth are shit. Am I putting you in the picture?'

Yes, he was, I said. But what I couldn't understand was why the Bish had sent for this Nick, and why he was coming here to the palace.

'You'll have to ask the Bish. On second thoughts, if you did ask the Bish he'd only answer, 'That would be telling,' and laugh, like he does when I ask him who Mrs sodding Danvers is. It's his mystery, Stephen. Nick's one of his quirks, his *whims*.'

What Nick and the Bish got up to together went far beyond sausage duty, Tonio said. The Bish could only stand the strain of Nick once in a blue moon . . . and the blue moon was in the sky once again, right above Wandsworth. 'It's like a mad turn he has, the Bish. "I must see Nick," he says. Which means that one of us – Brendan, this time – has to go to the filthy miserable hole in Finsbury Park where Nick dosses down and tell him that Alec, Bishop of Wandle, requests the pleasure of his company at the palace tomorrow evening. Nick never says no to the invitation.'

'I'm buzzing off,' said Jack as he walked into the refectory, which was where we were. 'I'm not staying in the palace with that dopey bastard.'

'Shall we buzz off, too?' This was me, to Tonio.

'We can't. We'll be needed to clean up, and clear up, afterwards.'

'Afterwards?'

'Yes, Stephen, afterwards. After Nick has slung his hook, alias vanished, for another year and a day. He always leaves a fine mess behind him.'

Jack snorted at Tonio's remark, and then Tonio suggested that we drop the nasty subject, and simply wait and see what good old fate had in store for us. 'We'll know the worst soon enough.'

The Bish was in an excitable state when the bell rang at ten past nine. 'It's him, it's him, Anthony. Nicholas has arrived.'

'What a surprise, Your Grace, and there was I expecting Mother Teresa.'

'Let him in, Anthony. Let him in.'

'Beg pardon, Your Grace, but might I suggest that Your Grace calms down a trifle? Your Grace's hands are in a tizzy and you're sweating something chronic.'

'Yes, yes, yes. Let him in, will you.'

'At the double, Your Grace,' said Tonio, taking off Brendan's manner of speaking. 'At the double.'

'Anthony is teasing me, I fear, Stephen. I do believe he is a little jealous of my – my relationship with Nicholas.'

'Is he, Your Grace?'

'I think so.'

The Bish dabbed his sweaty face with one of his funny handkerchiefs. It had lace round the edges, like they all had.

I heard a dog barking.

'Aha, Nicholas has brought Rotten to see me. Isn't that a *droll* name? Rotten!'

'Is he, Your Grace?'

'Is he what, Stephen?'

'The dog. Rotten.'

'When he's in a rotten mood, yes, he is.' And the Bish laughed his funny laugh, but a bit nervily.

The dog came running into the reception area, and when he saw me he stopped. He stopped dead in his tracks. He kept his eyes on me and growled, and went on growling.

'There's a nigger in the building,' said a voice I guessed was Nick's. 'I've trained that animal to frighten darkies. He only growls like that if there's a nigger around.'

In that moment, even before I'd seen him, I decided Nick, or Nicholas, was horrible.

'Just as I suspected.' This was Nick, once he was in the reception area. 'You've got a nig-nog working for you now, have you?'

'Stephen's a nice boy, a dear boy, Nicholas.'

'Stephen, is it? Picking them up in the jungle now, are you?'

'Stephen's from Halifax, Nicholas.'

'The fuck he is.'

'It's true,' I said. 'I am.'

'Was I talking to you, darkie? No, I wasn't. Take my advice and keep your thick-lipped trap shut.'

And all the while the dog, Rotten, was inches from my feet, and growling.

'You mustn't intimidate my boys, Nicholas.'

'Mustn't I? Who says? I'll intimidate who I fucking please. This is my country and I'm my own master in it.'

(I'm sorry about the language – the f-f-f-ing – but you can't say I didn't warn you, Doctor Lady and Mr Gabriel.)

'What with the dago wop here' – this was Nick, of course, pointing at Tonio – 'and the nigger here, and the freckled Paddy who brought your message over to Finsbury Park, you're becoming quite an international ponce, aren't you? You're spreading your global wings. What's wrong with English boys, then? Not sweet and juicy enough for you?'

'Always, always. There's always Jack, Nicholas. Jack's very special. And Ray and Wally have been back lately, splendid fellows, following their little spot of trouble.'

The Bish didn't mention the Honourable, or otherwise, Grenville.

Nick was as ugly as Tonio promised he would be. I couldn't see the squiggle pretending to be his hair because he had a leather cap on his head covering it. He wore a black leather waistcoat, which meant he was showing most of his hairy chest, and black leather trousers and black boots up to his knees. He had a scarf tied round his neck. It was of the Union Jack, the scarf. The national flag.

They say that people's pets look like their owners, and owners come to resemble their pets. Well, ugly as Rotten was, and he was ugly, he wasn't as ugly as Nick. Rotten's teeth were white at least, whereas Nick's were brown, with great gaps between them. Rotten, Nick said, was the pride of Staffordshire, the home of his breed. Staffordshire was welcome to the horrible *squatty* thing, I thought. *Squatty* was Tonio's word for him.

'A person could be dying of thirst in your fucking palace. Aren't you going to offer me some refreshment?'

'Forgive me, Nicholas. What a very *remiss* host I'm being.

200

Fetch Nicholas a can of his favourite beer, Anthony. Will you be requiring a glass?'

'You know fucking well I won't be requiring a glass. It's only old nancies like you drink beer out of glasses. Real men drink it straight from the can.'

'Of course they do, Nicholas. How forgetful of me.'

While Tonio was gone fetching the beer, the Bish smiled at Nick and said, 'It's lovely to see you, Nicholas. You're a sight for sore eyes.'

'You'll be sore in more places than your eyes by the time I've finished with you. A thorough duffing-up will cost you, you know.'

'I know perfectly well, Nicholas. I've set aside a generous sum for you.'

'Out of your immoral earnings, is it? Your cock and arsehole money?'

'There's no cause to be vulgar, Nicholas.'

'What you call vulgar, you great fat nancy of a ponce, I call the plain truth. Unvarnished.'

'That's it, Nicholas. Unvarnished.'

'As long as you pay me what's due to me, I don't give a toss where the money comes from.'

'I'll pay you, Nicholas.'

'I haven't come all the way here from Finsbury Park out of love, you know,' said Nick, undoing the black leather belt with a silver buckle on it which I forgot to say just now he was wearing too. Nick was.

'No, Nicholas, of course you haven't. Never out of love. Never, never.'

Tonio returned, and handed the horrible Nick a can of beer. Which he opened, and drank from, loudly.

'A couple more of these and I'll be ready for action.'

And still I couldn't move, Doctor Lady and Mr Gabriel, because of the dog, that Rotten, watching me and growling.

'Bring Nicholas another two, would you please, Anthony.'

'Anthony will bring Nicholas another six, at least, Anthony will. You and me have some private matters to sort out,

201

Bishop Nancy, and I'll need to refresh myself while we're doing it – minus the dago wop and the nigger.'

When Tonio came back, he had eight cans with him, which he slammed down on the table.

'Shall we retire to our quarters, Your Grace?'

'Retire! Quarters! Your Grace!' This was Nick, spitting out every single word. 'Listen to him!'

'The dear boy is being respectful, Nicholas.'

'The fuck the dear boy is. What's he respect you for? For teaching him to talk like a poncey nance, the same as you?'

'Of course not, Nicholas. Yes, Anthony, you and Stephen may retire.'

'Beg pardon, Your Grace, but Stephen can't, as of yet. On account of the dog won't let him.'

'Leave, Rotten,' said Nick. 'Leave the frightened nig-nog.'

And with that the dog stopped growling and stood up and walked across to his master, the horrible Nick, and sat down next to him, nice and friendly.

'Thank you, dear boys,' said the Bish. For once, we didn't kiss his hand and walk out backwards. It didn't seem the right thing to do, with Nick being there. We just left.

You should have heard the noise, the noises, we heard, the two of us, Tonio and me, as we sat crouched down in the refectory with our ears against the wall. You should have heard the Bish's 'Ooohs' and 'Aaahs'. You should have heard the Bish's screams, Doctor Lady and Mr Gabriel. Those, in particular.

'He's killing him, Tonio.'

'No, he's not. The Bish is loving it.'

It didn't sound as if he was loving it. It sounded as if he was in agony, in utter agony.

'That's what he's loving. The agony and the good old ecstasy, as somebody wrote in a book somewhere. Listen hard and take heed,' Tonio whispered, taking off my manner of speaking just as I'd taken off Mr Portman's. We both of us laughed.

Well, we did listen hard and we must have taken heed, because I remember – and Tonio would remember, if he was alive – that the Bish had to pretend to be a dog. That's what Nick ordered him to pretend to be. He made him undress, Nick did, and then he ordered him to get on all fours.

'Bark!' Nick shouted.

Rotten barked, and the Bish went, 'Woof, woof! Woof, woof!'

'That wouldn't scare the shit out of a babe in arms. You're a mutt, Mutt, so fucking bark like one.'

'Woof, woof! Woof, woof!'

'If you can't bark, you can howl instead.' Nick thrashed the Bish on the backside, we supposed, or on what Tonio called his 'wrinkled old peach', and the Bish howled as a result.

'Stay firm on your legs, Mutt. I want you to wag your tail.'

'I don't have a tail.'

'Wag what you've got, then.'

Whatever the Bish wagged, it didn't satisfy Nick. He thrashed the Bish some more, till the Bish screamed.

'Now do as Rotten does, when I say the magic word. Beg.'

We couldn't tell how Rotten begged, but Tonio thought he most likely had his front paws in the air.

'Beg, Mutt.'

The Bish's begging had the horrible Nick cackling in a horrible way.

'Now watch Rotten die for England, Mutt, and copy him. Lie down and die for England, Rotten.'

Tonio explained that when you said 'Lie down and die for England' to a clever dog, it rolled over on its back as if it was dying.

Rotten must have died for England, and the Bish too, because the next thing we heard was Nick shouting at the Bish that he was no match for Rotten, and that all his lousy fucking performance deserved was a boot in the guts.

Nick started kicking the Bish, and went on kicking him, and after that there was *pandemonium*, there was 'good old mayhem', what with Nick grunting and the Bish screaming and groaning, and Rotten barking – and I wondered at the horrible, horrible sound of it, and if the Bish really would die. Then I covered up my ears, I remember, and Tonio suddenly held me tight to him, like my mum used to hold me, long ago.

'It's over, Stephen,' Tonio said. (It wasn't Stephen. It was my mum's name for me he used, which no one else but Tonio's been allowed to.) 'It's over, Stephen. It's definitely over.'

Tonio still held me while we listened. That silence was really creepy, Doctor Lady and Mr Gabriel. You could hear nothing in it.

Someone began to whistle, and we guessed it had to be him, the horrible Nick. Then we heard the dog scampering down the stairs, and the tread of Nick's boots going after him. We didn't move, though. We waited until we heard the main door slam shut below until we moved at all.

'This could be the nastiest part – the clearing-up and the cleaning-up. It could be nastier than usual, Stephen. I hope your stomach's feeling strong.'

Which it wasn't – I'm sure I don't have to tell you.

'Let's stir ourselves,' Tonio said. 'Let's examine the wreckage.'

The Bish was on the floor of the reception area, curled up in a ball, stark naked. He was moaning to himself. He was whimpering.

I wanted to be sick at the sight of the blood on him. Tonio must have wanted to as well because he said, 'There's enough mess around here without us two adding to it.'

The Bish had a bloody back, including his bottom. We saw, when we shifted him a little, that he had a bloody mouth. There were bruises on his belly and on his face.

'It's your acolyte.'

'Oh, Anthony. Oh, Anthony.'

'Your Grace looks terrible.'

'Has he gone, Anthony?'

'He has, Your Grace.'

'He's not lurking anywhere? To do me more mischief?'

'No, no. He's vanished. He's *vamoosed*.'

'Who's that with you? It's not him?'

'That's Stephen, Your Grace. He's going to help me help you. Who's been a very silly Bishop?'

'I have, Anthony. I have.'

It was our luck, Tonio's and mine, that the bell rang soon after. We froze, but then we realised that whoever was outside had to be one of us because he was ringing the bell in our secret way.

It was Brendan I opened the main door to. 'I watched them leaving,' he said. 'Nick and the dog. I've been waiting for an hour or more to see them leaving. They've crossed the bridge. We're safe.'

With Brendan's two extra hands, we managed to lift the Bish up off the floor once Tonio had washed the worst of the Bish's wounds. We carried the Bish to his bed, and flopped him on it.

'Dear, dear boys,' he said.

'It's iodine for Your Grace. That is Dr Innocent's prescription. It's iodine for Your Grace's wounds.'

'Oh, no, Anthony.'

'Oh, yes, Your Grace. Iodine's only what Your Grace deserves for being such a silly Bishop.'

'It stings, Anthony. It smarts.'

We held him down, the Bish, Brendan and me, while Tonio dabbed his bruises with drops of iodine on cotton wool. The Bish winced and gasped and even screamed again, and Tonio said it was his own silly fault, and not to be a coward.

'Never again, Anthony.'

'Never again what, Your Grace?'

'That dreadful Nicholas. That beast. I shan't invite him to the palace again.'

'Beg pardon, Your Grace, and with respect, but Your Grace said that the last time Your Grace was beaten to a good pulp. And the time before that, too. And the time before that.'

'I am serious, Anthony.'

'Ditto myself, Your Grace. I'll believe your "never again" when it happens. No, when it *doesn't*.'

I'll spare you the dirty details about what we had to clear

up that night in the reception area. There was blood, of course, but there was other muck besides. The horrible Nick had relieved himself of his beer on the carpet and on the walls. That's putting it politely for you. And Rotten had also relieved himself – in a heap, on one of the Bish's prize Persian rugs. Which Tonio shoved straight into a plastic bag – the whole rug, I mean – to be thrown away. 'We'll tell him Nick thieved it, along with the candlesticks and the clock.'

Anyway, the clever Mr Gabriel, who has read the papers, will know and remember that the Bishop of Wandle, so-called, led what the papers said was 'a double life'. He played it close, he honestly did. He was plain Alec Wandle when he spoke on the radio or on the television about the problems of youth, which was his favourite topic of conversation. 'He's an expert on the good old problems of youth,' said Tonio while we watched him on the television in the Bish's office. 'It's the youth of this great country of ours who concern me most,' we heard the Bish say, in a very unBishy voice – very, very ordinary it was, his voice, with not a bit of wobbling in it. You couldn't picture him in his robes, in his regalia, doing his daft '*Dominus vobiscum*' stuff, when you saw him there, dead ordinary, talking to another fat man, who was done up like a real vicar. Which he was, apparently – a real vicar.

This time I'm telling you about, when the Bish was in the programme on the television, *Questions of Faith*, was the evening after he'd had his duffing-up by Nick. I helped Tonio all through the afternoon to bring the Bish back to the land of the living. He didn't look too bad when Tonio had finished with him, except there was this bruise on his face had gone a funny purple colour.

'Emergency measures, Anthony. Emergency measures.'

'Are you saying, Your Grace, that you wish me to apply a spot of make-up?'

'Yes, Anthony, I am. Precisely.'

Tonio rubbed some cream on to the bruise from a tube the Bish kept in his private medicine cabinet. While Tonio was rubbing, the Bish began to giggle to himself.

'Beg pardon, Your Grace, but would Your Grace like to share the joke with us?'

'I was only thinking, Anthony, that the church's one foundation is Max Factor.'

The Bish laughed his funny laugh as loud as he could, which wasn't as loud as usual because his wounds were still hurting him.

'Is that the joke, Your Grace?'

'It is, Anthony.'

'Very droll, Your Grace,' said Tonio, without a smile. 'It's really very droll. Isn't it, Stephen?'

'Yes, Your Grace,' I answered, though I couldn't see the joke myself. I still can't see it. I mean, is Max Factor like Horatio, and Heathcliff, and Mrs Danvers? I bet you two know who he is.

Anyway, when we watched him later on Tonio said that they must have applied more make-up and powder to the Bish's bruise in the studio. 'He told me he was going to tell them that he walked into a door when his mind was on higher things. Some door, I don't think. Some higher things!'

The Bish and the real vicar were discussing the problem of sex and the young. 'He's playing it close, the Bish.' This was Tonio. 'Are you listening hard to Alec Wandle, Stephen, and taking heed?'

I caught the Bish's drift, and so did Tonio, but I can't vouch for Jack, who was half-asleep. The Bish was saying to the other fat man that he thought men who loved men and women who loved women – 'in a purely physical sense' – were sinners, and as such should be *condemned*. He was quietly spoken for him, as I've said, but the other fat man, the proper vicar, lost his temper and appealed to what he called Mr Wandle's 'spirit of forgiveness'. 'I cannot forgive what is wicked,' said the Bish, alias Mr Alec Wandle. 'I cannot and will not tolerate it.' Then he mentioned Sodom and I lost him. I wasn't on his wavelength. It was Sodom this and Sodom that till in the end I had to ask Tonio if he knew what Sodom was.

'It's a place, Stephen, in the Bible, where people got up to wicked things. The Bish would have felt at home there, despite all that goody-goody flannel he's spewing right now.'

'He can be not dopey when he wants to be,' said Jack, who woke up for a minute and saw the Bish talking ordinary and acting normal. 'It only goes to prove.'

What it only goes to prove I can't divulge, Doctor Lady and Mr Gabriel, because Jack closed his eyes after his 'It only goes to prove' and was very soon snoring. He was out for the count for ages. Until the Bish returned to the palace, actually.

The Bish was well and truly down the road to losing his brain. He was trying to open the doors with all the wrong keys, and calling out to Mrs Danvers for assistance, and then laughing his funny laugh afterwards. He finally made it into the cleared-up reception area, eventually.

'Good evening, boys. I must apologise for being *tardy*. They opened the hospitality cupboard at the television studios and offered the Reverend Parker and myself a drink or two.'

'Or more, Your Grace.'

'Naughty Anthony, to tease your Bishop.'

'Beg pardon, Your Grace, but has Your Grace eaten?'

'A modicum, Anthony.'

'Would your Grace care for a nice snack of cold chicken with some green salad and mayonnaise?'

'I should, Anthony. I can imagine nothing more scrumptious.'

The Bish ate his meal in the office, and washed it down with white communion wine. He switched to the clear liquid once he'd had his fill.

'What did you dear boys make of me on the television this evening?'

'I'd say you were a filthy hypocrite, Your Grace, if I didn't know you better.'

'Needs must, Anthony. You have your camouflage and I must have mine.'

The Bish recruited all three of us – Tonio, Jack and me – to do sausage duty. 'In rota, of course, dear boys. Impossible otherwise. Jack will open the batting.'

Which Jack did, and while he was doing it, Tonio asked the Bish if the people in Sodom were acquainted with sausage duty. Was it one of their good old sins?

The Bish laughed so long and so loud that Jack had to stop for a while, with his hand in the air.

'I rather think the *Sod-o-mites* had a different name for it, Anthony. The sausage as we know it – the ever-popular banger – had not been invented then. Definitely not. The sausage as we know it dates from the Middle Ages. From the fifteenth century, to be absolutely accurate.'

'A person can learn something new and interesting from Your Grace every day of his life if he wants,' said Tonio. 'Your Grace has more facts at his fingertips than a – well, than a garden has flowers, in my honest opinion.'

Tonio winked at me, but I couldn't wink back, because the Bish was looking straight at me, and smiling.

'Come into my study, dearest,' said my father. 'I have something important to tell you.'

'Daddy, what is it?'

He closed the door behind us.

'Make yourself comfortable, because that's what I intend to be.'

I sat in my usual chair, facing him across his desk.

'You will start bleeding this year, and you must not be worried. It is best that you know of it in advance. It is nothing to be scared of.'

'Yes, Daddy.'

'Why "yes", dearest? Has your mother already alerted you? Spoken with you, woman to woman?'

'No, Daddy.'

'And your teachers? And the nuns? Have they said anything?'

No, they hadn't. No one had mentioned bleeding.

'Does your "yes" indicate faith in your father's advice?'

Of course it did. 'Yes, it does.'

'Let him advise you then. You will bleed, my dearest, as all women have bled before you. And you will continue to bleed, at a certain time in every month until you are well into middle age. You will menstruate, Esther.'

I repeated the strange new word.

He explained, in detail, where I would bleed from. He used other strange words – 'menses', 'uterus' – and told me their meanings. I was not yet twelve.

'This lesson is one of my birthday presents to you, dearest. You may not appreciate it for a few months, but there it is, it's yours.'

I appreciated it exactly five months later, when the very first trickle appeared.

My mother was alarmed by my calmness. 'You are not frightened, Esther?'

'No, Mummy. Should I be?'

'Yes, you should. I was. I was laid low. I thought the blood would never stop. I thought I was dying.'

'It's only nature, Mummy,' I remarked, with almost genuine confidence. Although I wasn't scared, I was in acute discomfort, and embarrassed.

'Only nature! You are not being a natural girl.'

I associate Tata's study now with the smell of those mild Havanas he was forbidden to smoke elsewhere in our large apartment. Their aroma suggests learning to me, the knowledge contained in the thousands of books that lined its walls. It was Tata's Hume I read, and Tata's Plato, in the heady unfemale days and nights of my self-educating adolescence. And it was there, in his cigar-scented library, that I discovered William Osler's *Aequanimitas*, a collection of the great doctor's addresses to medical students, nurses and practitioners that my father had bought off a stall for a shilling. In one of his addresses, entitled 'Internal Medicine as a Vocation', Osler informed the students at the New York Academy in 1897 that syphilis was the only disease they were required to study thoroughly. 'Know syphilis in all its manifestations and relations, and all other things will be added unto you.' He would be saying much the same today, in less quaint language, about the awful acronym.

210

When, in 1978, we decided to give our clinic at St Lucy's a name to match its new, inviting appearance, it was I who proposed Osler to replace the ubiquitous Special. And at the opening of the Osler Wing, I thought back to the lesson that was my father's premature birthday present to me, and thanked him for it, under my breath, and for all the knowledge, if not wisdom, that has accrued from it since.

The final side of Stephen's 'precious gift' is the shortest. It begins with Jack and Stephen at the breakfast table:

'It's dopey having a cock this big,' Jack said this morning, the same as he says most mornings, when he'd come out from having a shower. Usually, that's all he says – about his cock, I mean – being a man of few words, including 'dopey'. But today was different. Today he 'waxed philosophical', as Tonio said about him once when he allowed himself the luxury of speaking what was in his brain for longer than a minute. 'Wonder of wonders, Jack, you just waxed philosophical.'

'Did I, Ant?'

'You certainly did.'

Anyway, this morning he spoke the longest in one go I've ever heard him. I paid no attention when he made his typical Jack Saul remark, and carried on eating my toast, expecting him to gulp his tea down, which is his habit. But he actually spoke instead.

'Still, I mustn't grumble, Stephen.'

'Why's that?'

'Because I mustn't. I'd be worse off if I didn't have it. That's what I'm thinking.'

'I'm not,' I said to him, 'on your wavelength.'

'If I'd been born with a smaller one, like I see on everyone else, I'd never be in such demand as I am. And always have been. Nobody'd bother with me if I'd been born different.'

'Yes, they would, Jack.'

'No. No, they wouldn't. It was all the talk at my school, this dopey object was. It made me sort of famous. It made me sort of unique, really.'

'Did it?'

'Yes. Yes, it did. And still does.'

'Aren't you going to drink your tea?'

'When I'm through thinking, Stephen. I'll have it then. You on my wavelength yet?'

'Nearly,' I answered him. 'Almost.'

That's when it was that Jack began to talk a stream. He said the reason why he mustn't grumble is because of the bloke he met yesterday evening, who told him straight off that 'it' was wonderful, and Jack was offering me no prizes for guessing which 'it' the man was referring to. Then the bloke told him 'it' was tremendous, and Jack didn't know why but the bloke really started to annoy him. He got on his tits. He pissed Jack off. Jack said the reason why he didn't know why this bloke was annoying him was because the bloke was only saying to him what all the others had been saying to him since he went on the game, on the circuit, and that was coming up for sixteen years. Jack said he doesn't listen to them as a rule, because what they say is so dopey to him it goes in one ear and out the other, but yesterday evening he caught himself listening to the bloke saying he could worship 'it', and Jack was still offering no prizes for guessing which 'it' he could worship. Jack said he didn't know quite why, but he suddenly thought he was just a cock for this bloke, and it might have been anybody attached to the cock as far as the bloke was concerned. Jack Saul didn't exist for him, just Jack Saul's dopey cock. It was then that Jack got very annoyed. It came into his mind, Jack said, that he could count the punters who've been interested in him, Jack Saul, on the fingers of both hands, and he wasn't including the thumbs. No one ever says Jack has beautiful eyes or lovely blond hair. It's like they all go blind as soon as they look at his dopey cock – blind to the rest of him, was what he was saying. If he was as ugly as that dirty ugly bastard Nick who used to duff up His Grace, they wouldn't notice. If he was covered with great

212

big boils and blisters on every part of his body except there, they wouldn't see them. So, he didn't know why, Jack let this bloke have a piece of his mind yesterday evening. He gave the bloke the benefit of his thoughts. He said that he was a someone, and not just a wonderful, tremendous cock; that he was a person, and not just an attachment.

'Tell, me, Stephen, why did I say that to him, and not to the others?'

I hadn't an answer for him. I asked what happened next.

'Nothing. That's what happened. Nothing. I came home.'

'Your tea must be cold by now.'

It was. As I was making us a fresh pot, Jack explained why he mustn't grumble. 'It's not going to shrivel, is it, Stephen? If they're only interested in Jack Saul's dopey cock and not the Jack Saul it belongs to, I'm set up for life, aren't I? It won't matter when I grow old, will it, because my cock will still be wonderful and tremendous, like it is now. It'll go on being my breadwinner, and so I mustn't grumble. Everything turns out right in the end really. Me thinking about how that bloke got on my tits has made me realise I mustn't grumble. So I won't complain when the next bloke tells me it's wonderful and tremendous. I've let what I feel out of my system and I'm better already. Yes, Stephen, I mustn't grumble.'

And he hasn't. He hasn't said another word, apart from 'See you later' when he went out.

Anyway, Doctor Lady, Mr Gabriel, I am sitting here in my choicest ensemble – dark-blue cashmere wool sweater, pale-grey cords, brown I-talian leather lace-ups, darker-brown silk socks – waiting to *divulge* the rest of my story. I hope you're listening. It would be very rude of you if you aren't, after the trouble I've gone to giving you this precious gift.

When the Honourable Grenville was sent packing from the palace with Tonio's flea in his ear, we thought we were shot of him. That's what we reckoned. We were wrong. When he came back, it was from the grave. He caused even more harm as a ghost than he did alive, it was our opinion. He 'wreaked his revenge from beyond', as the Bish said at the time. He had the last laugh on the lot of us.

(Your clever sweetheart, your *darling* Mr Gabriel, Doctor Lady, most likely remembers the Bishop of Wandle scandal. He can go to his kitchen and cook you a meal – his spicy prawns, and so on, and so forth – while I run it through just for you. Is that *agreeable*?)

Well, it seems that Grenville – who wasn't a Honourable, actually; his dad made his fortune in cardboard boxes – tried to sell the papers (the newspapers, I mean) the low-down on the Bish and the palace in Wandsworth. None of the people at the papers' offices believed him. They thought he was spinning them a yarn just to get the money to buy drugs. Which he was too, of course, but it wasn't such a yarn he was spinning them. Some of it was the truth. As he saw it, but still the truth. The people at the papers told him his yarn was far-fetched. They told him it was his cocaine or whatever speaking. They told him to shove off.

Which Grenville did, and wrote it down, his so-called yarn, in a school exercise book. There it all was, in his words: how he'd been picked up late at night by the Bishop of Wandle and his assistant, Anthony, at Euston Station; how he'd been driven in a taxi to a building in Wandsworth with the name J.T. Montagu on the outside; how he'd stayed in the Bishop's palace, as the Bishop described it. There it all was, in Grenville's words: the dormitory and the refectory, the reception area, the chapel with pulpit and confessional and the Bish's bedroom. There it all was about the games of Naked Knowledge and the sausage duty, and there we were, too: the young black – yes, *black* – from Yorkshire; the blond boy who found everything 'dopey', and Tonio, alias Anthony, but with the Innocent bit missing from his name, because Grenville wasn't aware he was Anthony Innocent.

Grenville died – not in a hospital like Tonio, but on a doorstep in Brixton, from a drugs overdose. It was an accident rather than a suicide, the papers said. Now this is the really funny bit, Doctor Lady. On his body – in his jacket, actually – was an envelope with his mum's and his dad's address on it, and the school exercise book also. Grenville's father, Mr Smith – that was a surprise, Grenville being a plain, ordinary Smith; anyhow, Grenville's father, Mr Smith, identified his son and was given the book. Which he then went ahead, would you believe, and sold to one of those papers that had told him it was a far-fetched yarn. Mr Smith sold it for pots of money as an *exclusive*, and then reporters kept watch on the palace and tried to talk to the Bish whenever he came out, and us boys, and Tonio smelled a rat, he said to me. Anyway, first it was the papers and then it was the police, and then – on a Wednesday evening – the palace was raided. They caught the Bish in his full regalia, along with Brendan and Wally and two new recruits from King's Cross Station, Peter and Christopher, who don't mind if they're called 'Pete' and 'Chris'.

You're probably wondering where we were – Tonio, Jack and myself. We were in a hotel, actually – not the Ritz, the Savoy or the good old Dorchester, Doctor Lady. No, we were in that crummy hotel where Mr White took me, and we were lying low and waiting for the storm to break, as Tonio promised it would. This was the day before it did – the storm, broke. Tonio had warned the Bish that he'd smelled a rat – 'Six of them, Your Grace, and there's three of them out in the street this minute' – and that he thought there would be a storm breaking. But the Bish had answered, 'It will blow over, Anthony. Rest assured. I have powerful contacts. There will be no storm.'

'Let's *skedaddle*,' said Tonio. 'He refuses to budge. Let's leave him to it.' Which we did, in the middle of the night, with everything the three of us needed shoved into a single big suitcase, and even then – it was a quarter to four and pitch-black dark – there was a reporter on the prowl. 'Going somewhere, boys?' he asked us. 'To Her Majesty's good old shithouse, actually, my man,' Tonio replied to him, putting on a funny posh voice. 'We only plop where the china's finer.'

Tonio had the idea we might be being followed, though we couldn't hear anybody walking behind us. 'I don't trust those scum. They're as bad as Jennifers, in my opinion.' We each took turns carrying the suitcase, and it wasn't until we reached Fulham that the all-night bus arrived. There was no one else on it, so Tonio relaxed and lit a cigarette and said he felt safe again.

The storm did break, of course, and the papers went to town, as they say, with the Bish. Grenville's mum and dad, Mr and Mrs Smith, were in a photograph together standing in front of their super de luxe mansion in Surrey, with its indoor swimming pool, hand in hand, and above the photograph it said 'Our Sorrow'. We had some laughs at that – 'Our Sorrow'. Anyway, they'd had such hopes for Grenville – they revealed in their exclusive interview – and today those hopes were dashed, but it was some small consolation to them in their grief, they spewed, that Grenville had written down his painful story, which other unhappy youngsters out there could learn from. 'If one poor lad is saved from the evil clutches of the likes of Alec Wandle, then my beloved Grenville would not have died in vain.' Spew, spew. That was Mr David Smith, who was now twenty thousand pounds the richer, thanks to his beloved son, Grenville, who did not die in vain.

'Evil' – that was the word, the 'dopey word', in Jack's opinion, they used in the papers after the Bish was found guilty at the end of his trial. 'This evil monster', 'this evil impostor', 'the evil Bishop-who-never-was', 'the evil beast who preyed on youth' – and there he was, the Bish, in his regalia, in his complete ensemble, holding up his pastoral staff and smiling at the camera. Wally's face was in the papers, too, as the victim who had 'bravely bore witness against the' – you've guessed it – 'evil bishop'. It was Wally who gave the jury the details about sausage duty and Naked Knowledge.

'The Bish's powerful contacts weren't much help to him,' Tonio said. 'They kept very quiet.'

The Bish was sent to prison for five years twelve years ago, which means that he's back in the land of the living if he hasn't gone and died of drink. Where he is and what he's doing I don't know and there's been no actual news on the circuit for ages and ages.

Except for one funny, typical Bish thing I heard only the

other day. I bumped into Peter, the Bish's very last recruit from King's Cross Station, and we shook hands and agreed it was water under the bridge, and he told me he'd spent some time in a special home for young offenders but they'd let him out and business was hunky-dory 'for the nonce'. That 'for the nonce' got us going on the Bish, and it was in the Needle and Compass that Peter said that, when the police arrested the Bish, the Bish burst out laughing. And then, Peter said, the Bish pulled himself right up to his full height and shouted, 'I am Bishop of Wandle still!' and then he laughed, did the Bish, for so long and so loudly that the Jennifers could only stand around and wait for him to stop. He had hysterics.

The last of Stephen's long silences follows. Then in an altered, quieter voice, he resumes:

It's been a bit like he's been with me, my friend Tonio – with his 'good old' and his 'alias' coming out of my mouth for him, I mean. It's been almost as if he's been by my shoulder reminding me what to say to you, Doctor Lady – and you as well, Mr Gabriel – who never had the pleasure of his company.

With the Bish locked up, we had to fend for ourselves. We went freelance. That was Tonio's word – 'freelance'. It was a client of Tonio's who found this flat where Jack lives now, and where I store all my ensembles and stay when it suits me. Tonio and me were happy here, true pals together, and sometimes we'd be lovey-dovey, but he wasn't serious. Which I might have been, I have to say.

'Tonio' was his mother's name for him, like 'Sugar Cane' is my mum's for me. Mrs Innocent died from cancer when she was quite young, though not as young as Tonio was – when he died. Mr Innocent was of I-talian origin originally, Tonio said, but he couldn't claim to be a *bona fide* I-talian, 'alias the genuine article'. The Innocents had come over to Britain a hundred years ago, when they were Daily Something – those two names defeat me, Doctor Lady, they honestly do, but you know how to say them, in that funny voice of yours.

'He became a tyrant, my father, when my mum died.' This was Tonio. 'He became a bloody pig-headed bully. He made life hell for me and my sister. She's a martyr the way she puts up and copes with him.'

I went to his funeral, Tonio's, out of respect, in that blue suit you considered flash, Doctor Lady, and thought I was dressed in for a wedding. No, I've been to one wedding too many, thank you very much. Anyhow, I went to Tonio's funeral, to the church, and there was Mr Innocent, sobbing and sobbing and there she was, Tonio's sister, Gina, and her eyes were dry, and her face looked like it had froze.

You should have seen him crying, Tonio's father. You should have seen his tears, and how they wouldn't stop falling. And you should have heard what I heard her say to him after, by the grave, his daughter.

She said, 'You disgust me. Your crying is disgusting. You didn't tell me he was dying, because you were ashamed of his illness. You didn't tell me he was dying in hospital, alone. You didn't tell me. You didn't let me say goodbye to my own brother.'

And then she spat on him, and walked away, and I'm sure she walked away for ever.

Tonio *stumbled*, Doctor Lady. 'Stumbled' was Tonio's word for falling in love. The man Tonio stumbled for is Dutch. Was Dutch, actually. I met him just the once, when Tonio and him were head over heels, and Tonio wasn't to know that Jan was ill, for the simple reason that Jan didn't even know himself, not then.

Thank God, if there is such a person, I heard from Graham on the circuit that Tonio was back in London from abroad. 'Tony Innocent's been sighted,' he said. 'He's dying from the dreaded,' he said, 'and he's in hospital. Nobody knows which.'

Which I found out, Doctor Lady. The hospital. Yours.

Thank God, if there is a God, I reached him in time. There isn't much to thank God for, if there is such a person, but

I do thank God. I sat by Tonio, and touched him, and held his hand, and saw my friend, my one true friend, go out of this world.

You heard Tonio call me Sugar Cane, didn't you, Doctor Lady? Of course you did. I was hoping you hadn't, but then you said it to me and I told you, in no uncertain terms, that I couldn't allow it. 'I can't allow that,' I remember I said. 'I'm Stephen to you and nothing else. Understand?'

You understood.

Well then, since I shan't be seeing you and your sweetheart, your darling Mr Gabriel, again, it doesn't matter much any more. You won't be getting the chance to call me Sugar Cane anyway. Which is why it doesn't matter much any more that you know now that my mum first, and then Tonio, called me – Stephen Eccles – by my secret, alias *clandestine*, name of Sugar Cane.

It was when my mum came back to Halifax, to her new nice home, from her short honeymoon with him, that she made it up for me. I was in my room, and she came in, and she must have seen how sick and miserable I was in myself, and she came over to the bed and she held me in her arms, and when I cried into her blouse she told me there was no love, no real lasting love, between herself and Stanley, and that I had to believe her when she said that there were only two men in her life and only ever would be. 'Just your daddy and you, my little Sugar Cane.'

'Your who, Mum?'

'Sugar Cane. I've just this minute made it up for you. You are my very own sweet little stick of sugar cane.'

Well, anyway, she never called me Sugar Cane again. She most likely forgot that she made it up for me that night. She most likely forgot because she didn't mean what she said. She most likely forgot, in my opinion, because the words you say and don't really mean are the words that leave you easiest, the words you don't remember.

And as for words, Doctor Lady and Mr Gabriel, I've had enough of them. I've had my say. There's masses more I could tell you, masses and masses, but enough's enough. I've had my say.

After a short pause, though, Stephen continues:

Are you wondering, you two, how Tonio became the Bish's acolyte? Let me put you out of your misery. It's a simple story. Tonio was standing on Wandsworth Bridge, staring down at the mighty Thames, and wondering to himself should he go home to his father, who would bash the good old living daylights out of him for running away, or should he brave it out, like the man his father said he wasn't, when all of a sudden the Bishop of Wandle was effecting an introduction, and asking Tonio if he would care to visit his palace, which was a mere stone's throw from where they were. And Anthony Innocent said, 'Why not?' and went with the Bish, and stayed.

So there you are. Well, Doctor Lady, it was an honour making your acquaintance and allowing you to admire my ensembles. And Mr Gabriel, too. You are a funny couple, in my opinion.

For what it's worth, and if you want it.

Anyway, please accept this precious gift from me.

Goodbye.

I said goodbye and I mean it.

I never could have said any of this to your faces.

I have before me the obituary of Alec Morrison, who died six months ago, on the 15th of March, 1986:

Alec Edward Morrison, whose death was announced on Monday, was at the centre of one of the most notorious scandals of recent years. Under his bizarre sobriquet, the Bishop of Wandle, he has already entered popular mythology.

His criminal activities came to light in 1973 when a youth, Grenville Smith, was discovered dead from an overdose of heroin. Smith had been procured by Morrison for immoral purposes and had lived for a short period in his Wandsworth residence, a disused furniture depository. Smith wrote an account of his stay at the 'Palace of Wandle' which was found on his body and subsequently published in a Sunday newspaper. The manner of the Bishop of Wandle's exposure was as strange as anything in Morrison's strange life.

He was born in 1917, the only son of the Right Reverend Percival Morrison and his wife Irene. He was educated at a London grammar school, since demolished, and at Oxford, where he attained a First Class degree, with honours, in medieval history and religion. After distinguished wartime service in the Royal Air Force, he became a journalist. Writing as Alec Wandle, he expressed fiercely reactionary views in a weekly column that earned him a large number of prominent enemies. His assumed stance was that of a man of the highest moral principles. In the early seventies, he made frequent appearances on the television religious affairs programme *Questions of Faith*.

In reality Alec Morrison, alias Alec Wandle, was a pimp and a blackmailer. He was sentenced to five years' imprisonment in February 1974, but was released in January 1978, following good conduct. He married, in 1981, the portrait painter Priscilla Reynolds, who bore him a daughter, Serena. They both survive him.

Mrs Morrison informed the press on Monday that she will be editing the volume of memoirs her husband had almost completed.

I shall read Mr Morrison's book in the hope of finding a reference, at least, to Stephen Eccles, the boy he bequeathed the curious legacy of a rag-bag of words and phrases – of 'for the nonce' and '*Dominus vobiscum*' and 'Stradivarius'; of 'sausage duty' and 'nectarine'; and of phantoms like Heathcliff and Horatio and Mrs Danvers.

I see Stephen now as I saw him a few nights ago, on the stage at the opera house, diminished in size, a small boy again, on the very verge of life. And then the image vanishes and is replaced by the tall and handsome boy-man himself, in a striking ensemble of cashmere wool and corduroy. And between the two I sense only waste and emptiness, and a fragile need for enchantment sustained against a mountain of terrible odds.

CODA

This afternoon, on an impulse, I took our week-old son to meet his grandmother.

'He's beautiful,' cooed the matron, Miss Lavelle. 'He's bonny. If Mrs Potocka could only know who he is, what a wonderful surprise she'd have.'

'Hello, Mummy.' My mother didn't respond to the forbidden word. 'This is Stephen. This is your grandchild.'

She stared beyond him.

Would she be offended, I asked her, if I breast-fed him here and now? He was obviously hungry.

I went on with my mad chatter as I fed Stephen. Could she remember being pregnant with me? Was her pregnancy as hellish as mine had been?

'I expected morning sickness, Mummy, but not sickness round the clock. I thought you stopped throwing up towards the end, but it wasn't like that at all. I was vomiting just hours before he arrived.'

I smiled at my insane courage. To talk of vomiting in the presence of Countess Potocka!

'Stephen's my first and my last, Mummy. I couldn't endure that agony again. And besides, I'm about to be too old. I shall be forty-three in November.'

My madness persisted. I reminded her that she had never told me the facts of a woman's life. It was Tata who had done that. It was Tata who explained to me what she and the teachers and that vile trio of nuns had been too scared or disgusted to explain. It was Tata who prepared me for the real world.

And then, as if to confirm my temporary derangement, I recalled the woman with the foul breath who had mocked me in the street when I was a girl, calling me a princess and a rich little pampered missy. Tata had persuaded me, I revealed, that the woman wasn't mad as I'd supposed, but desperate and wretched. She belonged to that frightening vastness outside the polite confines of our apartment. 'Our *appartement*,' I said, echoing my mother's French pronunciation.

My madness grew in me, and I talked of Sammy, he of the 'too-pronounced' nose, and dear sweet Maureen − 'Esther's Mr Elkin's mother' − and the grief I felt for each of their vanished lives. I described *A Song, A Dance* to my mother − scene after luminous scene − and as I spoke I realised that Sammy had said everything he wanted and needed to say in that one perfect film, and that when he had finished it there was nothing else but a lasting silence to fill. 'With drink, Mummy. He filled it with drink.'

I mentioned Gabriel next, and the dress that has to be discarded before he can make love to me. 'He's casting off his mother every time,' I heard myself confide. 'Isn't that funny?'

My mother suddenly sat up in bed. She pointed a finger at Stephen and glared at him.

'Mummy? Mummy?'

This was the look of hate and rage I had seen, years earlier, on the Sunday afternoon I walked into Anna Pavlova and smashed her to pieces. 'It was an accident,' I screamed, as the glass cracked and broke around me. 'Please believe me. It was an accident. It was an accident, I swear.'

'You clumsy bitch. You clumsy bitch with your so great hands and feet. You clumsy unfemale bitch, you have destroyed her. She cannot be replaced, and you have destroyed her for me.'

My mother was no longer glaring at Stephen, but her finger remained pointed in his direction.

'*Kurwa nać*,' she said. Her eyes met mine. '*Kurwa. Kurwa. Kurwa nać*.'

Miss Lavelle came into the room.

'*Kurwa*,' said my mother, whose smiling face I saw through tears. '*Kurwa nač.*'

'I think she's calling me a whore, Miss Lavelle.'

'Is it Polish she's speaking?'

'Yes, it is. The language she lost as a child, when her family fled from the Russians. The language she left behind.'

'Would you like to tidy your face?' Miss Lavelle handed me a paper tissue.

'Yes, I would.'

I tidied my face, and stood up, and kissed my mother's forehead, as Tata had so often kissed mine.

Then Stephen began to bawl, and it was time to go.

Discover more about our forthcoming books through Penguin's FREE newspaper...

Penguin

Quarterly

It's packed with:

- exciting features
- author interviews
- previews & reviews
- books from your favourite films & TV series
- exclusive competitions & much, much more...

Write off for your free copy today to:
Dept JC
Penguin Books Ltd
FREEPOST
West Drayton
Middlesex
UB7 0BR
NO STAMP REQUIRED

READ MORE IN PENGUIN

In every corner of the world, on every subject under the sun, Penguin represents quality and variety – the very best in publishing today.

For complete information about books available from Penguin – including Puffins, Penguin Classics and Arkana – and how to order them, write to us at the appropriate address below. Please note that for copyright reasons the selection of books varies from country to country.

In the United Kingdom: Please write to *Dept. JC, Penguin Books Ltd, FREEPOST, West Drayton, Middlesex UB7 0BR*

If you have any difficulty in obtaining a title, please send your order with the correct money, plus ten per cent for postage and packaging, to *PO Box No. 11, West Drayton, Middlesex UB7 0BR*

In the United States: Please write to *Penguin USA Inc., 375 Hudson Street, New York, NY 10014*

In Canada: Please write to *Penguin Books Canada Ltd, 10 Alcorn Avenue, Suite 300, Toronto, Ontario M4V 3B2*

In Australia: Please write to *Penguin Books Australia Ltd, 487 Maroondah Highway, Ringwood, Victoria 3134*

In New Zealand: Please write to *Penguin Books (NZ) Ltd,182–190 Wairau Road, Private Bag, Takapuna, Auckland 9*

In India: Please write to *Penguin Books India Pvt Ltd, 706 Eros Apartments, 56 Nehru Place, New Delhi 110 019*

In the Netherlands: Please write to *Penguin Books Netherlands B.V., Keizersgracht 231 NL–1016 DV Amsterdam*

In Germany: Please write to *Penguin Books Deutschland GmbH, Friedrichstrasse 10–12, W–6000 Frankfurt/Main 1*

In Spain: Please write to *Penguin Books S. A., C. San Bernardo 117–6° E–28015 Madrid*

In Italy: Please write to *Penguin Italia s.r.l., Via Felice Casati 20, I–20124 Milano*

In France: Please write to *Penguin France S. A., 17 rue Lejeune, F–31000 Toulouse*

In Japan: Please write to *Penguin Books Japan, Ishikiribashi Building, 2–5–4, Suido, Bunkyo-ku, Tokyo 112*

In Greece: Please write to *Penguin Hellas Ltd, Dimocritou 3, GR–106 71 Athens*

In South Africa: Please write to *Longman Penguin Southern Africa (Pty) Ltd, Private Bag X08, Bertsham 2013*

BY THE SAME AUTHOR

Gabriel's Lament

'Gabriel Harvey's mother wanted an angel, and her son was happy to oblige. But she mysteriously abandoned him and he remained trapped in a twenty-eight-year adolescence and fettered to an unexpressed grief. The discovery and naming of that grief is the subject of this most original novel ... touching, beautifully paced and quite unforgettable' – *Literary Review*

'At once comic and desperately tragic ... a novel which draws you with a strong, sure touch into its web of family life, deceit and counter-deceit, love in spite of all' – *Sunday Telegraph*

An Immaculate Mistake

Paul Bailey's unusual and evocative memoir of childhood and adolescence is set mainly in the working-class London of the 1940s and 1950s.

'If only more memoirs could be written like *An Immaculate Mistake* ... unsentimental yet touching ... a funny, sad way of coming to terms with the experience of childhood' – *Sunday Times*